THE
EXPLORERS
THE
RECKLESS
RESCUE

Books by ADRIENNE KRESS

THE EXPLORERS

THE DOOR IN THE ALLEY

THE RECKLESS RESCUE

THE QUEST FOR THE KID

THE EXPLORERS

THE RECKLESS RESCUE

ADRIENNE KRESS

Illustrated by Matthew C. Rockefeller

A YEARLING BOOK

Text copyright © 2018 by Adrienne Kress
Cover art and interior illustrations copyright © 2018 by Matthew C. Rockefeller
Logo art copyright © 2018 by Caldwell Bosch

All rights reserved. Published in the United States by Yearling, an imprint of Random House Children's Books, a division of Penguin Random House LLC, New York. Originally published in hardcover in the United States by Delacorte Press, an imprint of Random House Children's Books, a division of Penguin Random House LLC, New York, in 2018.

Yearling and the jumping horse design
are registered trademarks of Penguin Random House LLC.

Visit us on the Web! rhcbooks.com

Educators and librarians, for a variety of teaching tools,
visit us at RHTeachersLibrarians.com

The Library of Congress has cataloged the hardcover edition of this work as follows:
Names: Kress, Adrienne, author. | Rockefeller, Matt, illustrator.
Title: The Explorers : the reckless rescue / Adrienne Kress ;
illustrated by Matthew C. Rockefeller.
Other titles: Reckless rescue
Description: First edition. | New York : Delacorte Press, [2018] | Summary: "After nefarious, nameless thugs have separated Sebastian and Evie, the pair must travel the globe to reunite and piece together the remaining clues about the missing explorers from the Filipendulous Five"— Provided by publisher.
Identifiers: LCCN 2017020662 | ISBN 978-1-101-94009-9 (hc) |
ISBN 978-1-101-94011-2 (ebook)
Subjects: | CYAC: Adventure and adventurers—Fiction. | Secret societies—Fiction. |
Missing persons—Fiction. | Voyages and travels—Fiction.
Classification: LCC PZ7.K8838 Eym 2018 | DDC [Fic]—dc23

ISBN 978-1-101-94012-9 (pbk.)

Printed in the United States of America
10 9 8 7 6 5 4 3 2
First Yearling Edition 2019

To readers—who are the ultimate explorers.

. . . frustrating. But you know what's even worse than a cliff-hanger? Waiting to read what happens, then finally getting your hands on the next book, and the author decides to begin the story with a character you've never met doing something in a place you've barely heard of. That's totally the worst.

Benedict sat staring at the vista before him. The whole world was laid bare, vulnerable, it seemed, sprawling from the base of the active volcano he was sitting high atop. Which, he had to admit, it was. Vulnerable. Though in such a peaceful moment, it felt highly absurd to picture flows of lava, clouds of black ash, or anything violent, really. The sun was setting over the sea in the distance, and there wasn't a single cloud in the sky. The birds were calmly chatting to each other, having gotten over the unfortunate misunderstanding from that morning. From this vantage point he could almost imagine he was the only human on earth. The town that he knew lay beneath him was masked from view by lush green foliage.

He had given himself two months. A short leave that even the university had suggested be extended because of some kind of affection for him, or maybe because two months really messed with their scheduling. But he hadn't wanted more. He had just needed some space, a little room to clear his head. And he'd been wanting to photograph the isolated Vertiginous Volcano for years. Yet six weeks had already passed and he hadn't taken a single picture. Sure, he'd looked through the scope, he'd set up shots, he'd paced back and forth. But pressing down his finger, hearing that satisfying click . . . there was something that was preventing him. He let go of his camera, letting it dangle from his neck on its strap, and stared at his hands. It was surprising that in such a humid climate they could be so cracked. But days spent climbing up and down the side of a volcano had worn away at his palms, and the wind at this height had dried out his skin. He balled his right hand into a fist and squeezed it with his left until he heard and felt the pleasing pop of his knuckles. Then he pulled up the collar of his green windbreaker and buffered his neck against the sharp wind.

Not one single photograph.

Why?

What was he waiting for?

"Mr. . . . Barnes?" asked a warm, happy voice slowly, haltingly.

"Why so hesitant, Peter?" asked Benedict, turning to the young man. Peter grinned and sat beside him. Benedict smiled back. He had met Peter on his first day in the town. The local teenager was fascinated with photography, had started a club at his school, and had wanted to be Benedict's apprentice. Benedict wasn't comfortable with the term—there wasn't much he could offer the boy. He liked to work alone. But he'd allowed Peter to follow him a few times. To watch. Right now, evidently, to stare.

"Was there something you wanted?" asked Benedict.

"Oh yes, this came for you." Peter reached into his pocket and pulled out a letter.

"A letter?" Benedict was charmed. He couldn't think of the last time someone had written him a letter. He took it from Peter and looked at it. "Urgent" was handwritten in red across the front, and it had been sent to the university. He supposed they had decided to forward it to him despite his request that they not do that with his mail. Mostly because all he got were bills and magazines, nothing he wanted to deal with on top of a volcano.

Urgent.

Hmm.

He flipped it over. A red wax blob sealed the letter closed. Stamped onto it was an unusual-looking symbol. Benedict furrowed his brow. Then he shoved the letter into his pocket.

"You're not going to read it?" asked Peter.

Benedict gazed out at the setting sun bleeding over the landscape.

"Not today, Peter." He cracked the knuckles on his right hand again. "Not today."

➤ CHAPTER 1 ◄

In which we resume
our story.

There is a difference between fact and opinion. It's hard to tell sometimes because opinions like to dress up as facts, and their costumes have gotten quite impressive lately.[1] There is a way, however, to easily tell the difference between them. You have to weigh them. Because, you see, facts have more substance. So they're heavier. This is how one can know for a fact, for example, that being kidnapped for your brain is scary. Because when this fact is placed on the scale, man, does it ever tip the balance!

---

[1] I once saw an opinion wearing the most spectacular curly mustache that distracted me so much, I totally let him come into my head, even though I found his footwear suspicious.

There are other facts one can be certain of. Like that private planes are cool. That traveling long distances gets boring. And that not knowing where you are going or what's going to happen to you is exhaustingly stressful.

And if you don't believe me, just ask Sebastian, who was sitting in his seat and staring out the window of the private jet, feeling precisely all those things.

It was odd to feel bored. Not that feeling bored is a rare or weird feeling. It's a very common part of life, after all. But it just felt so strange to feel bored in his particular situation. He should have been feeling terrified, possibly even a little excited. And he knew this because he'd felt those things initially when he'd been snatched out of the Explorers Society headquarters and held captive in a helicopter. But that felt like forever ago now. After flying to the private airport, getting on the private plane, flying over the ocean, and continuing to fly over the ocean. And yet more flying over the ocean . . .

Things had started to get just a little boring.

And now the boredom was turning into sleepiness.

Which was really quite simply all kinds of wrong.

"You could sleep," said Mr. M.

Sebastian shifted his gaze from the window to the man sitting across from him wearing a patch over his left eye. Mr. M appeared very relaxed, but of course he would be. *His* life wasn't in danger, now, was it?

"So could you," Sebastian pointed out.

"Nah, gotta keep one eye open," replied Mr. M, laughing at his own joke. Sebastian didn't laugh. "Get it? One eye? Get it?"

Sebastian got it. He just didn't find it particularly funny. Suddenly he had a flash of his parents at the dinner table and his mother telling that joke about the salamander and how not-funny the joke was and—

Oh, there was that pain in his gut again. He wondered if his parents were looking for him. They must be.

He wondered if Evie was looking for him.

Like she'd promised.

"It's because I only have one eye, that's the joke," continued Mr. M. "Because keeping one eye open is an expression." He paused. "But also I only have one eye. It works on two levels."

"I get the joke!" snapped Sebastian in exasperation.

"Whoa, okay, okay. Jeez, relax."

"Easy for you to say," muttered Sebastian under his breath.

"It's true. It's very easy for me to say. I've completed my task; I have the key. Which is you." He stared at Sebastian for a moment. And then as if by way of explanation: "You're the key."

"I know I'm the key," Sebastian replied curtly. What on earth was going on? Before this week, everyone had always treated him like the highly intelligent boy he was. Now everyone seemed to be second-guessing his smarts. And it was seriously annoying.

"So anyway, with my job well done, I feel as cool as a cucumber." Mr. M paused. "Why do they say that? Are cucumbers cooler than other vegetables?"

"I don't know why they say that." Another wave of sleepiness was washing over Sebastian. He was tired of dealing with Mr. M, who had this frustrating ability to be both extraordinarily terrifying and completely tedious at the same time. And weirder still: if he hadn't known any better, Sebastian would have sworn that Mr. M wanted to be his friend. Not that there was anything wrong with friends, of course. It's just that people who want to hurt you are not the best choice for friends.[2]

Just as Sebastian finally gave in to his exhaustion and closed his eyes, he was rudely drawn back to the horror of his situation by a guttural grunt. He started and looked up. Mr. I, with his gruesomely wired-shut jaw, was towering over him. The man gazed at him hard for a moment and then turned to Mr. M. He grunted again.

"What is it now?" asked Mr. M, seemingly sincerely annoyed that his conversation with Sebastian had been interrupted.

Mr. I pointed toward the cockpit, and Mr. M sighed. Mr. M gave Sebastian an apologetic glance, then stood up, adjusting the old-fashioned-looking gun in its holster as he did, and made his way to the front of the plane. Mr. I replaced him in the seat and

---

[2] Unless, of course, you're part of the "We want to hurt each other for fun" club, which, from my understanding, is currently down to one member.

stared at Sebastian. Or at least, seemed to stare. He was still wearing those sunglasses of his.

Staring, Sebastian could handle. It was a quiet activity and required nothing of him. But as he stared back defiantly, gazing at his own reflection in the man's glasses, Sebastian found his boredom seeping away. There was something about Mr. I that just so completely reminded him of the danger he was in. Maybe it was how worn Sebastian looked, reflected in the dark, unforgiving glasses; maybe it was that Mr. I had very recently been this close to ending his life; maybe it was the bits of wire sticking out between the man's teeth and poking through the flesh of his cheek. Whatever it was, Sebastian was officially scared again. But more than that, he was reinvigorated.

His plan to sleep would have to wait while he formulated another one. It was time for that marvelous brain of his to take charge.

Yes.

It was time to plot a daring escape.

➤ CHAPTER 2 ◄

In which a meeting
takes place.

There was a pig-in-a-teeny-hat-shaped lump under a sheet.

It snorted.

"Oh, sorry!" said Evie, quickly removing the sheet, balling it up, and tossing it into the corner. The pig sat and stared at her with a look of disappointment. A look that said, "I've been taking such good care of you ever since your friend was kidnapped, and this is how you treat me?"

"I really am sorry," Evie said.

The pig snorted again.

Evie bent over and gave it a little scratch behind its right ear before straightening the teeny hat on its head.

Then she quickly stood and grabbed the next sheet and pulled it off the table in one determined motion. Unlike the pig, Evie didn't snort. But she did sneeze loudly as the dust tickled the back of her throat and nostrils. The large white sheet in her hands billowed out impressively before her, then fell limply to the floor as the pig took one step to the left, neatly avoiding it. She gathered the sheet up in her arms and added it to the pile in the corner. Then she turned and took stock of the room.

The Emergency Meeting Room for Emergencies meeting room hadn't seen a lot of activity in recent years. Myrtle, the Explorers Society president and general rememberer of dates and things, had told Evie it hadn't been used since the great sea horse rescue almost fifteen years ago. Evie supposed that was a good thing. Emergencies generally were not events one relished. She'd encountered a great many in her short eleven years on this planet.

Still, there was some small comfort that the society was taking this seriously. That they cared so much for Sebastian. He'd been kidnapped only a few hours ago through the window of her brand-new bedroom at the society, yet they'd already arranged the important meeting. The use of the room could be described as both upsetting and comforting.[3] Though, of course, very little was able to comfort Evie at the moment.

Myrtle had rounded up the members of the board who were currently in the city to come and discuss the matter. Evie wasn't so sure what there was to talk about. It was simple: They needed to rescue Sebastian. They needed to do it now. She had read somewhere that after two days, it was much less likely to find a missing person ever. Time wasn't on their side.[4]

"What about the rest of the table?" asked Catherine Lind, animal expert and former member of the infamous explorer team the Filipendulous Five, as she added to the stack the white sheet she'd just pulled off a row of chairs.

"We won't need it," replied Myrtle, placing her hands on her hips and looking off into the dark far end of the room.

Evie wished there were windows to open, or some kind of natural light, but they were deep underneath the society building. The roots of the large tree that grew up through the central library of the building

---

[3] Which is also how I describe the new duvet cover I just got for my bed.

[4] Time wasn't not on their side either. Time just generally likes to maintain a neutral opinion on most subjects.

twisted along the ceiling and dove into the ground at inconvenient intervals. They created floor-to-ceiling pillars around which the large meeting table had to bend and turn. The table was so long that it vanished into the darkness. Evie assumed it, too, was draped in yet more white sheets to protect it from the dirt and soil. Lanterns along the opposite wall lit half of the room. It was all so dark and oppressive. And it added to Evie's general sense of doom and fear.

"I don't understand why we can't just go after him now," said Evie again in frustration.

"Because rushing into things at the beginning often ends up making things take longer in the end," replied a melodious voice from behind her.

Evie turned to see a tall man with a meticulously groomed goatee standing in the entrance. He walked inside, followed by two other members of the society: an elegant brown-haired woman in a flowing dress, and a short, stout man in a checkered suit. Evie didn't know any of them, though she did think she might have seen the woman before, in the leather chair room. Their presence only made her more nervous.

As they took their seats at the table, Catherine leaned in and whispered into Evie's ear, "The members of the board of directors. They've always intimidated me."

Evie could see why. They all looked so stern. And as she sat down beside Catherine, she had the distinct impression they were judging her quite harshly. What they were judging her on, she had no idea. And considering they were the ones who had approved her moving into the society headquarters and being educated there, Evie found their attitude a little unfair, really. The pig made a soft snort beside her, and she scooped it up into her lap. She hugged it maybe a bit too closely, but it seemed to understand that its role was to take care of her and accepted the squeeze with grace and dignity.

Myrtle sat herself at the head of the table. "Evie, meet Llewellyn Tracy, Lady Trill, and the Hopper. The four of us represent the board of directors for the Explorers Society, and we are now going to discuss what is to be done about Sebastian."

"And my grandfather," added Evie quickly.

Myrtle furrowed her brow at that.

"Your grandfather? Myrtle, no one said anything about a grandfather," said Lady Trill carefully.

"Ah, well, yes," said Myrtle awkwardly. It was the first time Evie had ever seen the Ice Queen less than composed.

"He's the reason all this is happening in the first place." Evie looked at the confused expressions the members of the board were wearing, unique in their own special ways: Llewellyn Tracy narrowed his eyes and scratched his goatee; Lady Trill raised her eyebrows so high, they disappeared behind her bangs; and the Hopper bounced in his seat. "Um . . . didn't Myrtle tell you when you agreed to take me in?" asked Evie. She was starting to get that fluttery feeling in her chest that happened when she was on the verge of becoming emotional.

"Myrtle told us everything was taken care of and that you were an orphan who needed help and a proper education. We trust her, and we enjoy helping and properly educating people," said Lady Trill.

"Oh. Oh dear," Evie said quietly to herself.

"Does this have something to do with the Filipendulous Five?" asked the Hopper, stopping his bouncing for a moment and giving Myrtle a hard look. "Is that why *she's* here?" He indicated Catherine as if she were a distasteful painting or an unpleasant smell.[5]

Myrtle sighed hard. Finally she conceded the point and admitted to the board that "the members of the Filipendulous Five are in danger. Someone is after their pieces of the map from their last expedition." She didn't explain further. From the expressions on

---

[5] Or a distasteful painting of an unpleasant smell.

the board members' faces it seemed they were all too familiar with the story, or at least the part of it that ended with the Filipendulous Five causing a tsunami from deep below the ocean waves in their submarine, and all the destruction that ensued. It was harder to tell if the board members were aware of what the team had been after: the secret waterfall down in the Mariana Trench, the one that seemed to be some kind of fountain of youth. Evie felt that maybe she should just keep silent, not adding to Myrtle's story. Catherine certainly didn't speak up either.

"That bloody map!" said the Hopper with so much ferocity that he fell off his chair. Quickly he clambered back onto it and looked at the others as if nothing had happened.

"That's why those men came here. That's why Sebastian was kidnapped," said Evie carefully.

"Are you saying that the Filipendulous Five are responsible for the extreme damage that was done to society headquarters the other day? The damage that will take months to repair, and at quite a high expense?" asked Lady Trill slowly.

"Uh," replied Evie.

"In a manner of speaking," replied Myrtle, not looking very pleased.

"Well . . . ," said Evie, thinking as fast as she could.

The last thing she wanted was for the board to refuse to help rescue Sebastian and find her grandfather because of some evil men showing up and causing mass chaos in the society building.

"Yes?" asked Lady Trill.

"Well, I mean, sort of yes," said Evie. "But also no. They would have come no matter what any of us or Catherine did. They wanted the map. And I don't think it's fair to place all the blame on the Filipendulous Five when they did everything the society asked them to do by hiding the map. Really, if we play the blame game, surely the society would have to take some of it."

There was a long silence as Evie collected herself. The pig snuggled more deeply into her arms.

"And," Evie said, starting up again, "whatever happened, I don't think Sebastian deserves to just be left to his fate. He only wanted to help." Her voice cracked on that last word. "None of this had anything to do with him, and now he's in serious danger." She had to stop now. She had to stop before she burst into tears.

There was another silence. And then finally it was broken by someone other than Evie.

"Poor lad," said Llewellyn Tracy.

Evie nodded. Poor lad indeed. Poor lovely, logical Sebastian with the photographic memory that could memorize a key to a map in a mere moment. And now

he was all that remained of that key. And so they took him. And it was all her fault. She took in a deep breath and squeezed the pig even tighter.

"We think these men are going after Benedict Barnes next," said Catherine, finally speaking up. Evie understood why she'd kept quiet until now. It didn't seem like anyone at the table was particularly fond of her. Except Evie, that is.

"Oh, is that what you think?" sneered the Hopper.

Catherine looked at him hard, as if she wanted to say something very particular to the man, but instead she turned her gaze to the others, leaned forward, and said, "Yes. He and I are the only remaining members who have a somewhat public profile, even if Benedict changed his last name. I myself know only Benedict's address and Alistair's post office box address. I have no idea where the others are, and, very likely, neither do these men."

"How can you be so sure they know where Benedict is?" said the Hopper, crossing his arms over his chest.

"They know it the same way I know it," interrupted Evie, tired of the Hopper's attitude. "They went to the university to find him, and when they learned he wasn't there, they found out where he was."

"How do you know that?" asked Lady Trill.

"Our paths crossed while I was at the university campus myself." Evie didn't want to go into the details of her harrowing escape from Mr. K. It was all still too fresh—she flinched at the memory of jumping out of the bell tower.

"So where is Benedict?" asked Lady Trill.

"The Vertiginous Volcano," replied Evie.

There was a charged silence after she said the name. Evie didn't understand why. The name didn't seem all that scary. Sure, volcanoes could be very dangerous, but many people visited them, even active ones. It wasn't like they were always erupting all over the place or anything.

"He always did want to visit it," said Llewellyn Tracy. "But that does make things difficult, doesn't it?"

"It does?" asked Evie.

"The Vertiginous Volcano is a very tricky mountain. There is only one way to its base, located in the small town that is situated in the volcano's shadow," explained Catherine.

"What's so tricky about that?" asked Evie.

"The town is hidden. There's a secret entrance to it, and only a few people know of its whereabouts," said Catherine.

"Oh," said Evie. She understood now the charged silence. Or at least, thought she did. To be fair, there were many reasons for a silence to be charged, but a secret entrance seemed as good as any.

"The good news is that I know someone who can help," said Catherine, speaking a little more loudly, almost as if she was making a pronouncement.

"You do?" asked Myrtle. Everyone else around the table looked as shocked as the president.

"Yes. Benedict worked for a time with a man named Thom Walker in Creaky Cove, Australia. He was a cartographer, responsible for mapping out some of the harder-to-reach areas of the rain forest in the northern parts of Australia. Thom was the one who told Benedict about the volcano originally, of its existence on Newish Isle, a small island country located a couple thousand miles east of the Queensland coastline. And I assume it was Thom who went with Benedict to Newish Isle and showed him the secret entrance to the town." Catherine looked very sure of herself, and Evie was grateful. Her confidence made it seem all the more possible to do what they had to do. Not that Evie actually knew yet what they were going to do. But "had" and "going to" were two separate things. They had to rescue Sebastian. They had to warn Benedict about the dangerous men. They had to rescue her grandfather. How were they going to do any of that? That was still up in the air.

"I see. So you're going to find Benedict Barnes, are you?" said the Hopper.

"Evie and I will, yes," replied Catherine, looking over at Evie with a small smile that Evie returned.

"You think it wise to bring a child with you on such an expedition?" asked Lady Trill. But it wasn't a rhetorical question; she seemed sincerely curious about whether Catherine did find it wise or not.

"I do. Evie and I have discussed it, and I think, considering the promise she made to Sebastian to rescue him and her need to find her grandfather, considering also how well she handled herself recently opposite these men—"

Evie interrupted her. "And she couldn't leave me behind anyway. I'd find a way to join her."

"It could be dangerous," said Lady Trill.

"It would be dangerous if I was a grown-up too, and yet that doesn't seem to be an issue you have with Catherine." Evie liked the logic there. Sebastian would have been proud.

Sebastian.

Every time she thought of him, her heart hurt.

"So the two of you want to go to Australia to find this man, and then go to Newish Isle, find the town, and find Benedict. Which will in turn lead you to Sebastian. Which will for some reason lead you to this young lady's grandfather," said Llewellyn Tracy slowly, putting the pieces together.

"Yes. We have to assume that those men are heading to the volcano as we speak. We have to assume that time is of the essence," said Catherine.

"But how will finding Sebastian help her grandfather?" asked Lady Trill, her eyebrows still hidden behind her bangs.

Evie looked at Lady Trill with the same level of confusion with which Lady Trill was looking at her. It seemed pretty obvious, didn't it? "Because they are all in danger—Sebastian, Benedict, and anyone who is with them—but my grandfather most of all. We don't know why, but we know that his life is on the line. And the only way to find my grandfather is to find the others in the Filipendulous Five. My grandfather sent each of them a letter like the one Catherine got. When we put them all together, we'll be able to figure out where he is."

"We *think*," Catherine corrected her gently. "We don't know for certain that they received letters, and we don't know, even if they did, if the letters are a clue to finding him."

Evie looked at her for a moment. Catherine was right. It was just a guess that the letters would help her find her grandfather, but some guesses were better guesses than others. Some were more like hypotheses—guesses made after a lot of thinking and putting ideas together. Like when you guess that if you jump off a table, you'll go downward. Wasn't this one like that? Wasn't it?

"Yes," Evie said firmly. "We *think,* but we're pretty sure."

Catherine smiled. "We're pretty sure."

Evie smiled too.

"I don't understand," said the Hopper, annoyed. "Why does your grandfather have such a close relationship with the Filipendulous Five?"

And that was when Evie finally understood the confused looks and strange questions. In all this, Evie and Catherine had neglected somehow to share one important connecting piece of information. She glanced at Myrtle, who was examining the surface of the boardroom table with the kind of fascination normally reserved for a newly uncovered fossil.

It was up to Evie, then. She looked at the members of the board, and with her chin up proudly, she said, "My grandfather is Alistair Drake."

➤ CHAPTER 3 ➤

In which we experience
a bit of turbulence.

The problem with Sebastian's planning a daring escape from a plane populated with dangerous men was the part where he was in a plane and it was populated with dangerous men. Also the part where he was up in the air with nowhere to escape to. Still, this didn't stop Sebastian from thinking hard, trying to solve the puzzle.

The solution, Sebastian pretty quickly realized, came in not being in the air. His best shot, he figured, was, once they'd landed and left the plane, somehow slipping out and away. But that was tricky because of the second part of the problem: the dangerous men.

Sebastian sighed hard, so hard, in fact, that Mr. I looked at him with a slightly different expression.

"I hate long flights," explained Sebastian.

Thud.

Sebastian and Mr. I were both tossed violently about in their seats. Sebastian, shocked, glanced out the window. Darkness. Just black darkness of dark.

Thud.

"What's going on?" asked Sebastian, looking at Mr. I—not that the man could answer even if he knew.

The expression Mr. I wore on his face now was one Sebastian had not seen on him before. He had known the man to look menacing, and also menacing, and sometimes menacing, but he had never seen him worried before. Or . . . now that he looked more closely . . . frightened? This, in turn, had the effect of making Sebastian even more frightened himself.

"What's going on?" asked Sebastian again, his voice shaking a little this time. Just as he did, the plane lurched up and then down so violently that he was certain that had he not been wearing his seat belt, he would have hit his head on the ceiling. Possibly even been thrown straight through it toward the heavens.

The calming ding of the FASTEN SEAT BELTS light overhead sounded, completely unaware, it seemed, of the immediate situation. It felt almost more like a co-incidence and less like a reaction to the outside turbulence: *Oh, hey there, guys. I was thinking maybe you might want to fasten your seat belts. And also, what's going on? Anything new or interesting?*

The plane lurched again.

Sebastian's insides lurched as well.

Now, Sebastian was a very rational person and knew that, more often than not, not throwing up was a question of mind over matter. In this instance, though, the *Don't throw up, don't throw up* running through his head was not feeling as effective as it could have.

Lurch!

Don't throw up, don't throw up.

"Good evening. This is your captain speaking." The captain spoke in smooth, calm, even tones, almost as if she, like the little ding light, were oblivious to their situation. "We've hit a bit of turbulence, which is perfectly normal, no need for concern. Turbulence is a very common occurrence and something planes have been built for. Also, a bird flew into our right engine and that caused it to explode, so we're down an engine and we're going to have to make an emergency landing at Incheon International Airport."

"What?" asked Sebastian loudly.

Mr. I's grimace reflected a similar stunned response.

"Okay," said Mr. M, returning from the front and settling in across the aisle. He leaned toward Sebastian and Mr. I. "Look at me, Sebastian."

Sebastian did as he was told.

"We're landing in Seoul, South Korea. We're changing planes. I'm going to need you to be as helpful as possible, yes? We can't have you causing us any trouble, okay?"

Sebastian nodded. Why would he be any trouble? He was the least troublesome person he knew. And that included Sam Dunsmore, who had won the Least Troublesome Student award three times in a row now at school.[6]

Lurch!

Mr. M was flung back into his seat. Oh. Oh, wait. Sebastian now recalled his train of thought from before. Wasn't he supposed to escape? Wasn't that the plan he'd made? He really oughtn't to have made that "not causing any trouble" promise just now.

Then again, it had been a week of breaking rules and being inappropriate. And surely promises to kidnappers were meant to be broken. In fact, he now marveled that Mr. M would want him to make a promise

---

[6] A total popularity contest and not remotely accurate, in Sebastian's humble opinion.

in the first place. Surely the man knew that Sebastian was under no obligation to keep it. This was an every-man-for-himself situation. Every boy for himself too, for that matter.

Lurch!

Ding![7]

The door to the cockpit flew open, and Mr. K with the melted face staggered out, stumbling to a seat at the front of the plane. But not without giving Sebastian one of his trademark glares.

Sebastian wondered if they'd all taken a class in glaring or if maybe that was why they'd each gotten the job. For their glaring skills.

Suddenly he felt his head spin and his ears pop. Sebastian glanced out the window and expected to see more of that same blackness of water he'd become so familiar with. But wait. He could now see some lights of a city in the far distance. He pressed his face against the glass to see directly below them and could make out the dotted lights of a runway. Well, that was good, at least. It didn't make him feel any safer, but he liked that no one below was in danger of a plane landing on top of them or anything.

---

[7] Or, *Hey, guys, just an FYI here: Maybe you want to do that whole seat belt thing just about now? No pressure or anything, though.*

He took in a deep breath and tried to calm himself. *Don't throw up, don't throw up.*

Lurch!

The air pressure in the cabin was heavy. It almost felt like someone had his head between their hands and was squeezing. Hard. The lights of the airport were flying past now in a blur. He could tell the plane was getting lower and lower. It had to be slowing down for landing, but the proximity to objects flying by the window and not just blackness made the speed they were traveling at seem so much faster than before. Sebastian took quick stock of his surroundings. They hadn't had the usual safety instructions before taking off. He didn't know where the emergency exits were! He suddenly felt compelled to find out. Finding out was both rash and rational, considering the circumstances. He unbuckled his seat belt and stood.

"What do you think you're doing?" shouted Mr. K from the front of the plane.

Sebastian tottered forward and found that the exit nearest him was one row away. He didn't care that Mr. I had turned in his seat and was staring at him. Nor that Mr. M shouted out, "The ding! The ding happened! You can't ignore the ding!"

Sebastian stumbled up a row and fell into the chair beside the exit. The presence of the red lever that opened the door was like a lifesaver. Not even *like* a lifesaver. It actually *was* one. He felt so much better.

"Your seat belt!" said Mr. M, and Sebastian nodded. He quickly did up his new seat belt.

Lurch!

The world outside his window was almost parallel to them now. They were almost there.

"Brace yourself," said Mr. M from across the aisle.

Once more taking Mr. M's instructions to heart, Sebastian placed a hand on each armrest and pushed himself down into his seat as hard as he could.

He stared out the window in the door. He stared at the red lever. He thought about Evie for a moment. Then about Myrtle. Then he thought about his parents and if he'd ever see them again. About his brother and sister. About Arthur, his cousin and best friend. Then he thought about Alistair. About him being Evie's only family now that she was an orphan, the only child of two people who had passed away a few years earlier. About how before she'd discovered he was alive, she hadn't had anyone. What was it like to not have a family?

Then he thought about himself. About maybe not making it. About all the adventures he had never had because he had never known he'd wanted to have them. How unfair it was that just as he was starting to learn about himself in ways he had never expected, it was going to be all over. How maybe thrilling things weren't so thrilling if they stopped being. If they ended. Abruptly. Painfully.

Lurch!

Thud!

Sebastian's head snapped back, and his teeth knocked hard against each other as the plane made contact with the ground. It was amazing just how hard ground could be, when you thought about it. Way harder than air, that was for sure.

The plane raced forward while slowing down at the same time. The rush of sound that greeted the landing, of tires on cement and air whooshing past, and the one remaining engine overheating, was intensely terrifying. It was only as they slowed further that Sebastian realized how quiet everything was inside the plane itself. Not a sound from any of the Mr.'s. Not a sound from the pilot. Possibly, like Sebastian, they were all listening to the frantic thudding of their hearts, their elevated breathing rate. Possibly they too were thinking about themselves and adventures and things that they hadn't done. Like maybe getting Sebastian somewhere and making him decipher a mysterious map.

Or something.

The plane slowed down to the point where it felt

as if they were in a car, casually driving around the tarmac. Sebastian saw the airport, not so far off—curved, sleek, and modern, almost like a large alien spaceship had landed and decided to just stick around. A few larger planes sat quietly at their gates, waiting for their passengers. The bright lights illuminated the inside of the building, creating a tiny movie in the distance as small people-shaped silhouettes passed by the windows. Sebastian wondered if those people had seen them land, had seen the drama. If it had even looked dramatic from where they were standing.

The plane got slower and slower.

The plane stopped.

Ding!

Sebastian glanced up. The little seat belt light was off: *Hey, guys! Guess what. Just letting y'all know it's safe to undo your seat belts now!*

So he did.

"That was . . . something," said Mr. M. He sounded relieved. Probably was relieved.

Sebastian felt it too. He stared at the red emergency lever. Grateful he hadn't needed to use it. Not really sure he would have known what to do if he had had to. He leaned forward and read the little safety illustration stuck to the door. It gave step-by-step instructions.

"This is your captain speaking. Well, we're alive. So that's something."

We're alive.

"Kid, what are you doing?" Mr. K called from his seat in the front. Sebastian glanced up and saw the melted man stand and squint at him.

"Nothing." Which was not entirely true—he had been reading—but it didn't seem the moment to be so specific.

"You shouldn't have stood up like that," said Mr. M, unfastening his seat belt and stretching. "That was dangerous."

"Forget dangerous. Kid's gotta learn how to take orders. I'm tired of these rebellious youths who think they don't need to listen to authority," replied Mr. K.

Sebastian laughed.

"What was that?" asked Mr. K, his voice low and ominous. He took a step into the aisle.

"Oh, nothing. It's just funny," replied Sebastian.

"What is?" asked Mr. M, who sounded sincerely curious.

Sebastian was too overwhelmed, too exhilarated, and too alive to care if his words were a little disrespectful. "You guys thinking I don't listen to authority and everything. That's so not me."

"Until now," growled Mr. K.

"Well, I guess," said Sebastian thoughtfully. "Now that I think about it. I mean, what is 'authority,' anyway? Can one just be authoritative, or does one earn authority from others? You guys are scary, totally, and have weapons and can hurt me. But do I respect your authority? Do I think you have any authority over me? It's more like you guys are bullies than authority figures, really . . . when you think about it."

When you think about it.

"Okay, it's time to shut up now," said Mr. K.

Sebastian stood. He looked at Mr. K, who was halfway down the aisle, making his way toward Sebastian; at Mr. M sitting a row back, furrowing his one eyebrow. He couldn't see Mr. I, but he imagined that he would be giving the usual death glare from behind those mirrored glasses.

"No."

"I gave you an order, kid."

"I know you did. And I don't care."

"Sit down and shut up."

"Or maybe . . . ," said Sebastian calmly, "this."

He turned quickly, wrenched down the red lever, and pushed as hard as he could. The emergency door flew open.

➤ CHAPTER 4 ⤙

In which there is
an argument.

"No! Absolutely not!"

"It's madness!"

"No! No, no, no, no!"

The board members—aside from Myrtle—were on their feet, shouting at each other. Which Evie found both overwhelming and odd, since they were in agreement.

"It wasn't his fault!" said Catherine loudly. She too was on her feet, pleading with the board members.

"He's irresponsible!"

"A menace!"

"A disgrace to the profession of explorer!"

"That's not true!" Evie's little voice rang out above

the fray, and everyone was silent then. "That's not true. What happened twenty years ago was an accident. I don't know how you can support Benedict or Catherine but not my grandfather." She was out of breath but wasn't sure why.

Llewellyn Tracy looked at her hard. "I don't trust Catherine or Benedict. But I like them better."

"Oh, well, then let's only help out likable people. It's okay if someone we aren't personally fond of dies because—because—" Evie was white-hot with rage and stammered, not able to complete her thought. "This isn't fair. You don't even know him. You only know what happened, and you blame him because he was their leader. But I think it's noble that he took on the blame for the tsunami. Especially when everyone's to blame. They were all in the submarine. They all agreed to fire at the rock wall." She looked at Catherine for help, then realized that the timing of the look made it seem like she was accusing Catherine of something bad, and that wasn't her intention at all.

But Catherine nodded, accepting the accusation. "Everyone *was* to blame," she said, taking over for Evie. "And everyone was banned from the society. And either you help everyone or you help no one. You can't pick and choose. Not with this." She spoke calmly and with poise. Towering over the table as she was, she looked quite formidable.

Everyone slowly took their seats again, each person lost in their own thoughts.

"We need to discuss this," said Lady Trill, and she leaned in to talk with Llewellyn Tracy and the Hopper in enthusiastic whispers.

Evie was getting tired. She and Catherine didn't need permission from anyone to rescue Sebastian, Benedict, and her grandfather. She could do it with or without them. But with them would be better. With them, she and Catherine would have a fully funded expedition. Money, while annoying and tedious, was awfully helpful. How she wished she had some of her own! Then she wouldn't have to try to convince a group of people that her grandfather wasn't some horrible monster and that he was worth saving. Nobody should ever have to make such an argument in the first place. Not about their own family.

The only family she had left.

The board members pulled away from their huddle and sat, each one with their hands folded in front of them on the table.

"The board has come to a decision. We will fund this mission, the rescue of Sebastian, Benedict, and, yes, Alistair. But in no way are the Filipendulous Five allowed to be members of the society again. And once this whole operation is over and done with, the team will quietly disappear and stop making a nuisance of themselves," said Lady Trill.

Evie nodded and looked at Catherine, who sat stone-faced.

"Further to that point, we demand that the map, all five pieces of it plus the key, be destroyed once and for all. So that this nonsense never happens again." Lady Trill paused for a moment. "We will not, however, destroy the submarine's orb, as it is a remarkable piece of science. It shall instead be locked up and not be quite as easy to access as it evidently once was." She looked at Catherine for her response.

It took the explorer a moment before she replied. Then, slowly and with some effort, Catherine said: "Sounds fair. Evie?"

For a moment Evie didn't understand. It wasn't really up to her to agree or not agree. She wasn't a member of the Filipendulous Five. But then: "Oh, yes, the orb. I still have it. It's on my shelf in my room." She had managed to protect it even when they'd been chased through the society headquarters by the terrifying men. And even though it had been briefly taken from her by Mr. K, that was hardly her fault. Besides, he'd dropped it after Sebastian had burned the key, and she'd kept it safe since then. She felt more than capable of continuing to do so. But it was okay. She trusted the board, even if she wasn't entirely sure she liked them.

"Then it's settled. Let this meeting be adjourned," said Llewellyn Tracy, standing.

"I second the motion," said Myrtle, rising as well.

"Motion passed," said the Hopper, bouncing off his chair. "Now get me out of here. I need some tea."

In short order the three other board members had left, and Catherine, Myrtle, and Evie, still holding the pig in the teeny hat in her arms, were standing alone in the gloomy boardroom.

"That went well. Relatively," said Catherine quietly.

"All things are relative," replied Myrtle. She looked at the redhead and then placed her hand on Catherine's shoulder. Considering how much higher up her shoulders were than stout Myrtle's, it was a bit of a stretch.

Catherine gave her a small, sad smile, then turned to Evie. "I guess it's time to book a flight to Australia. Is your passport up-to-date?"

"It is," said Evie. "My parents always insisted." You never knew when it was going to be time for an adventure, her mother would always say. Thinking this made her feel both sad and hopeful. How she missed them.

"Oh, I've already booked a flight for the two of you. You'd better get packing. It leaves in three hours," said Myrtle.

"You booked us a flight?" asked Evie, astonished.

"And a bus from Cairns to Creaky Cove. And you have a reservation in a lovely-sounding little inn called the Outlook," added Myrtle. Myrtle glanced at the pig. "Of course, you'll have to leave that behind." The pig gave a tiny offended snort.

Evie looked down at it. It had been a great comfort, but of course, taking a pig in a teeny hat along on such an adventure didn't make sense. It would only be in the way. The pig stared up at her, and then, after a moment, its expression changed to one that meant either that it understood the situation or that it was feeling hungry.

Evie looked back to Myrtle, still confused. "But . . . how were you able to arrange all that?"

"I have some pocket change," said Myrtle, leading the way to the door. "If the board had said no, I still would have helped you out."

"But why? You hate the team more than anyone else does," said Evie.

"That's true."

"Then why?"

Myrtle held the door open for Evie and Catherine, and once they'd passed through, she turned out the light in the boardroom.

"Because it's the right thing to do."

➤ CHAPTER 5 ➤

In which there's a chase sequence.

A slide inflated immediately after the door handle had been activated, and Sebastian was grateful because he hadn't even waited to see how far down the ground was before he'd launched himself out through the door. Landing on the rubbery slide had felt almost like a miracle, and it was only then that he had realized how insane he'd been to leap before he looked.

But he didn't have much time to think about it, and certainly no time to look behind him. He landed at the bottom. The momentum brought him quickly to his feet, and then he was off running. He didn't know where he was going except toward the warmly lit airport in front of him, toward the glass walls and the large airplanes and the airport workers loading and unloading baggage. He ran as fast as he could, wondering if the three men in black were on his heels or if he looked like some crazy kid running around for no reason. He didn't really care. All he could think was, if he could lose them in the airport, he could find a flight back home. And all this would be a happy memory, some story he could tell Evie and Catherine when he got home. That time he was kidnapped and taken to South Korea.

He flew past a baggage handler, who stared at him. Then Sebastian ran through the sliding glass doors into the airport. He looked around, and it was at this moment that he finally glanced back. All three of the men were charging him fast, but he was relieved to see that they appeared to have left their weapons on the plane. Considering that airport security was so tight that having a too-big bottle of liquid was considered a threat, Sebastian wasn't surprised. But he was relieved.

Also he really had to start running again.

So he did. He ran to the left and through a solid-looking door into a service hallway, low and gray but wide enough to drive luggage trucks through. Like the truck that was coming for him right now. Sebastian flattened himself against the wall and watched as the truck sped past. That would hold up the men chasing him for a moment, at the very least.

And then he was running again.

As he searched for an escape from the tunnel, his mind flashed back to the battle at the Explorers Society, to running down hallways and around the glorious library, to fighting his way through a pit of foam pieces. He remembered himself and Evie at the university. At the zoo. He remembered it all. And the one thing he thought this moment as he finally spotted a staircase was *Man, you need to be in good shape to do this sort of thing.*

He took the stairs two at a time and burst out into a wide, brightly lit departures and arrivals lounge. It was full of travelers of all ages milling about, many looking bored or tired, except for the kids who were either extremely excited or extremely exhausted and having temper tantrums. Sound filled the hall completely. Announcements over the loudspeaker in Korean, English, and Chinese punctuated the noise at regular intervals. The beeping of little electric cars driving airport employees from one side of the facility to another was so constant that Sebastian hadn't realized it was meant as a warning to move out of the way until he was almost run over. And Sebastian maneuvered his way through it all, not running now. He didn't want to raise suspicions

or get jumped by any security guards, but he went as fast as he could walk.

He had no idea where to go from here, but he did know to follow the signs. Signs ... The Explorers Society ... Once again another flash, of seeing that sign in the alley oh so many moons ago.

How that sign had changed everything.

Now he needed only one: EXIT.

Finally he spotted it, and he picked up his pace, glancing behind him yet again. His heart flew up into his throat when he saw the three men in black crammed together on one of the little cars, speeding right for him. Sebastian had no choice but to run for it. He dashed forward and made his way through a large group of Italian tourists, all wearing colorful backpacks and speaking a mile a minute. They barely noticed him barrel through them toward the exit and baggage claim area. But they were awfully useful in blocking the little car.

Sebastian turned down the hallway and flew down the escalator, grateful that everyone in this particular airport seemed to appreciate the "stand right, walk left" rule.[8]

Of course, this meant it was just as easy for the men in black to chase him as it had been for him to run away, and Sebastian was now pretty sure he was about to be done for. Customs was fast approaching, and Sebastian had no idea what to do. He didn't have a passport with him; he didn't want to be stopped by police. He didn't want to be stopped at all. And he didn't generally enjoy the idea of starting his visit in a new country by breaking one of their laws. But considering he was trying to escape the clutches of some very dangerous men, he really hoped he would be forgiven.

Sebastian blended into the crowd waiting in line and then decided maybe his youth could work for him. He started to push through the crowd, apologizing. "My family is over there," he said, pointing. Though

---

[8] So few people really seem to understand it. And it's such a simple thing to follow, really. Stand on the right of the escalator if you want to ride it; walk on the left. Then everyone gets what they want! I don't know why it's that hard to do. I mean really, people! . . .

very few people seemed to understand the words, they seemed to understand the sentiment, and let him through. He eventually made it to the front and looked around. There, down the row, was a loud, boisterous American family unit. Hard to miss with the father laughing happily, to himself, it seemed, and the kids ignoring him, playing on their phones. Slowly, and hoping they wouldn't notice, Sebastian got in line behind them. Then, when they were called up to the customs official, he casually joined them as part of the group. As the customs officer was looking at their passports, Sebastian wandered through the family to the far side of the customs booth.

"Well, now. I don't recall having five kids," said the father, suddenly noticing Sebastian. Then he laughed at his own joke and turned back to the customs agent, who had looked up at that. "Hard to keep track of them all!" joked the father again, and the customs official sighed and looked back at the passports. As quickly as he could, Sebastian ducked around the desk and made his way toward the baggage claim area, trying to look like he totally belonged. Then he glanced over his shoulder, certain the men in black could not so easily get through customs.

No, it seemed they couldn't.

Instead they had just chosen sheer force, pushing

their way through the bodies and right past the customs booths.

Now not only were the men chasing Sebastian, but the border guards were chasing *them*!

Sebastian picked up his speed and ran into the large well-lit baggage claim area. He ran around a baggage carousel and looked behind him. There the men were, gaining ground. He turned just in time to career into a large trolley filled with giant suitcases. As if in slow motion, Sebastian flew into the luggage and over, doing a full flip by accident and crashing to the ground hard on his face.

The man pushing the cart came to his side and said something to him in Korean. Sebastian pushed himself up and apologized as the man stared at him with concern.

"Really, I'm okay," said Sebastian with a forced smile as he scrambled to his feet. "I just . . . I need to run." He pointed at the men in black closing in on him. The man turned and stared, and Sebastian took the moment to run for it.

Sebastian noticed a blur to his side and quickly glanced at it. A large security officer had broken off from chasing the men and was now chasing him, running right for him. Sebastian turned and looked ahead at the exit. Two other security guards were standing there, preparing to take him down as he approached the line of passengers pushing their luggage out through the arrivals gate. He was cornered. He was done for. There was nowhere for him to go, no escape.

He veered away from the exit and skirted another large carousel that obscured him from his pursuers. He skidded to a stop and looked around. To his right he saw a group of five teenagers. They were chatting loudly, while several larger men piled suitcase after suitcase onto a trolley. The men were about finished, and the boys started to make their way to the exit, each putting on a pair of sunglasses as they went. Without thinking, since evidently that was his new thing, Sebastian raced toward the wall of luggage on the trolley, leapt onto the side, and held on to it for dear life, ducking down low. He had no idea if any of the men on the other side had seen him; he just held fast and stared in front of him as he was pushed closer and closer to the exit. The security guards were on the other side of the luggage. They didn't seem to have seen him.

The man pushing the trolley itself, on the other hand . . .

Sebastian was forcefully wrenched upward and tossed to the side just in front of the exit doors, which swung open and then shut with each new exit. He skidded into an empty podium with no guard behind it and quickly jumped to his feet—only to turn and find himself face to face with Mr. M.

"Time to go," Mr. M said.

Mr. M grabbed for him, and Sebastian fled. He launched himself toward the doors as if somehow, if he got through them, he would find himself safely whisked through a magic portal far away from these tediously efficient men. There was something pathetically desperate about it all, and offensively illogical. The doors swung open, and he and the teenagers and their luggage pushers all passed through at the same time. Sebastian could feel a hand graze the back of his shirt. He took another giant leap. This time the hand caught his arm, and he struggled to keep moving forward.

He was through, but he was caught. The exit was not a portal to safety, as he had fantasized.

Suddenly there was a massive explosion of bright light. Mr. M released his grip, and Sebastian found himself tumbling into what looked and sounded like a screaming wall of fire.

➤ CHAPTER 6 ◄

In which Australia.

Evie stared out at the vast blackness before her. The bus driver had insisted that the view was fantastic during the day, a white sandy beach bordered by lush vegetation, stretching out to the Coral Sea. But right now, at the small bus stop where she and Catherine had been dropped off without much ceremony, it seemed like the end of the earth to Evie. She could smell salt in the air and hear waves somewhere off in the distance. Maybe the end of the earth was salty.

The stars were something, though. Bright pinpricks of light, a sweeping pattern caused by the overturning of the world's largest sugar container.

"Let's turn in," said Catherine. It was, like many

of Catherine's statements, more of an order than anything else, but Evie didn't want to argue. She was so tired she could barely stand, and so disoriented she could definitely have believed she was standing upside down here on the bottom of the world. She had no idea what day it was. If it hadn't been dark out, she wouldn't have even been sure it was night.

It didn't take long for them to "turn in." They just had to cross the street to a small two-story white-washed inn. The front veranda was lit, but no one was sitting in the chairs facing the sea. Evie and Catherine climbed the steps and went through the front door, over which hung a white sign with bright blue letters that read THE OUTLOOK. The foyer was compact, with a ceiling so low that Catherine had to bend a little. They walked over to the check-in desk, painted a gray-blue like the walls. Mounted behind it was a large yellow-and-red surfboard from which room keys were hanging. No one was there. But there was a little bell.

"May I ring the bell?" asked Evie.

Catherine looked at her in that way she did, with that puzzled expression, and Evie couldn't understand what she was confused about. Bells were fun to ring.

"You don't have to ask my permission," said Catherine.

Evie smiled and hit the bell. It made a very satisfying *ding*.

They stood there waiting for someone to come.

And continued to wait.

And wait.

Catherine cracked her neck and leaned her head to the right side to give the left a bit of a break.

Since no permission was required, Evie rang the bell again.

Suddenly a young woman, her dark, thick hair up in a messy bun, came flying down the stairs behind them near the entrance. She was out of breath and was wiping her hands on her apron. Though she seemed run ragged, she smiled brightly at them and dashed behind the desk, removing the apron and stashing it somewhere below.

"Hi! I'm Ruby. Welcome to the Outlook Inn. How can I help you?"

"I booked a room," said Catherine efficiently.

"You did?" Ruby looked shocked at that revelation. "Are you sure? With us? With the Outlook?"

Catherine's brow furrowed as she nodded. "Yes, my friend called the other day."

"Erik must have booked it, I guess," said Ruby, pulling out a black ledger almost as big as she was and dropping it with a thud on the desk. She opened it to the day's date and then stared, her eyes doubling in size. She then looked back up at the two of them. "Are you Catherine and Evie?" she asked.

"I'm Catherine, she's Evie," replied Catherine, making sure, Evie supposed, that Ruby didn't think she was both people.

"Well, I'll be. . . . A reservation. That's cool." Once more she grinned at them. Evie couldn't help but grin back. Ruby's energy was infectious.

"Yes, I suppose so. But we've been traveling a long time, and it would be nice to turn in," said Catherine.

"Of course!" said Ruby, closing the book. She looked at them for a moment. "Did you want only one room? I know mothers and daughters like to share, but we have so many rooms that if you wanted to each have your own . . . I have two that join each other with a door."

Ruby looked at Evie, and Evie didn't know what to say. She was still stuck on the "mothers and daughters" thing. She supposed it did make sense that Ruby would draw such a conclusion. After all, they were the right ages. And when did one see this particular pairing, really? An explorer and a granddaughter on a rescue mission? That wouldn't be nearly as common.

Still.

Mother.

Daughter.

She wasn't anyone's daughter. Not anymore.

When Evie didn't speak up, Catherine did. "Yes, that sounds nice."

Ruby nodded and grabbed two keys from the surf-board. "Follow me!"

And they did. They followed her back toward the entrance and then up the narrow staircase. The second-floor hallway was also narrow, but the ceiling was high and the walls painted a bright white. Hanging on them were photographs of the sea and surfers, and Evie looked at them with interest. If this was indeed what existed out in that blackness, then maybe their driver had been correct about the fantastic view.

"Here we go, rooms four and five," said Ruby, handing the keys to Catherine. "Please let me know if you need anything. There aren't . . . many of you . . . so you have my full attention. Breakfast is from seven to nine." Once more she smiled that broad smile of hers. And with a contented sigh that seemed to indicate she felt she'd done her job well, she turned on her heel and went back down the stairs.

"Here," said Catherine, handing Evie her key. After Evie took it, Catherine added, "Meet for breakfast at eight?"

Evie nodded, and then they split up, each slipping

a key into her respective door and going into her room.

Once inside, Evie felt a wave of exhaustion hit her. The bed looked so welcoming with its modern white duvet with a gray stripe across the bottom. A large black-and-white photograph of waves crashing on the shore hung over the headboard. The furniture was a hodgepodge of items you'd find on the seaside, all painted white. The bedside tables were covered with a mosaic of seashells, and the curtains looked like netting. A chair in one corner was made of driftwood, and the low table before it was made of half a surfboard.

It was all very pleasant and very cozy, and Evie dropped her little bag in the corner before flopping onto the bed. It was soft and enveloped her like a sigh. And then, not meaning to, and still in her clothes and shoes, Evie fell into a deep, dull sleep.

➤ CHAPTER 7 ⤛

In which we meet
the Lost Boys.

Now, here's a little-known fact: Screaming Wall of Fire was a not-so-famous metal band back in the eighties. They began their very short-lived career in a bar in Wisconsin, even though they were all from Detroit. After they struck their first chord, several customers had to be taken to the hospital for damage to their eardrums. And one unfortunate bartender went to a psychiatric hospital, the man being unable to understand how such a sound could exist in the universe, thus making him question his very existence.[9]

---

[9] This also happens to be the name of the documentary film about them, which was way more successful than the band itself. It even won an Oscar.

And that was it. One chord, one night, one bar in Wisconsin.

However. The band the Lost Boys had managed to play many chords so far in their rather short but hugely successful career. The only unfortunate souls ever sent to hospitals were fans who twisted ankles or wrists or whatever when trying to get a closer look at them. It was actually a miracle that none of the members of the Lost Boys ever got injured themselves. Especially since wherever they went, they were greeted by bright flashing cameras and walls of screaming fans.

Sebastian certainly found the experience utterly disorienting, and it took him a good moment before he understood what was going on: that what he'd thought was a screaming wall of fire was actually a throng of fans yelling and paparazzi taking pictures with flashes happening fast one after the other, and that he just happened to have exited the airport next to one of the most popular K-pop bands currently on the scene. He was lying at the feet of a particularly excited group of teenage girls who started furiously taking selfies with him as he tried to stand up.

"No, no," he said, waving his arms frantically. "I'm nobody."

But they didn't seem to care. One even gave him a kiss on the cheek, and that caused his entire face to go red. For a moment he felt even more disoriented than when he'd thought he was facing a screaming wall of fire.

Also, he really didn't have time for this.

He turned and saw Mr. M keeled over, holding his one eye, blinded by the flashes of a thousand cameras and phones, and he realized what was happening. He needed to take quick advantage. He bolted over to join the band, and that was when one of the teens, a boy with black hair that flopped over his left eye, finally noticed him. The boy asked him a question as Sebastian walked quickly beside him.

"I'm sorry. I don't understand," replied Sebastian.

"Oh, sorry about that!" replied the boy with almost no hint of an accent. "I asked who you were."

Sebastian knew he had to get the explanation out as quickly and as efficiently as possible before Mr. M regained his sight, and before the other men got to him too. "I'm Sebastian, I've been kidnapped, I'm trying to escape." There it was. As straightforward as he could be.

The boy thought for a moment as they quickly marched past the fans and paparazzi straining against the ropes holding them at bay. It was silly, really. The fans could easily have ducked underneath. But it was a kind of respectful chaos. One of the boys in the band up ahead decided to do a front flip just for laughs, and the crowd went wild.

"Okay. Well, let's help you escape, then," said the boy. He took off his sunglasses and passed them to Sebastian, who immediately put them on. Then, in a perfectly timed moment, a fan tossed a baseball hat toward the band. The boy caught it deftly, grinned, and passed that to Sebastian. Sebastian looked at it for a moment. It had a cartoon version of the boy on it with a giant heart drawn around that. The cartoon was winking.

"Put it on," said the boy.

Sebastian reluctantly did.

In the time it had taken them to effect his costume change, the band and their team had made it past the rope and were walking toward the exit to outside. This was making life a lot harder for the large guys pushing the luggage, who now had to do double duty as body-guards. It wasn't the fans who were the biggest issue. Sure, some were overly enthusiastic and tried to run up and touch the band members, but the press were the larger problem. They had no respect for personal space, or for the band in general, and they were liter-ally falling over themselves to get a shot of the teens or a sound bite. They kept shouting loud questions, shoving mikes around the luggage. None of the boys were talking, though. In fact, the boy with his hair to his shoulders actively attacked one of the cameras, pushing back against it and causing its owner to fall over onto his backside. His action caused a chain reaction of other camera operators and reporters tripping over each other until there was quite a pile left behind.

The boy who'd done the flip yelled back to the rest of the band, and everyone hastened their pace, including Sebastian, who was trying to keep his head down as much as he could. Then, all of a sudden, he could feel a cool breeze on his face, and he dared to look up. They were outside, being quickly escorted onto a large black bus. The band rushed on, and Sebastian had no choice but to follow. He was stunned as he stepped inside. This was not an ordinary bus like the one he took to school. He was walking into a high-tech apartment. The place was decked out with black leather couches and chairs. A giant TV hung on one side of the bus, with video game consoles attached. Right where he'd entered, behind the bus driver, there was a little kitchenette with snacks, and the boys had already grabbed some chips and sodas and were lounging on the couches as Sebastian walked toward them in awe. The floor was reflective metallic tile, and illuminating his path were two rows of lights that slowly changed colors.

The boy who'd helped him out gestured for him to join them just as the bus started moving, and Sebastian staggered over and sat down at the end of one of the couches. The other boys stared at him. This was clearly the first time they'd noticed him. The long-haired boy asked something, and the floppy-haired boy replied.

"Oh, you speak English," said the long-haired boy. He had a thicker accent, but Sebastian was just impressed that it seemed everyone knew at least two languages. He only knew the one himself.

"Yeah, sorry." He felt obligated to apologize for his ignorance. It wasn't something he often felt the need to do, as he rarely felt he didn't know stuff.

"Don't be sorry to speak English," replied the boy, confused.

Sebastian wasn't sure what to say, so he said the only thing that came to mind: "Sorry."

The long-haired boy shook his head, then turned back to the floppy-haired boy and asked a question. After a short conversation, the long-haired boy stared back at Sebastian, wide-eyed. "Kidnapped?" he said.

Sebastian now felt a little awkward. "Uh, yeah."

"Who kidnapped you?"

This felt like an almost impossible question to answer. Answering it literally would be meaningless to these boys: "Three gentlemen with different letters as their last names. Also, a pilot is involved, but I've never met her." And answering it more specifically would take a long time. Also, it was kind of private. After all, there was still a man's life at stake here. Not that Sebastian thought that this particular group of teenage pop stars were secret spies out to destroy Alistair Drake or anything.

But then again . . . maybe they were. Who could really know?

"It's a long story, but they want what's in my brain."

"Like, your hypothalamus?" asked the boy who had done the flip, sitting himself across from Sebastian.

"My . . . No . . . no, not my hypothalamus." Sebastian was startled by the boy's knowledge of the term in English.

"Ah. Your cerebral cortex, then?" The boy leaned forward, looking very serious.

"No, no, they don't want any part of my actual brain."

"You have knowledge of something," said the floppy-haired boy.

Sebastian looked back at him and nodded. "Well,

it's more like I saw something, and remembered that something, and then that something was destroyed."

"Got it," replied the floppy-haired boy. "Scary situation."

"Yeah," replied Sebastian, grateful for the empathy.

"Sounds exciting!" said the long-haired boy.

"It's really not," replied Sebastian, not entirely sure why he was lying. Because it was actually kind of exciting. And this was kind of exciting too. Being on this tour bus, being in South Korea, meeting these boys. But while he was beginning to be more honest with himself about this new appreciation of excitement, he certainly wasn't ready to be honest with everyone else.

"Well, we're heading home, and there we can talk more. Right now have some snacks. I'm Kwan," said the floppy-haired boy, and he stuck out his hand.

"Nice to meet you," said Sebastian as he took it. They shook.

"This is Ujin." Kwan pointed to the long-haired boy. "Toy." The boy who'd done the flip. His hair was cut so short he was almost bald. "That's Yejun."

A boy Sebastian hadn't met yet who was over by the kitchenette rifling through the snacks, he popped up and looked at Sebastian hard from over his glasses, then said, "Hey."

"And the silent one way down over there is Cheese."

Cheese was sitting down the bus on a bunk in what looked to be the sleeping area. Like the others, his hair was black, but the tips were a vibrant purple. He gave Sebastian a nod, and Sebastian returned it.

"Well, I'm Sebastian," Sebastian announced to the rest. "And you guys seem to be in a band of some kind. Uh, a pretty popular band," he continued, trying to make pleasant small talk.

Toy choked on his soda, and Ujin had to slap him on the back a few times.

Kwan laughed. "You could say that. I guess you've never heard of the Lost Boys."

"No. I'm sorry." Sebastian felt sincerely bad about that, though it wasn't exactly a surprise. At least, not to him. He tried to offer an explanation: "But really, I don't know anything about popular music anywhere. My parents prefer classical, and we listen to a lot of opera." Kwan's eyes went wide at that, and Sebastian wasn't sure if he was appalled or impressed. "Uh, sometimes if we're in a silly mood we listen to Gilbert and Sullivan."

"Who's that?" asked Ujin.

"Oh, it's a writer-and-composer team who wrote these funny operettas in the late eighteen hundreds in England. Um . . . *The Pirates of Penzance*?" asked Sebastian hopefully.

Ujin shook his head.

"Okay, well, they wrote these funny opera things. Um . . . they're pretty funny. . . ." Why oh why couldn't he think of a better descriptor?

" 'I am the very model of a modern major-general. I've information vegetable, animal, and mineral . . . ,' " recited Kwan slowly.

Sebastian turned and looked at him, surprised. "Yeah! Yeah, that's from *Pirates*, yeah. You know it?"

Kwan smiled. "A bit." He stood up and crossed over to Yejun, who passed him another soda. He tapped at it thoughtfully.

Suddenly the bus lurched to the left, sending both Yejun and Kwan flying, depositing them on the sofa nearby.

A voice came over the loudspeaker, explaining what had happened, Sebastian assumed.

"What's going on?" he asked as Kwan staggered back over to him.

"It looks like your kidnappers may have found us," he replied as he walked toward the rear of the bus. Sebastian stood and followed.

The bus's windows were so darkly tinted that it was hard to see anything outside except the lights of cars whooshing past. But the rear window was covered by a blind, not a tint, so they were able to pull it up and see what was going on. Cheese joined them, and the three boys stared at the car behind them.

"Our driver said they tried to run us off the on-ramp to the bridge. There." Kwan pointed. "I think that's them. What do you think?"

Sebastian thought Kwan was exactly correct. It wasn't hard to recognize his three pursuers staring at the bus, as menacing as always.

"Whoa, cool looks," said Ujin, materializing at his side.

Sebastian had never thought of it that way, but they were indeed very distinct-looking guys. "They should be in a band," Sebastian said quietly to himself.

Cheese snorted and gave Sebastian a hearty slap on the back. *I guess he liked that,* thought Sebastian. *Which is weird. I'm not normally the funny one.*

"I hate tailgating," said Sebastian as the car drove closer and closer, practically touching the bus's bumper.

"What's that?" asked Ujin.

"When people drive too close to you. It's usually meant to intimidate you. To get you to speed up, break the law. It's so disrespectful." Of course, in this case there was a little more to it, but still, the fundamentals of tailgating had always really upset Sebastian.

"Well, it's working on me," said Kwan. "Those guys mean business."

"Yeah."

They closed the blind and made their way back to the couches. The rest of the band gathered around. "What does everyone think?" asked Kwan.

"I think those guys are the bad guys," replied Toy.

"Me too," said Ujin.

"I think," said Yejun, carefully removing his glasses and giving them a wipe, "it's time for a car chase."

Sebastian wasn't entirely sure he agreed with them. He was feeling ridiculously guilty, pushing these really nice guys into such a dangerous situation. "You know, you could just drop me off, let me run for it."

"No way! You're an honorary member of the Lost Boys now!" said Kwan.

"Since when?" asked Sebastian, completely confused.

"Since just this second."

"Okay, but that doesn't make sense. You guys don't really know me. Plus, of course, there's the fact that I don't sing or dance—"

Kwan raised his hand, and Sebastian stopped talking. "And your band name is going to be . . ." He looked to his bandmates for help.

"Mr. Kidnap!" said Toy enthusiastically.

"English!" said Yejun.

"No. I know," said Kwan with a grin. "Opera Boy."

Sebastian furrowed his brow, not sure that was the best choice, and not too terribly happy about being given a nickname in the first place. He had always been suspicious of nicknames.

"Yes!" said Ujin. And everyone else nodded enthusiastically. Cheese even let out a small whoop.

Well, evidently Sebastian was outnumbered on that one.

Kwan stood and gestured for Sebastian to follow, which he did. They made their way to the front of the bus and stood next to the driver.

"Okay," said Kwan, "let's lose those guys."

The driver nodded and veered left sharply, sending Sebastian stumbling toward him. Sebastian grabbed onto the driver's seat for dear life. "Hang on!" said the driver, and smiled at Sebastian.

Probably should have said that first, thought Sebastian as he straightened up. He stared out the front window as the driver, with impressive dexterity, slalomed between various cars on the brightly lit suspension bridge. The bus was fast approaching a pair of inverted-Y-shaped towers from which cables ran down to street level. From Sebastian's angle they looked like gleaming translucent pyramids. He stared up in wonder as the bus passed under them.

"We are on the Incheon Bridge, the longest bridge

in South Korea, the sixth-longest cable bridge in the world," Kwan informed him with a smile. Sebastian could only nod in response. "We usually go a bit of a longer way around to Seoul, through Incheon, to avoid the reporters if we can," explained Kwan. It was hardly necessary for him to do so, as Sebastian had no idea what a direct route would look like anyway. But he did appreciate that Kwan cared to explain such things, and thus seemed to understand that going any route but direct was generally illogical. He was starting to really like this guy.

Despite the great length of the bridge they were driving so fast that they were soon across it and heading toward the lights in the distance approaching them quickly. The bus continued its dangerous dance, skipping past cars and even at times driving on the shoulder of the highway itself. It was a dance that seemed to take both forever and no time at all. Sebastian was shocked, when Kwan finally announced they'd made it into Seoul itself, to learn that they'd been driving for over an hour. Why had it seemed so fast? He supposed running for your life did make the time pass.

This was his first real view of the city. It looked very modern to Sebastian, with brightly lit signs and tall buildings everywhere. Best were the occasional glimpses of what he'd learned was called the N Seoul

Tower, standing on a mountain in the distance. It almost seemed like a beacon.

The bus whipped around corners, and still, every time Sebastian looked back at Toy, perched at the rear window, he'd see the boy shake his head. "Still on us!"

"Man, they are relentless!" said Sebastian. "Are you sure you don't want to just drop me off? I can make a run for it. In some ways it's harder to chase a person than a bus."

"No way," replied Kwan. "Anyway, we're almost there, and there's no way they'll find us then."

"What are you talking about? They're right behind us!"

"You'll see."

It seemed impossible. They were downtown, surrounded by tall buildings and stores and restaurants. There was no place to hide a bus. There was certainly no way to outrun their pursuers. The bus turned sharply then and immediately began its descent into an underground garage. Sebastian couldn't help but duck as they approached the low ceiling, as if somehow that would help the bus be less tall. The bus cleared the entrance, just barely. Sebastian turned around.

"They're still there!" shouted Toy.

"Don't worry," said Kwan, grinning from ear to ear, seeming to be thoroughly enjoying this.

"I think I will, actually," replied Sebastian, closing his eyes and bracing himself as they headed at top speed toward a wall. The bus veered suddenly, impossibly, to the left and made it around the corner. They were now heading up a tight narrow ramp. Then there was another wall, and another. As impressed as he was by their driver's skill, Sebastian couldn't help but start to feel a little nauseous, and more than ready for all the quick turns to stop.

"It's working. They're falling behind!" called Toy.

"We just need them to fall back a little more," said Kwan, almost to himself.

Sebastian stared out the front window as they drove up and up out of the garage and straight toward what seemed to be the edge of the parking platform.

"Uh, guys?" said Sebastian, staring at the railing and the roofs of various businesses across the street.

"Just a little farther . . . ," said Kwan.

They didn't seem to be slowing down. In fact, they seemed to be speeding up.

"Uh . . . guys . . . ?" repeated Sebastian, this time backing away slowly from the front window into the kitchenette area.

"Now!" called out Kwan. Sebastian watched the boy brace himself, and was reminded of that landing he'd experienced in the plane not so long ago. He grabbed on to whatever he could find, which unfortunately turned out to be the handle of the fridge. The refrigerator door swung open and threw him backward, skidding on the shiny floor. All he could see through the front window were stars, and all he could feel was a sense of weightlessness as his body rose into the air. Yejun grabbed his wrist and held him tight.

They landed with a thud, but the connection they made with the ground was not nearly as impactful as Sebastian had been anticipating. Instead, it still felt like they were falling, but much more slowly. Sebastian stood up and went to the front. There was nothing outside the window. Only blackness. No stars. No rooftops. He turned around and saw Toy walking toward the front.

"Are they gone?" Sebastian asked.

"Of course they are," replied Toy with a grin.

Nothing seemed particularly "of course" about the situation, but Sebastian was both too confused and too relieved to care. He stood next to Kwan. "Where are we?"

"We're at home base," replied Kwan, turning and giving him a smile.

"We are?"

Kwan nodded. "Yup. This is the secret bus entrance.

We don't use it unless we're being chased by the paparazzi. Or kidnappers." He grinned again.

"Oh."

"We're in an elevator right now," explained Toy. "We jumped onto the platform from the parking garage, and it's taking us down."

For a moment Sebastian thought back to the elevator in the Explorers Society, that platform he'd once thought was just an entrance but had turned out to be a lift instead. It was kind of like that now, he supposed. Just way bigger. And way darker.

His lack of response quieted down the rest of the boys. The other members of the band gathered round, and they all silently stood staring at the black wall in front of them, waiting.

A few more moments passed, and then a bright white light broke the darkness from below and rose until the entire front window was filled with it. Sebastian blinked a few times, and once he'd adjusted to the sight, he realized they were entering a large, immaculately kept garage. Not like the dark gray one they'd just left, but more like a showroom you'd see at a car dealership. From his vantage point Sebastian could see several sleek-looking cars in front of them, all different colors. When the bus clunked to a stop and the door was opened, Sebastian marveled as he stepped out.

"Cool, right?" said Kwan, walking up beside him.

Sebastian was not old enough to drive and had never really paid that much attention to cars, but he appreciated an attractive-looking object, and all these cars were definitely seriously pretty.

"Very cool."

"Come on," said Kwan. "I don't know about you, but I'm famished!"

➤ CHAPTER 8 ◄

In which creepy things
happen in the middle of the
night. Because, of course,
creepy things always happen
in the middle of the night
and not when it's bright and
cheerful outside.

Evie awoke suddenly. Her face was still smushed
into the duvet, and for a moment she had absolutely no idea where she was. She was so disoriented
that for the briefest second she thought she was home.
Not at the Explorers Society, not even at the Wayward
School, but home. Actually home. Home from two
years ago. Home in her room with her parents reading
downstairs. Home with her stuffed animals around
her, with her books on her shelves. Beneath the mural
her mother had painted over her bed.

But it was so quick, so fleeting, and soon she pushed
herself up to sit on the hotel bed in a daze. Australia.
She was in Australia. Though even telling herself that,

she couldn't quite register the information. It seemed the stuff of fantasy that she was on the other side of the world, but it wasn't. She was here.

She was awake.

Evie looked over her shoulder toward the curtains. Then she got up and crossed the room to pull them open. Still dark out. Still nighttime. Why had she woken up, then?

Another loud thud from below.

Another?

When had been the first?

Evie looked down to the street and saw a figure bent over something. It was trying to move what looked like a large box. No, not a box, a wagon. A wheel was caught, it seemed. Another thud as the figure tried to dislodge the wheel.

The thud. Yes, the thud had woken her up. The first one. The one that only her subconscious had heard.

For a moment Evie wondered if she should help the figure. But there was a strange urgency to its movements. It gave off the impression that it didn't want to be seen, let alone helped. It was looking around furtively, its head jerking at the slightest noise. Suddenly it turned and looked right up at her window, and Evie ducked out of sight, not certain why she felt like she had to hide but sure it was the right thing to

do. As she slowly rose and peeked over the edge of the windowsill at the figure, now back to doing whatever it was doing, she thought help was the last thing it wanted. But what was it doing, and why so late at night?

Evie felt uneasy now. She was witnessing something, and it felt like something not good. What was in the wagon? she wondered. Then she stopped wondering because her mind was going to some seriously dark places to answer the question.

Instead she thought of Sebastian. Alone, unsafe, with three scary men up to no good. Just like this figure. She hoped Sebastian was okay. She more than hoped. She wasn't sure what she would do if he wasn't. She hoped they'd find Benedict soon, and she hoped they were right—that the men who had taken Sebastian were heading to Benedict too.

She hoped she and Catherine would be able to protect Benedict and save Sebastian, and all would be well.

She hoped she wasn't being a little too optimistic.

Another thud, and the wheel came free. The figure moved to the front of the wagon and started pulling again. The wagon followed the figure, and Evie watched as they both disappeared down the street and around the corner. Evie kept watching, though, kept straining her eyes into the darkness to see if there was anything more. Or if the figure would return. After fifteen minutes she gave up and looked out directly before her to the blackness beyond. Then she drew the curtains and returned to the bed.

This time she changed into her pajamas and climbed under the soft down comforter. The room was pleasantly air-conditioned, and she felt downright cozy and safe. Funny that something made of down and cotton could make one feel safe. They were hardly protective materials. It would have made more sense to feel that way if she was sleeping under chain mail. Still. It was what it was. She curled up on her side and fell asleep.

Again.

➤ CHAPTER 9 ◄

In which we get
to know Kwan.

Dinner was fast and furious as each of the boys gulped down the food waiting for them on the glossy white dining table in the equally glossy white dining room. It was like they hadn't been fed in days, instead of having just stuffed their faces full with snacks on the bus. Sebastian wasn't exactly an exception to the behavior, though while he could easily shovel in the steamed dumplings and fried pancake, the spicy kimchi caught in his throat a little. The thing that truly slowed him down, however, was finding a moment to ask them for a phone or something so he could contact his parents now that he was safe and sound. He had tried once to ask the boys, when they had first sat down in the white dining chairs that seemed molded out of one solid piece of hard plastic, but the boys didn't seem to have heard him, in their excitement to eat dinner.

So Sebastian now sat there, slowly eating and watching the giant screens on all four glossy white walls of the dining room, showing a variety of the Lost Boys' videos. He wasn't sure if the videos played all the time or if it was for his benefit, but he was quite impressed by them. They were slick and well-made, clearly with big budgets and lots of special effects. And several of them were in English, which surprised Sebastian but helped explain why the boys were able to speak with him so easily. He supposed the Lost Boys were trying to break into the North American pop scene and had therefore learned the language. It also explained Cheese's nickname. Well, why it was an English word, at least, not so much why they called him that in the first place. At any rate, it was admirable that they were trying to break into a whole new market.

But even more than that, he was impressed with how talented his new friends were. Especially when it came to dancing. Toy was particularly athletic, but all the boys were able to perform intricate dance moves in sync with each other, always with Kwan standing front and center. Their singing was excellent as well, though Sebastian was aware that there were computers that helped make voices sound more on pitch, so he couldn't be certain of their skill level. The dancing, though, was obvious. There was no faking that.

"What do you think?" asked Kwan, noticing that Sebastian's eating pace had slowed.

"You guys are great. I wish I could do that." Sebastian wasn't sure exactly why he'd said that last part. At no point in his life had he ever had the desire to dance or perform. At least, not before now. But all that was beside the point. Finally he had a chance to ask his question. "So, this has all been great and all, but I really need to call home—"

"I bet you can!" said Ujin, pulling his hair back into a low ponytail and standing.

"Bet I can what?" asked Sebastian. The statement made no sense. Of course he knew he could call home. Ujin made his way into an empty area by the head of the table, moving the chair to one side.

"Come on, Opera Boy!" he said, gesturing for Sebastian to join him.

"Are we going to make a phone call?" asked Sebastian, still confused.

"We're going to dance!"

Oh! "No, no. This is very silly, and I'm pretty tired, and I really should call—"

Suddenly there was the sound of slow clapping, and Sebastian turned to see the rest of the boys with big grins on their faces encouraging him to stand. "No, really. I should . . ." But the clapping was getting louder and faster, drowning him out. This was ridiculous. The clapping got faster and faster. Okay, fine, he'd do it, and then hopefully they'd listen to him. With great reluctance Sebastian was up on his feet and joining Ujin at the head of the table.

"Stand next to me," said Ujin.

Sebastian did and stared at the remaining band members, who had now stopped clapping and were all smiling at him, thoroughly enjoying themselves.

"Let's start easy. Just follow me. One step to the left. One to the right. And then slide. . . ." Ujin took a wide step and dragged his other foot over to match it. "Then do it but toward the back. Then toward the left. Then toward the front." He repeated the footwork facing different directions.

Well, that didn't look too hard. Sebastian took one step to the left, then one to the right; then he attempted the slide. His rubber sole squeaked a little and caught on the floor, but otherwise he managed it okay. Ujin smiled encouragingly, and Sebastian continued with the rest of the directions, finding the footwork getting easier each time.

"Cool! Now with arms."

Sebastian had always assumed the key to dancing was the feet, but after watching the fast and intricate hand gestures Ujin did to match the footwork, he was starting to doubt that opinion.

"Uh, can you do that again?" asked Sebastian after a failed attempt had resulted in his punching his own nose.

"Totally!" Ujin showed him the moves again, and somehow Sebastian managed to punch himself in the nose again.

This time Cheese burst out laughing and Sebastian felt pretty embarrassed.

"It's all about practicing. Do it one more time," said Kwan, giving Cheese a firm look, making the boy stop mid-guffaw. "But do it half speed."

Sebastian was feeling pretty done with this. He couldn't even get three silly steps. But he nodded and did the hand gestures at half the speed, with Ujin doing the same.

"Hey, you did it!" said Toy, applauding.

It seemed like a small success, but he had indeed done it. At the very least he'd managed not to injure himself. Whether or not he looked nearly as cool as Ujin was something else.

"Okay, full speed now!" instructed Kwan, and Sebastian followed their instructions: once, twice, a third time. And he was starting to feel like he was getting the hang of it.

"Okay, so we're going to do that four times in a row, and then we end taking a pose," said Ujin.

"A pose?" Sebastian didn't like the sound of that.

"Just something cool," said Yejun.

Oh, well, that was easy, then.

"Let's do this!"

To Sebastian's horror, loud music started to play from somewhere, and the rest of the group leapt up to their feet and stood beside him and Ujin.

"Ready . . . and . . . go!" shouted Ujin. And they were dancing, all of them were dancing, and so was Sebastian, for that matter, even though he felt like he was a half beat behind everyone. To the right. To the back. To the left. To the front. And . . . pose.

The rest of the boys struck poses that clearly had been well practiced and definitely fit the mandate of "cool." Sebastian, on the other hand, just stood there awkwardly, kind of like he was waiting for the light to change so he could cross the street.

"Okay, we'll work on the pose later," said Kwan, "but that was awesome! You're a natural, Opera Boy!"

Sebastian was pretty sure he was neither awesome at dancing nor a natural, but it was nice of Kwan to say. Also, well, it had been pretty fun.

"Ah, we have a new member, I see!" said an unfamiliar voice.

Sebastian turned to see a tall balding man wearing yellow tinted sunglasses standing in the doorway, smiling at them all.

"Ah! Suwon hyung, meet Opera Boy!" said Kwan, noticing the man and heading over to him.

"Interesting name," replied Suwon, raising his eyebrows.

"Oh, it's not my real name. My real name is Sebastian." Yet again more proof that nicknames just made things more complicated and that really there wasn't much point to them.

Except, of course, when they kind of made you feel like you fit in with the group. And that it showed they cared enough about you to give you a neat name.

No. Nicknames were still inconvenient and pointless. Sebastian resisted thinking otherwise.

"Well, Sebastian, I hope you enjoy your stay with us," said Suwon.

"Thank you Mr. Hyung."

"Ah no," said Suwon with a small smile. "Suwon is my name. They call me Suwon hyung or just Hyung as a show of respect and also a sign of our closeness. You see, 'hyung' is . . . well, you don't have these where you are from. We have honorifics here in Korea that we put after the names of people depending on our relationship to them. It is like a title. Like father or mother, I suppose for you. Literally it means 'older brother,' but I am not actually their brother, of course." He looked at the boys fondly for a moment.

Sebastian thought this calm quiet was the perfect moment to finally ask. "Oh, I see, that's very interesting. Um . . . Suwon, I was hoping I could call my parents."

"Your parents." Suwon looked at him with an expression Sebastian couldn't read.

"Uh, yeah. As you might have guessed, I'm not local. My family's a full ocean away, and I need to tell them I'm okay."

"You're alone, here in South Korea?" asked Suwon. This didn't seem to be the real question, though.

"Yes."

There was a long pause. "Tomorrow. Tomorrow you can call. It is almost morning as it is. Right now it is time for sleep. You will find we stick to a very rigorous schedule here." Suwon gave Kwan a meaningful look.

"But—" started Sebastian.

He was interrupted by Kwan. "Time to turn in!" Kwan then said something in Korean, and the rest of the boys nodded and quickly made their way past Suwon, each giving him a high five as they did. "Come on, you can bunk with me," said Kwan to Sebastian, who nodded and followed, giving Suwon a reluctant high five, though it felt really weird to.

Soon they were separated from the other boys and in Kwan's massive bedroom, which was decorated a lot like the tour bus, dark walls with a large TV and gaming consoles and a huge bed and a large black leather sofa. Sebastian looked around for a computer or a phone. He couldn't find either.

"Hey, do you have a phone?"

Kwan shook his head, kicked off his shoes, and made his way across the room to where there was a variety of instruments hanging on the wall, including several electric guitars. There was a full drum kit sitting in front of them.

"What about a computer, or really anything so I can contact my parents?" said Sebastian as he wandered over to join Kwan by the instruments.

"Hyung said you could call tomorrow," replied Kwan. It felt like he wasn't really paying attention.

"I know. I just thought that maybe . . . if you had a phone. Why don't you have a phone?" It seemed weird that Kwan didn't have such commonplace objects. Especially given the wealth of other things he did have.

"Do you play an instrument?" asked Kwan.

"Oh, uh, no, not really." Sebastian touched the cymbal on the kit.

"You should. Playing music is really freeing."

"Well, I feel pretty free generally, I guess. . . ." Sebastian wasn't sure what to make of this conversation. Everything was confusing, and nothing made sense. Two of his least favorite things.

"You like the drums?" asked Kwan.

Sebastian felt the cool metal of the cymbal under his fingers. He didn't really know if he liked them or not. Music and the arts and all those things weren't really what people did in his family. He'd never tried an instrument. Had never thought to try.

"Maybe." Sebastian kept his hand on the cymbal for some reason. Possibly a symbolic one.

"We'll teach you the drums," said Kwan with a smile.

"I don't think we'll have time for that," replied Sebastian. A part of him thought it was a very kind and generous offer, but another part of him was just even more confused.

"Oh, we'll have time. And of course you can also learn singing and dancing."

"Again, I really don't think—"

"We have a big show the day after tomorrow. A big concert. Sold out. The last leg of our tour. You'll see how much fun it is then. You'll get a lot more into the idea, I bet."

"Okay."

Kwan sighed hard. Then he finally wandered away from the instruments and sat on the edge of his bed. "You don't know our band, do you?"

"Oh. Uh . . . well . . . no." What was Kwan talking about? Also why did Sebastian feel bad about saying no, for some reason?

"So I guess you don't know much about K-pop in general?"

"I don't." Where was Kwan going with this, Sebastian wondered.

"Well, it's really popular. And basically, some bands are formed organically. You know, friends and stuff."

"Yeah?" Sebastian was still holding on to the cymbal, he realized. He let it go, walked over to the couch, and sat down. Like Kwan, he sat on the edge. Unlike Kwan, he was *feeling* on edge.

"Yeah, and sometimes they're created. By the record labels. There's training when you're young, there's auditions, trying to find the right group balance."

"Sure." Sebastian knew of some American groups that had also been formed sort of that way.

"And then there's us. We're kind of a combination. Some of us knew each other and Suwon hyung, and some of us auditioned. When we were younger." Another pause.

"Okay." Sebastian felt obligated to fill every silence provided by Kwan.

"I'm sixteen."

"Yeah. I thought you were, maybe." He wasn't exactly sure why Kwan was telling him his age, but Sebastian was just going to go with it for now.

"When I was your age, I thought this was all I wanted."

"Right."

"But now . . . I don't know. . . ." Kwan stopped. He looked at his feet.

"Now you're not so sure?" Finally Sebastian was starting to figure it out.

Kwan nodded. He didn't look up.

"Well, that's normal. People change their minds about what they want to be when they grow up. Like, as of last month, all I wanted to be was a neuro-surgeon, and now . . ." Sebastian stopped.

Kwan looked at him. "Now?"

Sebastian wasn't sure he could say it out loud. He wasn't 100 percent sure he actually truly believed it. After all, there were still many things about being a brain surgeon that excited him. But none could hold a candle to the other thing.

To exploring.

Saying it out loud would make it real. Would make everything he'd ever wanted in his life vanish in one pronouncement. And he wasn't ready. Not for that. Not for the scary vastness of unknown dreams that lay ahead.

"Now I'm not sure," concluded Sebastian. "Any-way. The point is, you've tried the K-pop thing, you gave it a fair shot. Maybe it's time for something new?"

Kwan shook his head. "I can't. I have fans. I don't want to let people down."

"You're just a teenager. You're not a grown-up or anything," replied Sebastian, shocked that so much heavy responsibility lay on Kwan's shoulders. Except of course it wasn't like Sebastian didn't have his own share. He and Evie, that is.

"Yeah, well . . . I still have responsibilities. I mean, maybe, if they could find a replacement . . ." Kwan stopped talking and sighed. He looked up, and then, realizing maybe he'd gotten a bit too personal, he smiled that big smile of his. Then quite theatrically he stretched his arms way above his head and yawned. When he'd finished, he said, "Anyway, you can take the bed if you want. I'll sleep on the sofa."

"No, the sofa is fine," Sebastian replied.

"You sure? You're the guest."

"Yes. I'm also totally exhausted. I could sleep on the dining room table, I'm so tired." It was true. He was fading fast. The weight of everything that had happened to him up until this moment was suddenly overpowering.

"Okay, good night!" Kwan called out, and in one swift motion he tucked himself into the giant bed, virtually disappearing under a mass of covers and pillows.

"Good night," Sebastian replied, and lay back on the comfortable sofa.

In a few short minutes he could hear rhythmic breathing coming from the bed. It seemed Kwan had already fallen asleep. It had all happened rather quickly and abruptly.

Sebastian lay there staring at the dark shiny ceiling above him. Despite his exhaustion, he just couldn't follow Kwan's example. His brain just would not shut off. He wondered where the men in black were, if they were just outside somewhere, trying to find a way into the headquarters of the Lost Boys. Sebastian shuddered thinking about it, and then he realized that this place had to have been created so that no paparazzi or fans could find their way in. For now, he had to assume, logically, that he was safe.

Sebastian glanced over at Kwan's back. He felt pretty bad for him. For all the responsibilities he had. For not wanting to disappoint so many people. Sebastian understood the feeling. He'd always wanted to make his parents proud. So far he'd succeeded. But someday . . . someday he might not.

Sebastian sat up in a sudden rush of adrenaline. Today was not going to be that day. He wasn't going to give up that easily. Sebastian quickly climbed off the sofa and looked around the room one more time for some way to communicate with the outside world. But of course Kwan hadn't been lying to him. It would have been strange if he had. Still, it really was weird that Kwan didn't have a phone. It was something every teenager had these days. Heck, most kids Sebastian's age had one. Except for him. He'd never really known why it was necessary, and neither had his parents. Of course now—after having been kidnapped—was probably exactly the right time to have a phone.

Sebastian made his way over to the door of the room. Just as he went to reach for it, it swung wide open. Standing in the bright hallway light was Suwon.

He announced something loudly, then noticed Sebastian standing right there and looked down at him, confused. Then he said, "Lights-out!" by way of explanation.

"Okay," replied Sebastian. There was something a little intimidating about Suwon. Sebastian had no reason to think this way, but there was something about him Sebastian just didn't entirely trust. Which was illogical and a gut feeling, and while he was disappointed in himself, he knew Evie would be proud. "So I was just wondering if I could borrow a phone."

"Not tonight. We discussed this," replied Suwon, looking at him suspiciously.

"But I really should call my parents. They must be very worried about me."

"Parents."

"Yes." And because it seemed like the man didn't understand him, for some reason he explained, "You know, the people who raise you and stuff?"

"I know what parents are, Opera Boy," said Suwon, shaking his head. "Though I wouldn't necessarily agree with your definition. In all cases, that is."

"I suppose not," replied Sebastian, not certain he wanted to get into a philosophical conversation about parenting at the moment. "Uh, can I call mine?"

Suwon thought about it for a moment. "Call them tomorrow. Now it's lights-out. Time for sleeping." Suwon reached around the door and flipped a switch, throwing Sebastian into darkness. With one last look, Suwon closed the door firmly, and Sebastian just stared at it.

Slowly he wandered back to his couch and lay down reluctantly. His mind was swirling with thoughts. No, worse than that, fears. He feared what would happen to him if the men in black found him. He feared what would happen if he didn't get in touch with someone soon—his parents, anyone. Would they panic? Would they be really upset? He didn't want to upset anyone. He wondered if Evie was coming after him as she'd promised, and he feared both that she was and that she wasn't. He didn't want her to get in trouble, to get hurt, but he didn't want her to abandon him either. He knew how brave she was and that she could do anything she set her mind to, but he still felt terrible that she had to do this. Had to rescue him. Had to rescue her grandfather. Had to really save the day in so many ways. Talk about responsibilities.

If only he hadn't been in her room at the society. If only he had gone home.

If only.

No. Sebastian put aside such thoughts in a brusque manner. No. These men were determined. They knew he was the key. They would have found him one way or another. And it wasn't his fault. None of this was Evie and Sebastian's fault.

He rolled over onto his side. He should sleep. If he slept, time would move faster and then it would be morning, and then he could call his parents, and then he wouldn't feel like this anymore. Sleeping was the most logical thing to do in this moment.

And so, he slept.

➤ CHAPTER 10 ◄

In which breakfast
is enjoyed.

It was the second time Evie awoke with a start. But this time it wasn't because of some loud, mysterious thud, but because of a thought: *Breakfast.*

She rolled over and looked at the clock on the bed-side table: 8:30 a.m. Shoot. She whipped the covers off her body and got changed as quickly as she could, then practically flew out the door and down the stairs. She stopped then when she realized she had no idea where she was supposed to meet Catherine.

"Good morning!" said a happy voice, and Evie turned to see a tall man with bright orange hair and a face ruddy from the sun emerging from a small door just beyond the check-in desk.

"Good morning!" replied Evie.

"Hey, wanna see something neat?" he asked.

Evie wasn't sure if she did or didn't. Right now she needed to get to breakfast. "Uh . . ."

"Come, look at this!" said the man, and he beckoned to Evie. He looked so excited that she didn't have the heart to refuse. As she approached, Evie marveled at his tan lines. Or rather, burn lines. He was wearing a tank top but clearly had been out in a T-shirt the previous day. His shoulders were pale white, but from above his elbows down, his arms were a blistering red. They were painful just to look at. He had a similar red ring around his neck where the T-shirt's collar had been.

When she arrived at the desk, he pulled out a small fishbowl with a brilliantly colored purple-and-pink fish inside. "Isn't she beautiful? I found her yesterday."

"She is." Evie leaned in closer to look at the creature's delicate wispy fins, paper-thin. Up this close Evie could see a subtle black outline around the fish's eyes and along its back, almost like the creature had been outlined and then colored in.

"Adding it to my aquarium. It's just perfect." The man gazed at it fondly and sighed. He was clearly proud of it, and Evie could see why. She'd never seen a fish so beautiful before. But of course, she really didn't have the time to just stare at a fish like this. She was on a rescue mission, after all.

The man seemed to sense that she was getting impatient, and he smiled again. "Looking for breakfast?"

"I am, yes," replied Evie.

"You have to go outside and around the corner of the building to the left. Need help finding it?" asked the man.

"Oh, no! No, I'll find it, thanks," she said, and jogged to the front door. "And thanks for showing me the fish!" she called over her shoulder.

"No problem!"

In a rush she flung open the door, prepared to dash around the corner and apologize profusely to Catherine for being late. But instead she was stopped in her tracks. It was as if she'd been slapped hard in the face, though she wasn't entirely sure she knew what that would feel like. But the feeling she'd had at the view that greeted her had so taken her aback, her reaction felt physical.

The brilliant blue sea stretched out vast and wide before her, the caps of the waves sparkling in the morning sun. The white sand that came up to a bleached wooden boardwalk across the street was almost too bright to look at, but her eye was soothed by the emerald-green trees to her far left and right that curved along both distant sides of the cove emerging from the dense foliage.

The inn was located at the perfect center of the curving cove. It was a flawless view. The air was warm already and the water inviting. And the waves seemed the perfect kind for surfing, not that she really knew what kind of wave that was. And yet.

And yet.

No! No view admiring! Only rescue missions for now.

Evie walked purposefully down the steps and looked left, then right. The street she was on was full of brightly painted shops and cafés running parallel to the beach, with nothing on the other side of the road, for obvious reasons. But the whole town seemed deserted. There was only a handful of people out and about, and, Evie acknowledged, though it was still relatively early, the emptiness seemed off.

Well, she didn't have time to think about it at the moment. She was already late. Quickly she made her way around the side of the inn and came to a little street-level outdoor café that was pretty much empty except for one gray-haired couple and Catherine, who was sitting toward the front of the patio, with a view of the water, and was looking quite intently at a piece of paper. She didn't even notice as Evie waved, passed through the gate, and came to sit opposite her. Only when Evie sat down did Catherine look up, surprised, seeing her for the first time.

"You're late," said Catherine.

"I am. I'm sorry. I had an . . . odd night." Evie decided to say nothing further. It wasn't really like the mysterious figure mattered, and ultimately, in the warm light of day, it seemed far less creepy to think about. In fact, she felt a little silly. It was probably just some local coming home late from work. With a wagon.

Because people often brought wagons to work.

For . . . reasons . . .

"What's that?" asked Evie, shaking the thought out of her brain.

"Alistair's letter to me," replied Catherine, taking a sip of coffee.

"Oh, of course!" She had been so wrapped up in the events of the night before that she had completely forgotten about her grandfather's clue. "Have you figured it out yet?"

Catherine shook her head. "No. Not yet. Do you want to read it?"

Evie nodded, and Catherine spun the letter to face her. For a moment Evie just took in the sight of her grandfather's handwriting, traced it with her fingers. Then she focused on the actual words:

> Dear Catherine,
> I hope this letter finds you well.
> I am myself living, as always, day to day.
> The weather is getting colder and the north wind blows harshly.
> But I've always liked a bit of a chill.
> It makes me think.
> And I always can put on different layers if I must.
> I hope you're still having adventures. Though don't just do so at my request.
> I hope this letter helps.
>
> As ever yours,
> Alistair

"It's definitely an odd-sounding letter," said Evie.

"It is. A combination of normal- and strange-sounding, direct and indirect. Which makes it all the more weird, I think. Any thoughts?" asked Catherine.

Evie wanted to say yes, wanted to have some kind of deep connection with her grandfather that made it all so obvious. But the fact was, she was just as clueless as Catherine. It was her turn to shake her head.

"Okay." Catherine picked up the letter and pocketed it carefully. "Well, for now let's keep thinking about it, and meanwhile, I think we should go find Thom," she said, signaling for a waitress.

"Good idea. Do we have any idea where he might be?" asked Evie.

"No, but we can start by asking around. Seems like a small enough community."

"Really small. In fact, almost-deserted small," replied Evie.

"You noticed that too?"

Evie nodded just as Ruby came up to them. "Oh, hey! Are you our waitress?" asked Evie when she saw her.

Ruby smiled that great smile of hers again. "Your waitress, cook, housekeeper, tour guide, whatever you need! These days it's just me and my friend Erik running the joint. What can I get you?"

Evie was both hungry and also not hungry. The time difference made her stomach a little queasy, but the hours spent traveling had made her famished. She eventually decided on a bacon-and-egg roll and some orange juice. She and Catherine sat in a pleasant silence looking at the waves crashing against the shore as they waited for her food, which was brought to her relatively quickly. Well, quickly enough, considering Ruby also had to cook it.

"Say," Evie began as Ruby placed the dish in front of her, "how well do you know the people who live around here?"

Ruby laughed at the question. "Oh, I'd say pretty well. That is, if you want to know their shoe size and what grade they got in history when they were fifteen." Evie was confused, and her expression must have shown that, because Ruby then said, "Lived here my whole life. I know everyone. I know them almost too well."

"In that case," said Catherine, "maybe you could help us out. We're looking for a Thom Walker. Do you know him?"

"You could say that," replied Ruby with a grin.

"Yeah?" asked Evie. How perfect! Things were already going their way.

"Yeah, he's my dad." Ruby pushed her bangs up off her face. "Man, it's going to be a hot one today."

"Your . . . dad?" asked Catherine, and she looked as surprised as Evie felt.

"Yeah, but I have to warn you guys. He's stopped doing that."

"Stopped doing what?" asked Evie.

"Taking people to that volcano town."

Evie was startled. First at the fact that the man they'd been looking for would not be able to help them, and second that Ruby knew why they were looking for him in the first place. "How did you know that's what we wanted to talk to him about?" asked Evie.

Ruby shrugged. "I'm used to it. My whole life, people have been coming to find him. Not many, but enough. It was worse when I was a teenager and these cute guys would come up to me and act nice to me, and they only wanted to talk to my dad." She didn't seem upset about it, though. She just laughed again. "I'm sorry if you came all this way to ask him. I guess it makes sense."

"It does?" asked Catherine.

"No one has come here for the beach this season. It's been rough. You can probably tell. So my dad's as good a reason as any to come here instead."

Evie felt flushed; she felt overwhelmed. Surely they hadn't come all this way for nothing. Besides, it couldn't be true, not if Thom had helped Benedict Barnes.

"I think you're lying to us," said Evie, maybe a little more meanly than she'd intended.

Ruby's smile dropped, and she placed a hand on her hip. "I'm not, and that's pretty rude of you to say."

"But what you're saying isn't true. He helped Benedict, didn't he?" Evie said, not willing to let the matter drop, and really not caring if she was sounding rude.

"You guys know Benedict?" asked Ruby, her eyebrows rising to the top of her forehead.

"In a manner of speaking," answered Catherine quietly.

"Okay." Ruby placed her other hand on her other hip. "Who are you guys?"

Catherine glanced carefully over her shoulder, and Evie wondered then what it was like to be her. To be a former member of the Filipendulous Five, to always wonder who was listening, to carry secret maps on one's person, secret vials around one's neck, and secret secrets in one's mind.

"Maybe we should go for a walk," suggested Catherine.

Ruby squinted at Catherine for a moment. And then she nodded slowly. "Okay," she said. "Okay. I'll get Erik to take over." She untied the apron around her waist as she walked toward the building.

"But I haven't eaten my breakfast yet," said Evie quietly to Catherine. It was probably the least pressing issue at the moment, but she was hungry.

"Well, I'd guess you have about two minutes before she gets back," replied Catherine.

Evie sighed and quickly took a couple of bites of her bacon-and-egg roll and downed the whole glass of orange juice in one gulp before Ruby returned.

"The beach?" Ruby asked as Catherine and Evie stood.

"Sure," said Catherine.

They crossed the street, not needing to look both ways because no one was coming, and made their way onto the wooden boardwalk. They started to walk north along the shore. Evie couldn't help but gaze out at the water as they did.

"What do you know about Benedict?" asked Catherine.

"I know he's a professor. I know he wanted to photograph the volcano," replied Ruby. Evie glanced at her, and there was a look in Ruby's eyes that made Evie think something had been left unsaid.

Catherine seemed to think so too. "What else?"

Ruby was quiet for a moment. Then: "I know he and my father knew each other from before. I know . . . something about a team he used to work for."

"Work with," corrected Catherine. She said it again, only this time more quietly, to herself. "Work with."

"With," repeated Ruby. "I don't remember the name; it was a tongue twister. I just remember that there were five of them."

"The Filipendulous Five," said Catherine.

"That's it! Yes, that's the name." Ruby looked at Catherine, who kept her eyes trained forward. And Evie looked at Ruby and then back to Catherine. She wondered what Catherine was looking at. She kind of thought it likely wasn't the boardwalk or the dark green trees. It probably wasn't something even in the present. A memory, maybe, instead.

"I'm one of them," said Catherine. "*Was* one of them."

"Oh. Oh, wow," said Ruby softly.

"And we really need to talk to Benedict because he's in trouble!" blurted out Evie. Now Evie knew exactly what Catherine was looking at, because Catherine had turned her head and was staring at Evie hard. "Sorry. It's just . . . it's true."

It was, it was true. It might be true. If the men were on their way to find him. But even if it wasn't true right this instant, it would become true in time. They needed his piece of the map.

"Why? What's going on?" asked Ruby.

Catherine shook her head. "I've taken a big enough risk as it is; I can't share that information with you. Not yet."

"You want to speak to my dad," said Ruby.

"I do."

"I can't promise he'll be helpful. He has really isolated himself lately." Evie saw the sadness in Ruby's face and felt sorry for her.

"It's a start. We know you can't guarantee anything."

Ruby nodded. "I can take you there this afternoon."

They stopped walking then and gazed out into the water. "Thank you," said Catherine.

"Yes! Thank you so much!" added Evie. This was good. It was a small step. Besides, once they met with Thom, surely he'd understand and want to help them out. They weren't just tourists or anything. They were on a serious mission! Lifesaving, even, possibly. "Hey, is that a dolphin?" she asked, just then noticing a gray smudge quite a ways out to sea.

She pointed, and both women squinted to look. Then Ruby sighed. It was a hard sigh, a frustrated sigh. Almost angry, even. "No. No, that's not a dolphin. That's Steve."

"Who's Steve?" asked Evie.

"Steve is the great white shark that's been stalking our cove for the last two weeks."

Evie instinctively took a step backward even though they were very far away from it and on land, of course.

"Yeah, he showed up about eighteen days ago and

hasn't left," continued Ruby. "Had to shut down the beach, and word's got out. It was like someone closed an invisible door on us. No tourists, no hotel bookings. If this lasts much longer, the town's going to be in a lot of trouble."

"It's quite unusual that he's just sticking around like this," said Catherine. And with quite the opposite instinct from Evie, she took a step forward. "I wonder what he's looking for."

"We don't know. A marine biologist went to check him out and said he looks fed and healthy. Maybe he just likes it here. I hope not. I hope he gets tired soon."

Evie watched Catherine stare intently at the creature. Even though she didn't think Catherine was actually capable of talking to animals, since that wasn't a thing people could do, she remembered how effortlessly Catherine had communicated with the pig in the teeny hat and the other animals in the rather eccentric and scatterbrained Hubert's room at the Society headquarters. And then of course there was that huge snake at the zoo. . . .

Was Catherine thinking of taking a swim and having a little chat? No, that was too much risk, surely, even for her. Besides, they didn't have time for that.

"Look, I've got to get back to the inn," said Ruby,

glancing at her watch. "Let's meet in the foyer around two and I'll take you to Dad."

Catherine nodded. "Thank you."

Ruby smiled in reply, and gave Evie a smile as well. Then she turned and made her way up the boardwalk and back toward the inn.

"Well, that's good, uh, that she's going to . . . help . . . us. . . ." Evie slowly stopped speaking when she noticed that Catherine wasn't really listening. In fact, she was walking away from her onto the sand. Evie tried to catch up as the explorer stepped down to the edge of the water. The wind was still pretty strong, but the waves had calmed down a bit. Small ones broke against the shore, leaving a foamy trail upon their retreat. Evie didn't want to get too close. She wasn't sure exactly how close to shore sharks swam.

"Great white sharks are fascinating creatures. Mostly because we still know so little about them. They also have such unfortunate reputations. They so rarely attack humans, and when they do, it is even rarer that the attacks are fatal," said Catherine in a kind of soft low voice. It almost sounded dreamy.

"Well, but they are really scary-looking. They're huge, with these dark black eyes, and they have big teeth, so I mean, I get it," said Evie. Oh boy, how she got it.

"They have blue eyes when you see one close up. Looks can be deceiving."

Evie watched as the fin vanished beneath the surface. All that remained was the bright blue before her. It seemed so welcoming that she wanted to run right in and splash around. But lurking beneath the surface . . . Looks indeed could be deceiving. "But I mean, this shark's been stalking the beach, lying in wait for some unsuspecting surfer or at least local fish. It seems pretty cold-blooded to me." She really didn't get how Catherine couldn't understand this.

"Actually, great whites are endotherms."

Evie turned and looked at her. Catherine's short red hair was dancing in the wind, flying out behind her, then across her face, obscuring it, then out again. "What?"

"These kinds of sharks. They're partially warm-blooded."

"Oh, well, I just meant cold-blooded sort of more metaphorically . . . like they're stone-cold killers, but . . . okay . . . that's kind of interesting." Evie had forgotten that Catherine wasn't too up on sayings and rhetorical devices.

"They aren't, though. They're just like the rest of us: animals trying to survive."

Evie didn't have anything else to say at the moment.

She appreciated what Catherine was saying and knew deep down she was right. But that didn't make Evie feel any less scared and, certainly when the fin popped up much closer than last time, didn't make her rush away from the waterline any less quickly.

Catherine, of course, stayed in place.

"Hey," called Evie from farther up the beach now, "so, could I have my grandfather's letter again? I was thinking maybe I could have a closer look at it while we wait to meet back up with Ruby."

Catherine turned around and looked back at her. She nodded and walked up to Evie, handing her the letter. Then, without saying anything, she returned to her spot at the edge of the water.

Evie thought it was probably best to leave Catherine alone at this point. Sometimes conversation and other people weren't wanted. And that was okay.

So she held the letter close, shielding it from the wind, and made her way back up the beach toward the inn.

➤ CHAPTER 11 ◄

In which there are
some concerns.

As he did most things in his life, Sebastian also slept with great efficiency. Typically when his head hit the pillow, he immediately fell into a deep slumber. He went through the appropriate number of REM cycles before he woke up—just before his alarm clock went off—feeling refreshed and ready to face the day.[10] So it was no small surprise when Sebastian found himself being shaken quite hard out of what was the deepest part of the REM cycle into a state of not sleeping. That is to say, when Kwan shook him to wake him up.

---

[10] The alarm clock, on the other hand, started each day feeling rather bitter and resentful that it never got to do its job, thank you very much.

"What? What's going on?" asked Sebastian groggily. The world around him was hazy. His eyes wouldn't quite open wide enough to see beyond their lashes.

"Time to get up! Breakfast, then workout!" said Kwan with a perky smile. Sebastian sat up slowly on his sofa, still in a daze, marveling at how downright chipper Kwan seemed. And chipper was not a thing Sebastian normally marveled at people being.

"What time is it?" asked Sebastian, rubbing his eyes, then opening them wide and blinking a few times.

"Eight a.m.," replied Kwan. He was staring into his closet at the most impressive collection of sneakers Sebastian had ever seen. He had pairs in every color imaginable and also some in colors that weren't. They were stacked neatly row above row, like in a shoe store. Could one even wear that many shoes in a lifetime? Well, yes, probably, but it was still a lot of shoes. After an intense moment Kwan said, "Aha!" and with pleasure grabbed a pair of white-and-orange sneakers and sat down to put them on.

"Eight a.m. That's not so early," said Sebastian, more to himself. Why was he so tired, then?

"True. I bet you have a pretty bad case of jet lag, though," replied Kwan, tying his shoes and then bounding to standing.

Jet lag. Huh. Sebastian had never experienced that before. Then again, he'd never traveled outside his time zone before, so it made sense. Was jet lag part of exploring? If so, that definitely went on the con side of his mental pros-and-cons list.

"You ready?" asked Kwan. And seeing as Sebastian was still wearing his clothes from yesterday, seeing as his kidnappers hadn't given him a chance to pack before his kidnapping, Sebastian nodded. "Great! Come on! We don't want to be late."

Of course, Sebastian's nod had been to what he'd thought was the question "Are you ready to call home?" It had not, in fact, been a nod in response to whether he was prepared for the rigorous routine he was about to be thrust into. Which was what he had inadvertently said yes to.

It seemed that the Lost Boys had a very tight schedule that had to be maintained. Sebastian wasn't surprised. To become a top musical group, you need to put in the work. He was more than a little impressed, watching as they quickly ate breakfast before going to the gym located down the hall, one as large as the gym in Sebastian's school. All five of the boys seemed wide awake and ready for work.

"Impressive," said Sebastian to Suwon as the two of them stood to the side and watched.

"They're good boys. Hard workers," replied Suwon with a smile.

"They really are," agreed Sebastian. Then after a pause he said, "Uh, Suwon, about the phone . . ."

Suwon waved off his request. "Not now. Later!" He stepped forward and shouted something at the boys, who promptly put down the equipment they were working with and ran to the corner of the room. They stood in a line one behind the other, and then one by one they each performed a series of flips across the room. Of course Toy was the most skillful, able to revolve two, even three times, whereas the others could only do one. Still Sebastian was in awe of all of them. Watching them, he realized that, evidently, gravity was only a suggestion.

Then it was off to the schoolroom, and Sebastian once again asked after a phone but this time was completely ignored. This second refusal created a knot in his stomach as he sat at one of the desks toward the back of the room, marveling at the same time that this was what it looked like from the back of the room, compared to his usual spot up front. He stared down at the sheet of paper in front of him. It really did seem that these boys never used computers. They didn't appear to have *any* access to the Internet, actually. All their lessons were done on paper, though in this case it made sense. On the sheet in front of him were some relatively straightforward equations to solve, and though he was feeling more than a little antsy about his general situation, Sebastian nonetheless solved them quickly and with pleasure. That was a thing he'd always liked about math. It was a universal language.

"Well done!" said Suwon after he'd read over Sebastian's answers.

Sebastian couldn't help but smile at that. "Thank you!" Now that Suwon was pleased with him, he gave it yet another go: "I was thinking maybe while they all worked on history I could call my parents?"

Suwon continued to stare at the paper. "You're very smart. Very smart. And you get along well with the others." He looked up at Sebastian thoughtfully.

"I guess so, yeah," replied Sebastian. *That doesn't actually answer my question, though.* The knot in his stomach tightened even more.

And it only got worse as the day continued. The band members went on with their rigorous routine, lunch followed by singing classes, followed by more school, followed by rehearsing various dance routines they seemed to already know inside and out. As all this happened, and Sebastian followed them from room to room, from activity to activity, his stomach knot grew larger and larger. Or maybe it wasn't that; maybe it was turning into a row of really tight knots. Like when you tie a piece of fabric and it gets wet and is then impossible to untie. The kind of knot that could moor an entire cruise ship to its dock.

Because no matter how many different tactics Sebastian tried, whether it was being really friendly or more demanding, Suwon just kept ignoring his request to call home. Sebastian was beginning to think that maybe he hadn't been rescued at all. Maybe he'd only found a new set of kidnappers. And though these seemed very nice and were ridiculously talented, it didn't make much of a difference. He was being kept from going home. And he didn't like that; he didn't like that one bit.

After dinner the boys were allowed to relax for a couple of hours. They all sat together in the purple plush recreation room playing video games. But while it looked like they were having a very fun time, Sebastian couldn't participate. He didn't have the time for fun. What he needed to do was find a way to a phone, to a computer. A nest of carrier pigeons. To something, anything.

"Come on, play!" insisted Ujin from the floor in front of the TV, for what seemed like the hundredth time.

"I'm good, thanks," replied Sebastian with a small

forced smile. Ujin shook his head and returned to killing zombies.

Kwan came over and sat beside Sebastian on the soft squishy couch. "Something's wrong? What is it?" he asked.

Sebastian wanted to share all his thoughts with his new friend. He wanted to explain his concerns about Suwon, how weird it was that the band members weren't allowed phones or even access to the Internet. How this place was starting to feel more like a prison than a safe haven. But he also didn't really know Kwan. He didn't know where the boy's loyalties lay, and if Sebastian was to guess, he'd assume they'd be with the band and Suwon. Sebastian didn't want to upset Kwan. More than that, he didn't want Suwon to find out how uncomfortable he was. Sebastian had no idea what the man might do if he found out.

"Do you like Suwon?" asked Sebastian carefully.

Kwan laughed. "What's not to like?"

"Oh, nothing. It's just, I was wondering . . . he's the only adult here. Your bodyguards and the driver seem to have left and everything, and he's in charge of you guys, so I guess it's important you like him," said Sebastian, feeling a little awkward.

Kwan reached for the chip bowl. "Huh. Well, I

guess that's true. I do like him. He's been very good to me."

"That's good," replied Sebastian, accepting the handful of chips Kwan offered him. "So do you miss having a phone and getting to play on the Internet and stuff?"

Kwan looked at him funny and then shook his head. "Well, it's not like we never get to use the Internet. It's just when we're on tour or preparing for a concert that Hyung considers the Internet is too distracting. And also . . ." He stopped.

"Also what?" asked Sebastian, feeling like he was about to get some kind of answer about Suwon, something important.

Kwan sighed. "Well, when we first became a band and started to do performances and we started to get popular . . ."

"Yes?" Sebastian leaned in.

"We would go online and see what people were saying about us. And most of the time it was great. Some really great stuff."

"Okay?"

"Yeah, I mean, it *is* okay. It's really cool. But . . . it also can become a bit of a problem."

"Yeah?"

"Yeah. It's addictive. Reading all these things about

yourself, people loving you so much. You want more people to follow you, you want more people to like you, to click buttons, to tell you how amazing you are. And it's never good enough. You think there's a point where it will be enough, but there never is. The highs are so high. And then there are the lows. . . ." He paused and sat there, thinking. Then, as if he'd made up his mind about something, he started talking again. "Sometimes people said some really mean things. Hurtful things. Nasty things. People made fun of our music, called us names, and some of us"—Kwan glanced over at Cheese, then lowered his voice—"even got death threats."

"Oh!" said Sebastian, shocked. "Oh, I'm sorry."

"Yeah, it was bad. And Cheese got really upset. I mean . . . really, really upset."

Sebastian suddenly felt like he was prying, like he was getting too much personal information. "That's horrible," he said. It was all he could think to say.

Kwan nodded. "But hyung helped him get out of it. And then hyung told us we shouldn't go online. It wasn't worth it. And he was right, you know?"

Sebastian nodded, though he didn't really know. This was totally foreign to him. He barely spent any time online except to do research. He hadn't really cared to do anything else. Now he was kind of grateful for that. All of what Kwan had said sounded very reasonable, and yet Sebastian couldn't shake the thought. . . . "But no phones, either?"

"Who are we going to call?" asked Kwan.

"Your families!" said Sebastian, aghast.

"Oh, well. Yeah. I guess them. Yeah." Kwan stood up suddenly then and returned to the group, sitting on the floor and taking over playing one of the games. It was an abrupt change of attitude and surprised Sebastian, making him suspicious. Though the story about the Internet had made sense, he still was seriously doubting that everything was as wonderful here as it seemed.

Once again he came to a determination, one that maybe, when he thought about it, he ought to have tattooed on his arm or something, so that he'd remember it. He'd never really wanted to have a tattoo before; they were so . . . permanent.[11] But this one seemed maybe necessary. It was time, once again, for him to escape.

---

[11] Except for the nonpermanent kind, or the tattoos that get bored with sitting on your arm all day and decide to go visit friends.

➤ CHAPTER 12 ◄

In which we take
a long walk
and pondering happens.
Also a fish.

Evie lay on her stomach across the width of her bed, reading—no re-reading, no re-re-re-reading—her grandfather's letter to Catherine. She tried not looking at it as an actual letter with information she was supposed to understand, but more like there was something hidden in words themselves instead. She tried putting together the first word of every line to see if it made a message. Then she tried the last word. Staring at the words so much made her eyes a bit fuzzy, and the writing before her blurred a little bit. It was then she noticed that some of the letters appeared darker in some of the words, like the last two in "can" and the first two in "adventures." A couple of others as well.

It felt like something, like a little hint of something she should understand. Were those words in particular more important? Did the dark letters spell something? Neither seemed to be the case, and her frustration returned.

She sighed as she sat up and looked out the window. From the bed all she could see was the bright blue of the cove. She wasn't going to solve this mystery by staring hard at a piece of paper. She'd read the words so many times by now that she had them memorized. No, sometimes in order to solve a problem you had to do quite the opposite: ignore it.

Evie decided she'd go check out the town while her subconscious did some pondering. Of course, once she was back outside and standing on the steps of the inn, she had a new problem to solve. What exactly should she check out?

The beach was empty again. Catherine had returned to her room, and Evie had spent more than enough time close to Steve the shark, thank you very much. So she resolved instead to wander along the main road, venturing in and out of various stores, looking at their goods. She felt a little guilty that she didn't have any cash on her to help support the Steve-induced failing economy of the town. She noticed the eyes of the store owners widen with hope as she entered, and then get smaller and sadder as she left. Evie was starting to feel so terrible about producing this reaction that she decided to stop going into shops altogether, and instead walked up the road a bit to where the dense green forest began along the shoreline. She didn't venture into it, though. There weren't too many things Evie knew about Australia, but one thing she did know was that there were a lot of snakes and spiders and all kinds of other things that liked to kill humans. And considering that she was likely eventually to be facing some humans again who had no issue killing (or at the very least seriously maiming) humans, she wasn't in the mood to face that risk with nature as well.

As she walked alongside the lush greenery, she lost herself in thought. Long walks had always had that effect on her. Usually her thoughts were large and broad, about her life, her purpose, why we needed to have daylight saving time, that kind of thing. But today her long walk did only one thing: it made her miss Sebastian more than ever. It was hard not to feel horribly guilty. It didn't matter what any of the members of the society told her. How could she not blame herself? How was his predicament not completely 100 percent her fault? The key he'd memorized that he'd been kidnapped for had been to help her grandfather. *Her* grandfather, not his. She was the one who'd gotten him involved in all this. She was the one who had convinced him to go against his very nature to help her, and why? Because she'd been too scared to do it alone? How selfish! She had been truly unfair to him, and now because of her he was in danger.

The only thing that gave her hope, the only small thing, was that those nasty men couldn't do anything truly horrible to him. Because they needed him. They needed what he knew. That was the only thing that made any of this somewhat bearable. That and, she reminded herself, the fact that he wasn't entirely hopeless. Certainly he didn't like taking risks and he maybe overthought things a bit too much, but he was also brilliant, and a good problem-solver, and Evie liked to think that she'd helped him a bit with his ability to just go with his gut sometimes.

No, Sebastian was far from hopeless.

It was just Evie who was feeling that way.

The road seemed to go on forever, and after a while it made sense to turn around and head back to the inn. Once she was on the main strip next to the beach, she strolled out onto the sand and walked down to the water's edge. The water was a much richer blue now that the sun was higher overhead, the part closest to her a saturated turquoise. Of course, she dared not go any farther—Steve was out there somewhere—but she bent over and stuck her fingers into the water as a wave rushed up to meet her. It danced over and around them and then retreated calmly. *Hi there!* it seemed to say. Friendly and quite warm.

"Hi," Evie said aloud. Then she stood up and drifted back up to the road.

As she was crossing the street, she noticed something sparkle just a little to her left. It glinted in the sun, and Evie, never one to shy away from shiny objects, went over to it. It was a fish. A small fish. With scales that looked silver if you looked at them one way, but purple if you looked another. It was odd to see a fish just lying there in the middle of the street. It was too far away from the sea for the fish to have accidentally leapt in the wrong direction and landed there. It wasn't particularly close to any markets that sold fish either.

It seemed, well, as if the fish had been taking the road somewhere and then, alas, suddenly realized it wasn't in water and hadn't gotten to its destination. This made Evie surprisingly sad, even though she knew she was being fanciful, that there was no way a fish could ever be traveling along a road like that on its own, trying to get to another location. It didn't look as if it had been there that long, but it did look like it was starting to cook in the midday sun, and Evie thought it best to leave it where it was. A mystery for others to stumble upon. If indeed anyone else bothered to come this way at all.

So Evie left the fish behind and climbed the stairs into the inn[12] to find Catherine.

---

[12] Truly, going "into" something called an "inn" is a very reasonable thing to do in general.

⤜ CHAPTER 13 ⤛

In which we meet Thom.

"I saw a fish on the road," said Evie a few hours later, leaning forward so Catherine and Ruby could hear her. She was sitting squished in the tiny backseat of Ruby's dark green pickup truck. The windows were rolled all the way down, and though the warm wind felt amazing on her face, it did make it hard for the people in the front seats to hear her when she spoke.

"A what?" asked Ruby.

"A fish, a small fish. It was in the middle of the road near the inn," said Evie a little more loudly.

"Oh, a fish," said Ruby.

"Yeah. It was weird. I was wondering how it got there."

They sped around another corner of the hill, heading farther inland. The farther they got, the more lush the foliage grew. If eyes could taste, they likely would have found it delicious.

"Sometimes a bird drops a fish," said Catherine. She looked over her shoulder to speak, her short red hair whipping around her face.

"Really?" asked Evie. She'd never thought of that before, but she supposed it made sense.

"Yes, sometimes a bird catches a fish and then it takes off and flies, and then suddenly for some reason, maybe the fish is wiggling or it turns out to be too heavy—"

"Or the bird gets distracted by a neat-looking cloud," offered Evie.

"Sure," said Catherine. "Well, whatever it is, the bird drops it and the fish lands in the middle of somewhere where fish aren't normally meant to be."

Evie thought about this with wonder. It made sense, but how interesting. She now felt sorry for both the fish that had fallen and the bird that had lost its dinner.

"Has anyone ever been hurt? By falling fish?" asked Evie.

"Oh yes, it happens quite a bit, actually," replied Catherine.

Evie sat back in her seat and looked out at the foliage. She was able to glimpse the bright blue expanse of the sea every now and then through the trees. Great. Falling fish. Now she had something else to worry about.

"We're here!" Ruby called out just then.

She turned down a dirt driveway that wound its way still farther up the hillside. The trees now completely blocked out the blue sky. Instead the truck was surrounded by green as they slowed down to a stop at the base of Ruby's dad's house. After Catherine climbed out of the truck, she pulled her seat forward so Evie could scramble out as well. Once outside, Evie stretched a little and then stared at the house. It was up above them a little ways, with a narrow path that cut through the trees leading up to a wooden staircase. The house itself was supported on twenty-foot-high stilts, around which vines wound themselves. The building looked almost as if it had grown there in the jungle, as opposed to having been built.

Evie followed Ruby and Catherine up the stairs, looking around her all the while. The higher up they got, the brighter it got with the trees thinning out, and the more jungle she was able to see through the trees. To other trees. To the vastness that was trees.

The three of them eventually made it to a solid front porch underneath a low slanted roof, and without even bothering to knock, Ruby led them inside. It was a small place but full of mottled leafy light and shadows, with windows running along the front wall by the entrance, and a skylight above. The wood the house was made of was a warm amber color, and the floors were covered in beautiful throw rugs of red and blue and green. Evie gazed at one wall, on which hung a large painting of what seemed to be a silhouette of a lizard on a deep burnt-orange background, its head black and its body an intricate design done in a rainbow of colors.

"Aboriginal art," said Catherine, coming up behind her. "Just beautiful."

"Yes," said Evie. She knew it was wrong to touch. The painting was so tactile to look at that she had a hard time controlling herself. But she did.

"My dad made that!" announced Ruby from deeper within the house. Evie turned and saw Ruby poking her head around a corner. "This way!" she said, and gestured for them to follow.

"He did?" asked Evie as she walked over and turned the corner. They were now in a very pleasant great room. Evie found herself standing on a higher level, next to the open-concept kitchen. Down a few steps was a very comfortable-looking living room, with several plush couches and more art on the walls.

But even more beautiful than the art was what she saw before her. Like the front wall, the rear one was also floor-to-ceiling windows. Yet unlike the front room, the view outside the windows was just a little bit more than trees.

The sea spread out in front of them beyond the green jungle that separated them from it. The water stretched so wide and far that Evie wondered if she could see Newish Isle from here. But all she saw was blue, a dazzling blue, a blue that almost seemed as if it were showing off a bit, except for the fact that it just happened to be that fabulous.

Evie didn't realize her mouth was agape until the low rich voice beside her said, "I guess you approve."

Evie turned to see a man with graying black hair, wearing khaki shorts and a red Hawaiian shirt, standing by the stove next to a kettle. He looked at Evie with a small smile, and she felt a little embarrassed for just kind of staring like that.

"I do" was all Evie could say. Who wouldn't approve?

"It's a nice enough view, I suppose," said the man.

Nice enough? Evie was stunned. How could anyone use the word "nice" at a time like this? "Magnificent," maybe; "fantastic," absolutely; but "nice" . . .

Evie noticed the man's smile growing wider and realized he'd been teasing. Of course. Of course he had been. She smiled too.

"It's amazing. I, uh, I also like the artwork. Did you do all of these, too?" asked Evie.

The man nodded and returned to the kettle. "I did, I did. A hobby, though, nothing more. My grandmother taught me what little I know. She was the true talent. Became quite famous. And not just among the Kuku Yalanji." He looked at Evie's puzzled expression. "Our people, mine and Ruby's." He fiddled with the kettle for a moment and then stood back, looking at it. "You know, they say a watched pot never boils, but I have never found that to be the case." And just as he finished speaking, white steam rose from the mouth of the kettle. "Aha! See?" He turned to Evie triumphantly, and she nodded to demonstrate that she did indeed see.

"Come on, Evie. Let's go sit outside," said Ruby, coming up beside her and placing a warm hand on her shoulder. There was something in her tone that made it sound less like a friendly suggestion and more like an order. Which confused Evie as she was ushered down the stairs and out through the glass back door onto the veranda. Ruby's dad seemed very warm and friendly as far as she could tell, not someone who needed to be left alone or tiptoed around.

Outside, the vastness of the view was all the more encompassing. It almost felt like it was drawing Evie into it, making her part of the vista. Which really made no sense, as she was the one looking out onto it. She sighed.

"Have a seat!" said Ruby. She herself was already seated on a reclining wooden chair, and Catherine was sitting on a long outdoor couch, complete with water-resistant cushions.

"Okay," said Evie, sitting next to Catherine while trying to keep her focus on the view. It was almost as if she feared that if she turned around, it would vanish before she could look at it again.

"Your father seems like a pleasant man," said Catherine.

"Oh, he does. And he is. Especially when he knows what's going on and isn't going to be helpful," replied Ruby, closing her eyes and leaning back.

"What?" said Evie. That made no sense to her.

"Whenever he's sure of himself, whenever he's made up his mind about something, he gets pretty giddy," said Ruby, still with her eyes shut. "I think he just feels so secure and calm in the decision that he can really relax. I told him I was bringing you; he knew why immediately. All this happiness means he's not going to be particularly helpful."

Evie looked at Catherine, who wore a serious expression, but one Evie couldn't quite read. She hoped Catherine was feeling as worried as she was. What would they do if he refused to help them?

"He does make very good tea, though," added Ruby.

"It's so hot out," said Evie. It seemed more like a lemonade kind of day than a hot-beverage one.

"Drinking something hot actually helps the body stay cool," said Ruby.

Evie just couldn't believe that was right.

"Okay, we have tea for everyone!" said Thom as he

came outside to join them. He was carrying a large tea tray that wobbled as he brought it over.

Ruby was on her feet in an instant. "Dad! Let me help with that."

"No, no, little Ruby. Your father can manage just fine," replied Thom, refusing Ruby's offered hand and making his way slowly to the low table in front of the couch.

"You're so stubborn," said Ruby with a sigh, sitting back down.

"You noticed, did you?" Her dad finally put the tray down, the cups dancing slightly on their saucers but otherwise everything staying in place. Then he sat in the other reclining wooden chair with a contented sigh. "Please, please, help yourselves! Enjoy!"

There was a little awkward business as everyone tried to pour themselves tea and get comfy again, but eventually they all had a cup in hand and sat back to enjoy the view.

"How's the inn?" Thom asked.

"Oh, well, you know," replied Ruby with a sigh.

"Still no luck with Steve, then?" asked Thom.

"No luck. If it keeps up, I'm not sure what we're going to do. Maybe close the inn for the season. Maybe for good. I can't afford to keep it running without customers, and I owe rent."

Evie looked at Ruby. Her usually sunny disposition had faltered somewhat. Like the shadow of a cloud passing overhead.

"Oh, Ruby. That's terrible." Thom reached over and took her hand. Ruby gave his a quick squeeze and smiled.

"I'll be okay, Dad. I always am." She sounded not all that convinced of her own statement.

There was a long, sad silence then. But it was also charged. Evie felt a need to say something. To maybe get them talking about why they were there in the first place.

"This is just gorgeous," said Evie, indicating the view. Because it was.

"It is. It really is. You feel like you're on top of the world here," replied Thom, taking a sip of tea.

"I was just thinking that . . . that you feel like you could see all the way to Newish Isle from here," said Evie slowly.

Catherine sputtered on her tea, and Thom laughed.

"Oh my goodness, you aren't subtle at all, are you, child?" he said. "Well, there is something to admire about that, I suppose. Direct and straight to the point."

Evie felt her face get hot, and she looked down at her tea. She wasn't sure what was embarrassing her more—that he'd so easily caught on to her plan, or that she actually had been trying to be subtle.

"I know why you're here. There's only one reason why anyone comes to find me, and it isn't to buy my art," said Thom.

"I'd buy your art," said Evie. *If I had money. And a way to transport it home,* she thought.

"You're sweet. And you know, I actually believe you would. Thank you. But I think we all know why we're here, so it makes sense to just address it head-on. I'm done taking people to the volcano." He took another sip of tea and kept his gaze firmly out toward the horizon.

"But why?" asked Evie, her voice getting high and cracking a little.

"Evie, please, stay calm," said Catherine, jumping into the conversation.

Evie scowled at that. Had there ever been a person in the history of time who had been told to stay calm, or to calm down, or any kind of calming, where the result had been anything other than the person getting more frustrated?

"But it doesn't make sense," Evie said. "Why did he help Benedict but he won't help us? What makes Benedict so special?"

"He's a pretty special person," said Catherine.

"Indeed he is. You know Benedict Barnes?" asked Thom, finally turning away from the view and looking at them with interest for the first time.

"Yes!" said Evie. This maybe was their way in. Thom seemed at least a little receptive now. "And we're trying to find him because he's in danger!" *Possibly, maybe, hard to know. Actually, it's my friend Sebastian who's in greater danger, but we think that we can help him if we can find Benedict.* She finished all this in her head because she wasn't sure it would help and she wasn't sure it would matter to Thom.

"Is he?" asked Thom. "How so?"

At this point Catherine leaned forward and gave a look to Evie that suggested it was time for her to speak. "Thom, my name is Catherine Lind. I was once a member of the Filipendulous Five and consider Benedict to be one of my closest friends. We need your help to find him."

Thom looked back at her, long and hard. Then he shook his head slowly. "I have great respect for your team, and great respect for Benedict. But I have made up my mind. The good news is, since I've taken others there, they know the way as well. Where they are now, though . . . I'm not entirely sure."

"But time is of the essence," said Catherine.

"I don't get it. Why can't you just make an exception for us?" pleaded Evie.

Thom sighed and leaned forward, placing his empty teacup on the tray in front of them. "You make one exception, and then you make another. And then another. In this moment you think, 'Well, this isn't so bad. There is reason enough to help them.' But then there comes another moment with the same thought, and so on. I should know; I've been thinking that way for five years now. Finally I decided that after Benedict, that was it. I was done. I would help an old friend. What could be considered a better final exception? And then there would be no more."

Evie stared at Thom. She had run out of things to say. It wasn't like he was being reasonable, exactly. It felt like there ought to be some way to logically convince him he was wrong. But she couldn't think of one. Oh, how she wished Sebastian was here right now. He'd know what to say!

"We understand," said Catherine, though to Evie it sounded like maybe there was a hint of the same frustration she herself was feeling. "So you don't know of anyone else who could help us?"

Thom shook his head. "Not their whereabouts, no." He paused. "Wait! I had an old friend who made the trip with me several times in our youth. He moved to Canada a while ago."

"We can't go to Canada," said Evie.

"Why not? It's a lovely place," replied Thom.

"No, I meant it's far away, and we have . . . days . . . hours, even . . . ," said Evie, trailing off.

"Then maybe find a large city. Go to Sydney, start there? Brisbane, possibly?" It was impressive just how helpful someone who was being totally unhelpful could be.

"Thank you," said Catherine. She stood up in her efficient way and placed her teacup on the tray. "We really shouldn't take up any more of your time."

"Oh, no. Please! Take up as much as you'd like. Stay for dinner. I make a mean stew," Thom implored her as he rose to his feet.

Catherine didn't say anything. Evie understood how she was feeling. This man had let them down in a huge way, and accepting his hospitality in the face of such disappointment felt weird.

Then again, there was no real reason not to stay for stew.

"Thank you," said Catherine. "We will."

➤ CHAPTER 14 ⭠

In which Sebastian has a pair of intense conversations.

It was time for lights-out again. And as Sebastian lay there in the dark, the knots in his stomach seemed to fill him up almost to the point of choking him. Finally, when he couldn't handle it anymore, he got up and made a beeline for the door.

He opened it slowly, carefully, worried that Suwon would be standing on the other side like last night. But he wasn't. The hallway was dimly lit and empty. And very quiet. Some people would call it too quiet, but Sebastian wasn't those people. Quiet simply was a state. It couldn't be too much. It couldn't be more than quiet. Quiet was.

Sebastian really had no idea where any exits might

be except for the one he'd come in through with the bus. So he made his way toward the garage. Working his way through the maze of hallways, passing the recording studio, the dining room, the schoolroom, finally he made it into the white garage, lit as brightly as when he'd first seen it. He walked to the center of the room, where a large round circle was indented in the floor. Sebastian was pretty sure it was the lift. It definitely was large enough for an entire bus to fit onto. But how to turn it on? How to get it to do its lifting thing?

Sebastian turned around and saw Suwon standing in the doorway. Seeing the man took him by surprise. Sebastian hadn't even sensed that he was no longer alone. He wasn't really sure what to do, so he just stood there, on the giant white circle, staring.

"Why are you up? It's after lights-out," said Suwon.

"Oh, uh . . ." Sebastian's mind raced. "I couldn't sleep. I wanted to see the cars. They're very cool."

"They are. Most of them are gifts. And useless. Only Kwan is old enough to drive, but he doesn't have his license. Though, someday . . ." He smiled, and then stopped smiling. "You're lying to me."

"No, I'm not."

"That was also a lie."

"No, it wasn't." Yes, okay, it was, but he was still getting used to lying and wasn't sure what to do when he was called out on it.

Suwon raised one eyebrow, and Sebastian felt defeated. He could keep insisting, but where would it get him? Suwon knew the truth. Or at least knew that Sebastian wasn't speaking the truth.

"I want to go home," Sebastian said, deflating and feeling very tired.

"Do you think that's wise, Sebastian?" asked Suwon, walking toward him.

"What?" What a strange question. "Of course it is. It's very wise. And logical besides."

"I understand the desire to go home. I have had that desire myself. But sometimes home doesn't desire you."

What? "Uh . . . I don't understand."

"My dear Sebastian. It is very hard to come to terms with, I do know that. I know the feeling well. But sometimes in order to move on, we need to acknowledge very difficult truths."

Sebastian didn't know what to say to that. He was terribly confused, and really didn't enjoy that feeling.

Suwon approached him and put a gentle hand on his shoulder. "This story about you being kidnapped, it's quite a tale."

"It is," agreed Sebastian.

"A bit fanciful, wouldn't you say?"

And that was when Sebastian finally understood. He scolded himself for not getting there sooner. "You think I'm lying!" he said, completely stunned.

"Not lying in the bad way of lying. It's a pity, actually, that the word 'lying' always sounds so negative. A lie in and of itself isn't always a terrible thing."

This was something Sebastian had been slowly learning. Ever since he'd met Evie, really. But still . . .

"I'm not lying. It's the truth. I realize it sounds pretty crazy, but it's the truth." Sebastian was starting to feel flushed and warm all over. It was a familiar feeling, one he always felt when someone was trying to make him think he was wrong when he knew without question he was right. This had happened a few times growing up, at his old school before he'd transferred to his new one. Where some of the teachers would be angry because he knew more than they did, and when he corrected them, they'd insist he was wrong. It was like that all over again. But this time it was about his own personal experiences, not an answer to a math problem or some historical fact. His very own life.

"I think," said Suwon slowly and in a comforting voice, "that you ran away. I don't know why, but I think that's what happened. And now you feel guilty. So you want to run back. But are you sure that running back is the right choice?"

"What do you mean?"

"Sometimes families aren't the ones you are born into. Sometimes families are the people you choose. Like here. We're very much a family here."

"Well, I guess, but surely the band members have parents and stuff. Surely . . ." Sebastian stopped talking when he saw the look in Suwon's eyes.

Suwon released a long breath, so long that it was hard to call it a sigh. Then he said, "I am Toy and Ujin's uncle, so you could say they have family 'and stuff,' yes. Though their parents passed many years ago. Cheese was a small homeless child I took in when he was very young. He became their cousin. Yejun was Toy's best friend in school, a foster child going from home to home."

Sebastian hadn't quite expected such an answer.

"And Kwan?" he asked softly.

"Kwan came to me later. He came to audition when the boys decided they wanted to form a group. We needed a fifth, a lead singer. I put out an advertisement, and hundreds auditioned. But Kwan was the best."

"And what about his parents?" Sebastian asked carefully.

"His mother died when he was young. And his father signed away parental rights, disappeared immediately. Kwan came to us because he knew his father didn't want him anymore."

Oh. That was truly sad. "So," said Sebastian slowly, "you take care of them. You're like their parent."

"I'm everything. Father, manager, teacher. At first I was scared to take on so much. But I have learned. And so have the boys. And I can be the same to you. You are smart. You are thoughtful. You would make an excellent friend to the Lost Boys. You could help them, help me," he said with a smile.

"But I'm not running away. I'm trying to run home. I need you to believe me."

Suwon nodded sympathetically, but he still didn't seem to believe Sebastian. "How about you go to sleep and think about it?"

"I honestly don't need to," Sebastian answered. Because he really didn't.

"I think you should." Suwon said it bluntly with a serious look on his face, both of which together seemed almost threatening.

It was so strange. Here was a man who seemed truly to want to help Sebastian, to be his surrogate father even, evidently. He was someone who cared enough to take on that responsibility. And yet at the same time he was doing more harm than good. His good intentions were definitely like ones from the proverb, leading in quite the wrong direction, down the road away from helpful. How did one fight a person like that? Sebastian had gotten used to dealing with evil people, and people who didn't entirely trust him, like Catherine. He had gotten used to convincing people who were reasonable but stubborn, like Myrtle. And of course he'd gotten used to the unpredictably clever Evie. But someone who wanted to be kind and who was at the same time oddly menacing? Sebastian hadn't had any practice with that yet.

"I don't . . ." He stopped. He had nothing to say.

"Well, you have time to think about it. Especially tomorrow, when we are all away at the concert."

"Wait, you're leaving me behind tomorrow?" For a moment Sebastian had hope that on his own he might be able to escape. And then of course he realized that his situation was likely to have more in common with solitary confinement. Solitary confinement with all the comforts of home and a gym and everything, but alone and imprisoned nonetheless.

"Only band members and crew are allowed backstage," said Suwon with a shrug.

Now, it wasn't that Sebastian was really that keen on seeing the concert in the first place,[13] or that he couldn't handle a bit of alone time. But it was yet another day and night of not getting in touch with anyone, another day and night trapped like this. Of course, it wasn't like going to the concert would change things. . . .

Unless . . .

. . . going to the concert changed things.

Yes. The concert. The concert where there would be thousands of people, fans, paparazzi, technicians backstage. All the opportunities in the world to slip away, to escape. *That* was his chance.

"But can't I come, just this one time? You said I could help," said Sebastian.

"Rules are rules." It did certainly seem that Suwon was a firm believer in rules being exactly what they were.

Suwon smiled. It wasn't a victorious grin, or malicious. It seemed warm and kind. And full of some kind of understanding. Sebastian once again found himself

---

[13] If they had forbidden him to see a concert performance of *The Pirates of Penzance*, on the other hand . . .

incapable of knowing what to do with such a smile. Such a *person*. It made him all the more uneasy.

He returned to Kwan's room—what else could he possibly do?—and felt even more unnerved when he heard the sound of the door being locked behind him. He was tiptoeing across the room to return to his sofa when he heard Kwan speak up.

"What's going on?"

Sebastian thought maybe he shouldn't answer honestly. After all, he was getting pretty used to this lying thing. Plus he had a new escape plan. But there was something in him that wanted to share. And it wasn't for his own sake. It was for Kwan's. He wanted to protect him. To warn him about Suwon. It was a risk, but he felt it was worth taking: "I tried to leave so I could find a way home, but Suwon wouldn't let me."

Kwan sat up in bed. It was hard to read his expression in the dark, but Sebastian really hoped the boy was on his side.

"He won't let you?"

"He doesn't believe I was kidnapped. He thinks I ran away. My guess is that he wants to adopt me. As your band's helper." For a brief moment Sebastian contemplated that scenario. Well, it would be better than being one of the Lost Boys, that was for sure. The feeling of sheer horror at the possibility of performing in front of huge crowds was too much for him. He barely enjoyed doing short presentations at school, for crying out loud. (And in fact, he had—cried out loud—over having to do his very first presentation ever in kindergarten, a show-and-tell involving a compass.)

"Oh. Well, I suppose that's nice of him."

"Is it? Is it nice of him? He's basically holding me prisoner!" Sebastian's unease was turning quickly to anger.

"Well, no, I suppose that's a problem. But he tries so hard. When he took me in . . ." Once again Kwan stopped midthought. Sebastian didn't feel it was the right moment to tell him he now knew the story. "Well, when he took me in, he was encouraging about my singing, about my dancing, and was so excited about how talented I was and that I was going to be a big star. He was so proud of me."

"And yet you don't want to tell him that maybe you want to do something more with your life and leave the band."

"Of course not," Kwan said quickly. Sebastian stayed quiet, fuming a little to himself. "What? What is it?" asked Kwan, noticing.

"I was just thinking how wrong that is. And it's frustrating that you can't see it. You don't want him to know that you want to leave the band because you're scared of what he'll do, and that's not right!"

Kwan was silent. The kind of silent that was so charged, it could power a small town. "I think that's personal."

"Well, I think it's wrong. I think Suwon is wrong. He's wrong to hold you back from pursuing your dreams, to force you to be a pop star. He's wrong to forbid you from using the Internet and from having phones. How are you going to ever learn what you want? To get to live the life you truly want? How are you ever going to learn how to take care of yourselves? It doesn't matter if it comes from a good, protective, proud place. It's wrong." Sebastian was pacing the room now, though he'd only just noticed he was doing it.

"He's not holding me back. He doesn't even know I have these dreams," Kwan said slowly.

Sebastian stopped pacing and placed his hands on his hips. He was angry now. Not at Kwan but at Suwon, at his own situation. "Well, why don't you tell him, then? Because you're afraid of him! You're afraid he'll do something if you leave the band! Because you're really his prisoner and—"

"No!" Kwan was up on his feet and turned on the light. He looked at Sebastian, staring him down.

Sebastian blinked for a moment at how bright it now was and also at Kwan's sudden fury. "I don't tell him because I don't want to disappoint him. Because he's done so much for me. Because he's the closest thing to a father I've ever had, and that includes my biological father!"

Sebastian hadn't quite been expecting that answer. He had been so focused on the warden side of Suwon that he'd forgotten the parent side.

"But what about me?" Sebastian asked. "I get that this is your home, but it's not mine. And I want to go back to mine." He felt physically weak all of a sudden; he felt sad.

"You should tell Suwon hyung—"

"I've tried to!"

"Then . . ." Kwan stopped talking and furrowed his eyebrows, thinking hard. "You need to find a way home."

Sebastian nodded. Yes, of course he had to. That was the point. "But I can't get out of the compound. Unless . . . you can help me out?" Sebastian looked at Kwan with faint hope.

Kwan shook his head. "We don't know the code to the lock. It's for our—"

"Protection. Of course." Sebastian sighed hard. "The key is the concert."

"The concert?" asked Kwan.

"Yes, all those people, all the chaos, it's the perfect time to slip away," Sebastian said.

"You can't come to the concert," said Kwan matter-of-factly.

"Yes, I know, it's a rule. Band only." Sebastian flopped onto the couch and sighed hard as he lay back, looking up at the dark ceiling. He sat up again. "Unless . . ."

"What?"

"Unless maybe by helping me I could be helping you." Sebastian wasn't sure his plan made sense yet, but it felt right.

Kwan looked both confused and a little excited. "What do you mean?"

"I join the band," said Sebastian with a grin.

"No, you can't. It's five members. It's us. It's just us. We're irreplaceable." Kwan said it matter-of-factly, so it didn't come across as arrogant, despite his word choice.

"But what if you weren't?" asked Sebastian, sliding to the edge of the sofa in excitement. "What if you were replaceable? What if we showed Suwon that? What if he realized that you could be replaced, and then you would be free to figure out what it is you want to do with your life? If you could train someone in a day to be a Lost Boy . . . if you trained me . . ."

"Impossible to do that in one day." Kwan was looking very serious now.

"Or at least train someone like me to be someone an audience would enjoy, maybe not as skilled or as good or as talented . . ." Sebastian stopped talking. It was then that he fully grasped the reality of what he was suggesting. He was suggesting that he, Sebastian, be trained at something he was, quite frankly, terrible at. Worse, he might have to perform in front of thousands. . . . No. No, if his plan actually worked, it would never come to that. He'd be gone before the curtain rose. Did curtains rise at K-pop performances?

Kwan was thinking hard now, though. He stood, and it was his turn to pace the room, back and forth. Sebastian watched him intently.

"This feels impossible. You're a terrible dancer," said Kwan as he paced.

"And an awful singer," added Sebastian. "But maybe there's something else I could do?"

Kwan stopped and gazed at the wall of instruments. "You are good at math. I saw you today, in school."

"I am, yes." What did math have to do with anything?

"Music and dancing are like math. Beats per bar, divided, multiplied. But there are added challenges. Music has notes. Dancing has grace. But keeping time, a beat, rhythm. That might be the most like math of all of them."

"I guess. . . ." Sebastian was starting to feel sincerely nervous, even though all this had been his idea.

Kwan turned and looked at Sebastian hard. "I think I know what we can do."

➤ CHAPTER 15 ➤

In which we go in search of a late-night snack.

Evie lay tucked in her comfy bed in her comfy room, but she felt anything but comfy. She felt frustrated and angry, and she turned onto one side in a huff. It didn't seem right that that was it. That Thom wasn't going to help them. He'd helped Benedict, after all. What was wrong with helping them? Why was Thom being so stubborn, and why was he so pleasant when he was being so stubborn? It was wrong. If you weren't going to be helpful, at least be an unlikable person. At least.

It wasn't the end of the world, she supposed, as she drew her blanket up under her chin. There had to be others out there who could help them, but knowing where to start, where to look, that felt almost impossible right now. Australia was a pretty big place, a country and a continent combined, with millions of people. Should they just go to Newish Isle, maybe? Would someone there know how to find the mysterious town?

And, of course, on top of all of that, there was her grandfather's letter. A riddle that remained unsolved. Or maybe not a riddle at all. Maybe he was just a weird letter writer. Maybe this was all so pointless and there was no one who could help them and everything was just impossible.

Evie sat up. She couldn't sleep. It was too much, too many thoughts, too much fear and resentment and . . . She wanted a snack. Yes, she ought to be full of stew, and she was. But this wasn't about hunger. A snack always calmed her down. When she was little and couldn't sleep, she would go downstairs after bedtime while her parents were still awake reading or watching TV, and they would make a snack for her. And at the Wayward School she used to sneak down to the kitchens after everyone else had gone to bed. She'd never run into anyone, which on the one hand she thought was weird because she knew that kids sneaked to the kitchens all the time at boarding schools, but on the other hand she kind of understood—the Wayward kitchens were deep in the basement, down a dark unlit hallway where mice scurried out of the way as you walked along it. Well, some of the mice; some seemed to want to join you as you went.

There was also the jet lag. It just messed with her system completely. Her brain had no idea what time it was at home, but her body was telling her it was eating time. *It wouldn't be stealing*, thought Evie as she got out of bed. She'd tell Catherine about it in the morning and they'd pay for whatever she had. Besides, she didn't want much. Maybe a piece of toast and some warm milk? A bowl of cereal? Something small. She slipped her shoes on and then quietly opened her door. The hallway had a small light glowing and was far friendlier than any of the hallways at Wayward. This was going to be easy.

She walked down the stairs and made it into the foyer. The front desk was shut down, and Evie assumed they'd locked up for the night. It made sense. Why bother having a twenty-four-hour concierge when you only had a couple of guests and weren't expecting more? This made it even easier for Evie.

Except of course now she realized that she didn't know how to get to the kitchen from inside the hotel. She stood in the foyer, feeling a little silly in her pajamas and running shoes. Her tummy grumbled.

Okay, brain, the tummy commanded, *let's think, let's think. . . .*

Yes! Evie remembered when she'd first met Erik at the front desk that morning. He'd come out of some door just around the corner from the desk. That had to be it!

She quickly darted around the desk and found the door, painted the same shade as the wall and almost invisible except for the doorknob. Evie opened it. It led downstairs into some kind of basement. Okay, well, sometimes kitchens were in basements. Like at Wayward. This felt perfectly normal. Of course, perfectly normal things did not require one to remind oneself that they felt perfectly normal, but . . .

Evie felt around for a light switch and found one near the top of the stairs. Though, when she turned it on, the light was not exactly impressive. Still, it was better than nothing, and Evie went down the rickety staircase. Downstairs was blackness, and it rose up to meet her on the last couple of steps. She squinted into it, and judging by the damp smell and the generally low ceiling, Evie guessed that this probably was not where the kitchens were located. She stepped onto the ground, a dirt floor. No, this definitely would not be the kitchen. A dirt floor could not possibly be up to code for the health department. She sighed. She had found the basement, that was all. She'd have to either try again or just go back to bed. Of course, now she was totally wired and wide awake, and her stomach was extra rumbly. And darn it, it was such a pity there was no food to be found.

Evie turned to go back up the stairs, and squish.

She raised her shoe and looked down at what she'd stepped on. It was hard to tell in the darkness, but the limited light from the staircase glinted off something silver. She bent down to have a closer look. And smell.

It was a fish. Very similar to the kind of fish she'd seen lying in the middle of the street earlier that day, actually. And now that she thought about it, the general smell in the basement was a fishy one. She stood upright. Maybe she had been wrong. Maybe this was the kitchen after all and they had different health standards in Australia or something. She took a step into the darkness and squinted. But the light from the staircase seemed to have come up against an invisible wall, or maybe it, as she did, found the basement just a little bit creepy.

Okay, if she took a few more steps forward, maybe her eyes would get used to the blackness. She took a step and another, leaving the light behind. Soon she was engulfed in black, and her eyes did adjust a little bit. She could see very basic shapes and outlines. Before her was something large and rectangular. Maybe a fridge? Or one of those low freezers? She reached with outstretched arms toward it, taking each step an inch at a time.

Her hands touched something cold and hard. She ran her hand up and came to an edge, the tips of her fingers going over and into a box. It had to be one of those freezers! Well, maybe there were Popsicles or something. But it seemed like it was open already, so maybe everything would be melted. Maybe all this was pointless and she should go to bed. She wasn't sure if she just wanted to reach inside the freezer without seeing what was in it. What if there was raw meat? Or, as the smell suggested, rotting fish? She felt a shiver run up her spine. A midnight snack wasn't worth it, not this much. Besides, if she went to sleep now, she'd wake up soon and it would be breakfast time.

She turned around.

Something tickled her face, and she jumped back. Her heart was in her throat, and she leaned against the fridge, panting. Carefully she extended her arm before her and waved it at around head height. There it was! The thing! She calmed herself down and grabbed for it. She realized then that it was a string, hanging from the ceiling. A wave of relief washed over her. Not only was the thing not some creepy insect or spider's web, but she had a funny feeling she knew exactly what it was. She pulled on the string. And the basement burst into light.

Okay, so she definitely wasn't in a kitchen. She was in what looked like a storage room, full of old junk, a lamp here, a desk there, a wagon against two large doors that Evie imagined must be a separate loading entrance for the inn.

Evie turned around to check out the fridge, just to see if maybe there actually were Popsicles after all.

Wild thrashing and big sharp teeth and—oh my goodness!

Evie ran as fast as she could out of the basement, tripping on the bottom stair and having to help herself climb up with her hands. Once out, she closed the door behind her and leaned against it. If her heart had been beating fast when the string for the light had tickled her, it was nothing compared to how berserk her heart was now.

Evie didn't know how, didn't know why, and almost didn't believe she'd seen what she'd seen. She shook out her whole body, trying to free it from the terror. Trying to free it from the realization that she had almost put her hand right into not a fridge, as she'd thought, but rather a large aquarium tank full of water.

Not that the water had particularly scared her. No.

It was the shark in the water that had been the terrifying part.

➤CHAPTER 16◄

In which Sebastian
shows off his skills.

Sebastian didn't so much wake up the next morning as put down the drumsticks and blink a few times. That was as awake as he was going to be, it seemed, but working all night with Kwan, pounding away on his drum kit (it was a good thing the walls in the compound were so thick, no one was woken up by his efforts), had produced somewhat decent results. At first it had felt impossible, because while singing required being on key and having a nice voice, and dancing required grace, drumming still required something more than just math to beat out a rhythm: coordination. It had taken two hours for Sebastian just to feel somewhat comfortable holding two drumsticks, hitting the drums and the cymbal, and tapping the bass drum with his foot. The rhythm part after that was a lot easier.

In the end, it turned out he wasn't exactly a child prodigy. His rhythms were basic and slow. But they still were something. And, he reminded himself, it wasn't like he'd actually have to perform onstage. This was just to get him to the concert, after all. It was something to share with the others. And they had to hope, with Kwan's leadership role in the group, that Suwon would give this a chance. Because otherwise, well . . . otherwise Sebastian really didn't want to know what would happen. Would he just have to be Suwon's helper for the rest of time?

With such fears weighing heavily on his shoulders, blisters on his fingers, and exhaustion swirling around his brain, Sebastian began the daily routine again. This time, though, he refrained from asking for a phone and instead explained that he'd thought long and hard about it and that he wanted to stay.

Suwon smiled knowingly, though what he knew and what there was to be known were worlds apart, and Sebastian waited patiently through breakfast and tumbling practice and schoolwork for Kwan to make the proposition. Even though it was still before noon, Sebastian was starting to get just a little bit antsy.

Finally, at dance rehearsal, Kwan made the suggestion.

"No," said Suwon. "There can only be five of you."

"But he won't dance or sing! He'll play!" said Kwan. Sebastian watched as the teen nervously fiddled with a loose thread on his T-shirt, but otherwise he was doing a good job and being the calm, happy Kwan that Sebastian had grown to know.

"This is ridiculous." Suwon turned to Sebastian apologetically. "Kwan clearly likes you, and that's good, now that you are family. But you can't be a Lost Boy. I am sure you understand that."

"But I want to be," said Sebastian, not at all convinced by his attempt to sound convincing.

"He can play the drums. Let him show you!" said Kwan with a smile. Sebastian felt his heart drop. He glanced around the room at the other boys watching the conversation with curiosity. He gave them a small smile, which they returned with bright, beaming ones of their own.

"I want to see!" said Ujin.

There were sounds of agreement from the other boys, and even though Suwon looked really suspicious about the whole situation, they all ran off with Kwan to fetch the kit from his room.

"Please don't mistake me," said Suwon when Sebastian and he were alone. "I'm very happy you'll be joining our family. But the Lost Boys are special. They've trained for years. They are irreplaceable."

Yes, I know. That's the problem, thought Sebastian. Of course, he didn't say that. Instead he just smiled as reassuringly as he could.

When the boys returned, Sebastian noticed something a little different about them. They put the drum kit together while whispering to each other. Cheese looked at Sebastian briefly and gave him a quick wink. Suddenly Sebastian had the impression that maybe this secret of his and Kwan's was no longer quite so private.

Had Kwan told them the plan? He couldn't have said the part about Kwan wanting to leave the band. They'd surely have been upset at that news. But he probably did tell them about Sebastian's plan to escape. It would explain why they all looked a bit . . . sneaky.

Great. Now he had to hope all five of them wouldn't give the plan away, not just Kwan.

"Okay, Opera Boy! Show them what you can do!" said Kwan with a bit too much enthusiasm.

"Sure, but maybe now you need to call me Drummer Boy or something," joked Sebastian poorly as he made his way around the kit and took the sticks off the small stool. Even holding them lightly like this, he could feel the rawness of his fingertips. This was not going to be fun.

"I still like 'Opera Boy,' " said Toy, but Sebastian really didn't care. He was too focused on the drums in front of him.

Slowly he sat down and stared at the drums. Then he took in a deep breath and raised the drumsticks into the air. It seemed in that moment that his fingers had swollen in size, fumbling the sticks even before he struck a beat. He glanced at Kwan, who gave him an encouraging nod, and then he started playing.

It was extremely rough at first. The bass was hardly keeping time, and each hit on a drum was distinct and awkward. But he kept going, warming up, and eventually he was able to tap out a pretty basic rhythm. It was hardly impressive. Sebastian looked at Suwon, who looked both confused and disappointed, and as Sebastian looked, he suddenly lost the beat. He stopped and stared at the drums for a moment, feeling pretty pathetic.

Silence descended on the dance studio.

"That was great!" said Ujin, a little too loudly, it seemed.

"I bet we could choreograph something to that," added Kwan. He gestured to the boys and then to Sebastian. And even though Sebastian was feeling a little numb inside and even more numb in his fingers, he smiled bravely and started the rhythm up again.

This time with the boys improvising choreography and gymnastics to his beats, Sebastian started to feel a bit more confident. So confident, even, that he attempted a couple of improvised moments of his own. And by the time he just had to stop because his hands hurt too much, a smile had grown on Suwon's face. It wasn't the usual smile either. It wasn't knowing or even proud. It was . . . it was surprised.

"That was great!" said Yejun, panting a bit.

"The fans will love it!" added Toy.

"I must agree. It *is* a great idea, and once perfected—" started Suwon, approaching the group.

"Let's perform it tonight!" Kwan interrupted with a big charming grin. "We can practice all afternoon and get a really good routine down. Besides, it'll be a great way to end the tour."

Suwon looked at him for a moment, then looked at Sebastian, who tried to grin just as charmingly but was pretty sure it looked more like he had gas or something. Finally Suwon sighed.

"Okay," he said. "Okay. As a way of introducing the latest Lost Boy. Okay. But then we have a lot of practice to do before the next album if we are to make this drumming idea work."

Sebastian nodded, wholeheartedly agreeing even though he had no intention of joining the band. If in theory he was to join it, far more practice indeed was required. He thought for a moment, and then watched as Suwon approached the boys, looking pleased as they enthusiastically thanked him. It was weird. Despite his need to control everyone and everything, Suwon was actually surprisingly open to suggestions. Sebastian now started to wonder: Was Kwan really afraid of telling him the truth, or was it more that Kwan was afraid of the truth itself? Of leaving the band, of leaving his family?

You're still being kept prisoner, reminded Sebastian's brain.

Right. Yes. Right. Focus, Sebastian, focus.

He made eye contact with Kwan, who winked at him.

Sebastian tried to wink back and did a strange sort of blink instead.

He could do this. He would do this. Tonight he was going home.

➤ CHAPTER 17 ◄

In which things start to get weird. Er.

No snack could have willed Evie to sleep that night. There was really nothing except maybe some kind of a sleeping pill that would have done it. Her adrenaline was surging fast, and she lay awake all night, staring up at the ceiling, waiting for the dawn. She listened as the waves crashed against the shore, as a car rumbled loudly past, and as the birds started to wake up and sing.[14] Eventually she sensed the light, and not knowing what else to do and feeling antsy just lying there still, she got dressed quickly and ran downstairs

---

[14] Interestingly, the wake-up song sung by birds in Australia was banned by the bird population in North America for being just way too perky, even for morning birds.

and outside, carefully avoiding even looking in the direction of the basement door.

She stood on the front veranda and stared in front of her. Sunrise over the sea. A fine line of light blue rising and turning whiter and whiter, until the sun popped up its head and yawned, spreading brilliant orange across the horizon. Maybe not sleeping had its perks. She sat down on a step and kept watching. The air was cool, but she could sense it warming up fast. It was going to be another hot day. Perfect for swimming. If only she was allowed to be a tourist and not a girl on a rescue mission. If only also there wasn't Steve out there in the dark depths . . .

Steve.

Evie leaned forward for a moment, placing her elbows on her knees and resting her chin in her hands.

Steve.

Steve the great white shark.

Stalking the sea.

She stood up in a rush of energy and looked back toward the door of the inn. It was still so early, and yet . . . yet surely this was exactly the kind of thing Catherine wanted to hear about. Surely this was the kind of thing you woke up the animal expert of the former Filipendulous Five for.

Evie turned back and looked at the sea once more.

There, so much closer than she'd expected, right in the middle of the cove itself, was a dark fin silhouetted against the sunrise. It glided along the surface and then disappeared for a moment.

A sign. It had to be.

Evie swung open the door to the inn and ran upstairs. She skidded to a stop in front of Catherine's room and banged on her door hard. Harder, really, than she had anticipated, but clearly she was not entirely in control of her body right now.

She stood impatiently waiting and placed an ear to the door to see if she could hear any rustling, any movement at all.

And then she fell into Catherine's room.

"What the . . . ?" said the sleepy explorer as Evie staggered upright. Catherine had opened the door so quickly that Evie hadn't had a chance to correct her balance, and now she was blinking a few times from the shock.

"Hey, Catherine," said Evie, then stopped. She found herself suddenly unsure what to say next.

"What's going on? Are you okay?" Catherine looked deeply concerned, and Evie immediately felt guilty for waking her so abruptly.

"Oh, I'm fine, I'm fine. I, uh, watched the sunrise!"

"Great," said Catherine, sitting down on her bed.

It was only then that Evie noticed her pajamas, flannel bottoms and a tank top, both covered in drawings of lions, tigers, and bears. Oh my, thought Evie, those are pretty cool-looking.

"I'm so sorry for waking you, but I suddenly realized something and I thought you should know," said Evie, starting to pace around the room, trying to release some of the energy she was feeling.

"Okay . . ."

"I think I know why Steve is hanging out in the cove!" she said.

"Yes?"

"Yes! I think he is looking for his kid. Or his niece or nephew. Or maybe a smallish younger sister, perhaps," added Evie, realizing she wasn't any kind of shark expert. It was just that she knew that the shark in the basement was way smaller than the average-sized great white, so it probably wasn't an adult.

"What are you talking about?" asked Catherine with a sigh. She reached up and pinched the bridge of her nose with her fingers.

"There's a little shark in the basement, and I think maybe that the little shark is related to the big shark."

At that, Catherine finally made eye contact. She stared at Evie hard. And for a long time. She was clearly processing the information she'd just been given. Evie wondered about the kind of conclusions she was drawing, the thoughts she had about the whole situation.

Finally Catherine spoke. "What?"

Evie sighed hard. "Last night I got up to try to find the kitchen because I was hungry. I went through the basement door, and I didn't find the kitchen. Instead I found a shark in a tank. It had these sharp pointy teeth and was thrashing around. It scared me half to death. Anyway, this morning I got up and saw Steve swimming outside, and suddenly I put two and two together. You yourself said it was odd for a shark to just stake out a cove for this long. And I think this is why. He's looking for his . . . relative." Evie didn't feel like making up another hypothetical list of possible relations.

Catherine rose and then sat down again. She looked at Evie. "There's a shark in the basement."

"Yes!"

Catherine sighed. "Evie, that's not possible. You can't keep a shark in a basement. Not a great white, that's for sure. They need to swim all the time. Not one has lasted in captivity longer than sixteen days. And also, they're huge." Despite what Catherine was saying, Evie didn't think Catherine sounded 100 percent like she didn't believe her. That was good at least.

"Well, it wasn't huge. It was little. Like I said. I mean, it felt huge at the time because it surprised me, but it wasn't. It was little. Little*r*, at least." Why was she explaining when she could simply show Catherine? "Please just come with me!" It really made the most sense. Seeing is believing. At least, that's what she'd heard someone say once.

Catherine nodded and quickly changed into her usual khaki pants, boots, and tan shirt. Then she followed Evie down to the foyer. Erik was standing behind the desk and smiled at them as they approached. And then watched as they walked right by him.

"Uh . . . you aren't allowed back here," he said with surprise as Evie completely ignored him and opened the door. She turned on the light and walked with purpose down the stairs, Catherine at her heels, and Erik behind her. "Seriously, mates, you can't be down there. It's dangerous."

"Yeah?" asked Evie, whipping around and reaching for the string. "Or maybe you're hiding something you don't want us to see!" With that, she pulled on the string and smiled in triumph.

"It's more just a safety issue. There's a lot of old junk down here," explained Erik after the lights came on.

Evie furrowed her eyebrows. Why was no one else reacting like she had to the shark?

"Okay, so where is it?" asked Catherine, placing her hands on her hips.

What? Evie spun around. The giant tank was gone. And so was the shark. Evie rushed over to the spot, as if maybe she was standing at an odd angle that made the tank invisible. Or . . . something.

Nothing.

She looked around. Not even a squished dead fish on the floor. She looked at Catherine. "I swear," she said, her voice shaking a little. "I swear there was a shark in here. Last night. It was here."

Catherine looked at her funny and then looked at Erik. "Sorry about that. We'll get out of here," she said. She turned back to Evie. "Come on, Evie. Time for some breakfast."

Evie stammered and sputtered and then fell silent. There was nothing she could do but nod sadly and follow Catherine back up the stairs, avoiding Erik's stunned expression. She walked with Catherine out the front door and around the side to where Ruby was just starting to set the tables. Ruby saw them both and smiled broadly.

"Wow, you guys are early! I guess you're ready for something to eat."

Evie sat down at a table. Her tummy stayed silent. *Oh, so now you're not hungry,* thought Evie. *Great. Just great.*

⋙ CHAPTER 18 ⋘

In which Sebastian attends his first K-pop concert.

Sebastian sat on the bus, fiddling with the drumsticks in his bandaged hands. After a full afternoon working on a routine they would never actually perform, his raw fingers had gotten even more roughed up from working the drumsticks, so much so that his left index finger had actually started to bleed. They'd wrapped up the wound and decided they might as well protect the rest of his fingers as well. Now he looked a bit like a boxer, his hands all wrapped up in white. The boys assured him bandages made him look pretty cool, but Sebastian was more worried about whether he'd ever be able to feel anything in the tips of his fingers again. Fortunately, this concern was a distant second to the rushing chaotic feeling of butterflies dive-bombing in his stomach. He was, quite frankly, a bundle of nerves.

On top of the throbbing fingers and the fear at the thought of trying to escape, he was also just plain physically uncomfortable. The band had insisted that if he was now a Lost Boy, then he should look the part. Kwan had loaned him a black sports jacket that had this sparkle to it under the light. Then Sebastian had borrowed equally sparkly black jeans from Toy. And Ujin had given him a designer T-shirt that really just looked like a plain white T-shirt that had gone through a paper shredder. All of the items were surprisingly tight, and the jacket itched around his neck. But more than that, he was wearing eyeliner. Cheese had carefully applied it to his face, and even though it wasn't heavy or anything, Sebastian could still feel it on himself, almost as if it was weighing down his eyelids. And he was fairly sure he'd been blinking more than normal ever since it had been applied.

So yeah, he was physically uncomfortable and mentally uncomfortable. Not only did he need to worry about his imminent escape, about how on earth he was planning to slip out of the stadium, but he had a small slight fear, a tiny independent moth among the butterflies: What if something went wrong?

"We'll get you out, don't worry," whispered Kwan

reassuringly as he sat next to Sebastian, resplendent in his sparkling blue suit.

Sebastian nodded, listening but not. He glanced up at the bus, where the rest of the band members were lounging and laughing, totally happy and excited to perform. "When are you going to tell Suwon that you're thinking of leaving?"

Kwan shook his head and clenched his jaw. "I don't know. I'm too scared. What if hyung throws me out of the band right away? Out of my home?" asked Kwan, his face forlorn.

"He won't! You're more than just a band member," said Sebastian, really hoping that it was true.

"What are you two talking about?"

Sebastian would have jumped at the sudden presence of Suwon if his pants hadn't been so tight.

"Oh, um," said Kwan, and then he fell silent. Suwon looked at him, puzzled.

"He's giving me tips on the drumming. I think I'm going to seriously rock this thing," said Sebastian. *Rock this thing?* Was that something that people said? He hoped so.

Suwon smiled a little tentatively. It was actually rather impressive how many different kinds of smiles the man had available to him. "Well, in time. With more practice. Tonight will be . . . for fun." He was trying so hard not to make Sebastian feel bad. It was almost nice of him.

"Oh yeah, of course. I just think in time I'm going to . . . rock . . . this . . . thing. . . ." Surely, *surely*, there was a better turn of phrase he could come up with?

Suwon sighed and leaned back. "You're really going to enjoy this. The show tonight." He smiled at Sebastian, who smiled back.

"Yeah," added Kwan. "Our concerts are kind of amazing."

"I'm sure they are," replied Sebastian, feeling unbelievably awkward sitting squished between the two of them. He was trapped, like he'd been trapped the whole time. It didn't really matter that he was starting to grow fond of both of them. Yes, even Suwon was becoming less evil than Sebastian had originally thought. But still. It was time. *Let this be over soon, please.*

The bus had been flying through the streets of Seoul as fast as when they had been pursued two nights earlier. Sebastian was waiting for it to pull to a stop outside the stadium. The stadium surrounded by fans. Where the band would disembark in a mob of camera flashes and screams, and where Sebastian would just take off, bolt down the street, go in whatever direction, just so long as he could get away. He kept a close watch through the window, absentmindedly tapping the drumsticks against his legs. Then, there it was! Bright lights flooding the street, making the world seem like day. The large sign on the stadium, advertising the Lost Boys in letters ten feet tall both in Korean and English. Swarms of fans entering the building. It was time. It was now!

And then . . .

They turned a corner, and in a flash they were suddenly driving into an underground tunnel. It happened so quickly, it felt almost dreamlike. Truly this entire experience had been dreamlike. He pinched himself on the leg, just in case. But that was silly. Of course he was awake. Unless, that is, in his dream he dreamed he was pinching himself.

The bus rolled to a stop, and Suwon got up to take charge. Sebastian turned to Kwan. "I thought I'd have a chance to escape," he whispered fiercely.

"Yes, certainly—after the concert, when we go and sign autographs by the gate," replied Kwan, looking at him, confused.

And that was when Sebastian realized it. All this time he'd been thinking he was only *saying* he was going to perform. But had he actually communicated that thought to Kwan? He couldn't remember. It seemed like although they'd shared a plan, they hadn't shared all the hows and wheres and, most important, whens. Kwan thought Sebastian was actually going to perform. Onstage. In front of thousands.

"I can't perform!" squeaked Sebastian as Kwan stood up to follow the other Lost Boys disembarking from the bus.

"Absolutely you can. The routine is great," said Kwan with a smile. And then he turned and left the bus. Sebastian sat there for a moment alone. Wondering if maybe he could just hide out and wait till everyone had gone and then run back up the tunnel.

"Sebastian?" called Suwon, sticking his head back into the bus.

Sebastian took a deep breath. He was not going to have a panic attack. Not here, not now. He didn't have the time. Even though he could feel his breath getting shallow, his pulse rate increasing, he was determined. He closed his eyes for a moment. *Breathe in, breathe out.* He tried to picture Evie sitting next to him, saying calming words. Saying anything: "I think it sounds like it could be really fun! What an opportunity!" Sebastian smiled, imagining it. Yes, that was a thing she'd say.

"Sebastian?" Suwon's voice broke through his imagining, and Sebastian opened his eyes again.

"I'm . . . I'm coming," he said with a gulp. Slowly,

as if he was walking on a ship during a storm, Sebastian teetered his way down the bus and to the door. Suwon smiled again at him as he stepped down the stairs and joined the Lost Boys. They had been greeted by a flurry of techies and the stage manager, who started speaking with Suwon in Korean. Then they were ushered quickly down a series of cement tunnels underground, and Sebastian got more and more concerned that escape might not be possible at all, even after the show, that he might actually have to become a Lost Boy. And while the horror of never seeing his family, Evie, or anyone from the Explorers Society again was high, right now the greatest fear of all was *I was not made to be a performer.* The knots in his stomach tied themselves into one giant über-knot and pulled taut. Maybe he should have simply jumped from the moving bus. He was feeling desperate enough to have tried that.

As they continued to wend their way through the elaborate labyrinth, Sebastian heard the sound of rumbling, and he stopped short, causing Cheese to crash into him.

"What's wrong?" asked Yejun, darting around the two of them and looking back toward Sebastian.

"I think it's an earthquake," Sebastian said. He'd never experienced an earthquake before, but the way the ground was shaking, the little dust particles that were falling from the ceiling, it all seemed to suggest that one was happening right now. And he really couldn't handle such a thing, not on top of all the other things.

Yejun laughed, and then Cheese joined him. Soon all the Lost Boys were laughing and starting to walk again. "That's no earthquake," said Yejun.

"No?" asked Sebastian, not entirely believing him.

"No."

Of course no explanation was offered, and so Sebastian's fears did not go away. In fact they only increased as the rumbling got louder and louder. If it wasn't an earthquake, then maybe it was a giant train barreling toward them in the tunnel? Right now it seemed the only possible answer.

Until a more plausible answer presented itself.

Suddenly they were no longer underground but instead were heading on an upward angle, their hallway turning into a kind of ramp. In front of Sebastian was darkness, and soon he was engulfed in it and the sound of rumbling. It took a moment for his eyes to adjust, and for him to realize he was backstage. And then, of course, the rumbling made perfect sense. It wasn't just rumbling. It was feet. Thousands of feet stomping the floor. And voices, too. Voices chanting in perfect unison what Sebastian now knew was the Korean for

"Lost Boys, Lost Boys, Lost Boys." All this just there, just beyond the blackness.

Sebastian was maneuvered by Suwon a little farther along and then around a corner. There was nowhere for Sebastian to go, to run to. He was just pushed forward toward his doom. Suddenly there was light again, and Sebastian could see the stage. He could see the entire vastness and the darkness beyond the other side of the stage. He still couldn't see the audience, but my goodness could he hear them! The stage was lit by shafts of light in purple and blue. Covering the back wall were over a dozen huge monitors that together created one giant screen. Right now they were showing images that dissolved into one another, images from some of the music videos Sebastian had seen. On occasion, the face of one of the boys would materialize, and then the crowd would stop its chanting for a moment to shriek and scream. It was kind of terrifying and awe inspiring. But mostly terrifying.

"Opera Boy! Over here!" called out Kwan, and Sebastian turned to see that the band and Suwon were standing in a tight huddle. He ran over to join them, holding the drumsticks tight to his chest almost like a security blanket. Once they had drawn him into the huddle, Kwan started to speak, first in Korean and then in English: "Here's to an amazing show. To an amazing band. To an amazing family. Play well and have fun!" He put his hand in the middle of the circle, and the others did as well, including Sebastian. "Lost Boys," said Kwan. And then the other boys said it too, and then, much like the audience, they chanted the band's name, getting faster and faster, louder and louder, until they all whooped together and raised their hands as one. Sebastian couldn't help but laugh with the rest of them, the energy was crazy-infectious.

And then, suddenly, the boys were off, darting away from the stage and into the darkness.

"What's happening? Where are they going?" asked Sebastian, turning to Suwon, who grinned back at him.

"You'll see," he replied. Suwon placed what in any other set of circumstances would have been a comforting hand on Sebastian's shoulder, but to Sebastian it felt like the kind of clamp the parking police put on the wheels of cars parked in the wrong place.

Sebastian stared ahead at the stage. The cheering of the audience had gotten louder and louder. It was a frenzy out there. On the giant screen, slowly, one by one, a picture of each of the boys materialized, until all five of their giant faces were grinning at the audience.

And then sudden darkness.

And then the crowd went wild.

➤ CHAPTER 19 ➤

In which a plan is made.

"Thank you for this," said Catherine as she sat in front of the small computer on the small desk in Ruby's small office.

"Oh, it's the least I could do. Again, I'm really sorry about my dad," replied Ruby.

"It's okay," said Catherine, logging on to the Internet and staring intently at the screen.

Ruby smiled and looked around the room. Then she looked at Evie. "I don't have much in here that's entertaining. Uh . . ." She picked a book up off the corner of the desk and handed it to Evie. "One of Erik's. I have no idea if it's interesting or really boring."

Evie nodded and took the book. She wasn't sure

why she needed it. After all, she was there to help Catherine find someone who could help them. But sometimes adults didn't realize how important a kid was to the team, so she didn't feel a need to say anything. She just stared at the book. *The Care and Consideration of Fish and Other Aquatic Animals.*

With a title like that, how could the book possibly be boring? thought Evie sarcastically.

She absentmindedly opened its cover while leaning over to see what Catherine had found.

"Any luck?" she asked.

Catherine shook her head. "The difficulty is that so many people don't believe the town exists in the first place. They compare it to Brigadoon."

"Where's that?"

"I'm not sure. But it looks fictional and . . ." Catherine leaned closer. "Musical." She sighed and then clicked the mouse a bit more. "What would be simplest is to hire a helicopter like those horrible men, but you can't legally fly over the volcano."

"Those men won't care if it's allowed or not. They'll fight anyone who tries to stop them," said Evie with resentment.

"Yeah, that's the problem." Catherine's clicking was getting louder and harder, and though her face stayed the same calm version of itself, Evie got the impression the animal expert was getting frustrated.

Time to leave her alone, thought Evie. Or maybe it was more like it was time for Evie to be alone. Catherine's anxiety wasn't exactly helping Evie's worried thoughts about Sebastian, and she was also still reeling from the lack of shark in the basement. Besides, she did her best problem-solving on her own. "Hey, I'm just going to sit outside for a bit, get some fresh air."

Catherine nodded but didn't say anything. She just kept clicking. Faster and faster, harder and harder. Evie backed away slowly through the open door, hugging Erik's book to her chest.

Then she turned and walked down the hall, down the stairs, and out the front door. She paused for a moment and then decided to cross the street to the beach. This time there were actually people walking along the boardwalk, that older couple from breakfast the day before. Evie waved, and they waved back. As she stepped onto the sand, she heard a little gasp, and she turned around. The woman had her hand over her mouth. She looked scared.

"Be careful, dear!" said her husband. "There's a shark."

"I know," replied Evie. Sharks don't swim on sand,

she wanted to point out, but it wasn't really worth it. The couple was just being concerned.

And then she had to double-check her memory. *Sharks don't swim on sand, do they?*

No, replied her memory.

Yeah, I thought not.

Evie strolled over to where the jungle spilled out onto the sand, and sat in the shade of a tall tree, facing the sea. She gazed out as far as she could, going over her grandfather's letter in her mind, trying to solve the riddle. But her thoughts kept wandering to the little shark from the night before. Could it all have been a dream? Had any of it actually happened? It certainly had felt very real. No. Evie refused to think she hadn't seen what she had seen. What would Sebastian have thought at a time like this? He'd have known he hadn't been seeing things. There was a shark. And now it was gone. There was no such thing as magic, so the only reasonable conclusion was that somehow, at some point, the little shark had been moved. And now that she thought about it, maybe it had been moved because someone had seen her downstairs. She hadn't exactly been quiet racing up out of the basement.

Yes. That's what had happened. Someone had gotten rid of the shark, removed all evidence, including the little fish. . . .

Fish.

A shark was a fish.

Evie slowly looked down at the book on her lap.

She opened the cover and flipped through the pages. It was as boring to look at on the inside as the title had been on the outside. For a book all about some of the most colorful and exotic creatures on the planet, the little black-and-white drawings every few pages hardly did them justice. The writing did even less—dry, purely scientific, with no effort to capture the reader's attention or imagination, or really with any interest in whether a reader read the book or not. But as Evie flipped through it, she did find one very interesting thing. Notes in the margins. And paragraphs circled here and there. And as she flipped on, a story was unfolding, told not by the author of the book but by its reader. Someone was interested in how, in very practical terms, to take care of fish. Transport them. Keep them comfortable and safe.

Evie slowly looked up from the book.

In a flash her memories categorized everything of relevance very nicely for her: the figure outside at night, Erik and his purple-and-pink fish, the little silver fish in the street, the little silver fish in the basement. And the little shark. The *relatively* little shark.

And now the book. "One of Erik's."

Erik.

Evie stood up abruptly. This time she knew she was right. Well, she had known she was right before, but this time she had evidence. Tenuous evidence, but the book . . . the book was good evidence. Solid. Factual. Boring-but-exciting-at-the-same-time kind of evidence.

She tore through the front door, up the steps, and into the little office. Catherine was still sitting exactly as Evie had left her, though her face was less intense, wearier. She looked up at Evie and gave her a sad smile.

"I figured it out!" announced Evie, breathless.

"You found someone to take us to the town?" Catherine's eyes got bright and wide.

"Oh. Oh, no. No, I didn't do that," said Evie.

"Oh! You solved Alistair's riddle!" Catherine's eyes got even brighter and wider.

"Um. No. Uh . . . not that either." Evie was now wondering if maybe her attentions were not exactly as focused on what they ought to have been.

Now Catherine furrowed her eyebrows. Her eyes were no longer wide nor sparkly. "Then what did you figure out, exactly?"

Okay, well, now it just felt kind of . . . unimportant. "Where the little shark went, or at least who removed it. I guess . . . I guess really this is all kinds of silly. This isn't something I should be focusing on." She sat, deflated, on her small chair again.

"Okay, tell me," said Catherine. Her eyebrows remained furrowed, and she still didn't look like she believed her, but Evie appreciated being humored. Especially because Catherine wasn't the humoring type.

"I think Steve is looking for his little shark. I think Steve is trying to find him. That's why he's not leaving the cove. I think the little shark was taken, and I think Erik took him. I think he really likes fish and I think he's been feeding the shark at night, bringing it fish in a wagon. And I think he moved the little shark when he realized I saw it last night." Saying it out loud like that did suddenly make it all sound a bit far-fetched, but it wasn't, Evie knew. It really wasn't.

Or even if it was, that didn't make it any less true.

Catherine thought for a moment. "Well, I don't know. Sharks aren't known for their caregiving skills. Normally when they give birth, they leave the baby to take care of itself from that point on."

"Really?" asked Evie. She tried to imagine that, being abandoned by one's parents the moment you were born, no one to teach you or care for you. Just making your own way. Then again it wasn't so far off from her own lonely situation, but that thought hurt a bit too much, so she pushed it out of her head.

"Then again," continued Catherine, "nature does constantly surprise us. And great whites do travel in schools. And there doesn't seem to be any other reason to explain Steve's presence. So . . . maybe . . . I don't know. . . . I suppose that could be true. But if it is, I don't fully understand how Erik could possibly contain a great white in a tank. More than that, I'm not sure it's the best use of our time to investigate it." She swiveled slowly back to the computer.

"I guess not," said Evie. "But . . . don't you care about Steve at all? And what about the trapped little shark? That's so sad! Don't you care about them being reunited?"

Catherine seemed to soften at that, but she didn't look back at Evie. "I do care. I worry a great deal. It's something I've been thinking about a lot. Do we sacrifice helping our friend to help the shark? It's hard for me to make such decisions, but I tried to do what I thought Alistair would do: help the team first. I wasn't always very good at that in the past. . . ." She trailed off.

Evie didn't want to pry, and she now felt guilty using Catherine's love of animals as a way to convince her to seek out the little shark. Of course Benedict's and Sebastian's safety was worth more. Of course it was.

And then a thought.

"Or maybe . . ." Evie stopped and pondered for a moment.

Catherine glanced over. "Yes?"

Suddenly Evie looked up at her, grinning widely, her eyes bright and shiny. "Maybe there's a way to do both!"

"How so?" asked Catherine.

"Steve has ruined this tourist season for the cove, right? You heard Ruby talking to her dad, how she might have to even give up the inn. And her dad obviously was upset for her."

Evie didn't need to connect the dots any further. Catherine stood upright in one quick movement. "Evie, you're right! Helping Steve could very well help us. As it so often does, helping animals ends up helping humans! If we get Steve and this little shark back together, Steve will be happy and hopefully will leave the cove."

"And," added Evie, "when Steve leaves the cove, the tourists will come back and Ruby's business will be saved. . . ."

"And then maybe her father . . ."

"Yes! Maybe then he'll help us, to say thank you!"

"So we need to find the shark!" said Catherine. She seemed excited, which was not something Catherine seemed that often.

"What do you mean, 'Find the shark'?" asked Ruby, standing in the doorway.

➤ CHAPTER 20 ◄

In which shark stuff happens.

"You think Erik has a little shark and that's why Steve has been stalking our cove?" Ruby repeated the words slowly after Evie had explained it all to her. She mulled over each of them, as if one might reveal whether Evie was totally crazy or not.

"Yes, we do. I think he's been keeping it in the basement and feeding it fish in the middle of the night, and I think he saw me last night, and I think he took it somewhere," said Evie, breathless.

"If this is true . . . If this is true . . . ," said Ruby to herself. "Is it true?" She looked at Catherine. It was one of those annoying things adults did on occasion, a need to verify the truth of something with another adult, as if all kids were liars or something. Evie really didn't like it, but right now she just wanted to convince Ruby, regardless of how she did it.

"I believe it's true," Catherine answered. "I believe Evie."

Evie smiled.

"Okay. Then we need to find this little shark and return it to the ocean," said Ruby, sounding suddenly very sure of herself. "And we need to do it now."

"We agree," said Evie.

"Erik gets afternoons off. I guess we just have to go pay him a visit," said Ruby.

"I guess so," replied Evie. Besides, she figured wherever Erik was, very likely the little shark was there too.

In no time at all they were piling back into Ruby's truck and speeding down the highway in the opposite direction from Thom's place. Evie's hair whipped around her face, and she felt both exhilarated and scared. What if Erik didn't have the little shark? What if it had all been a dream after all, the shark in the basement? What if all this helping out didn't end with Thom helping them?

Then again, what if Erik *did* have the shark? What then?

So many what-ifs.

Evie held tightly to the seat of the truck as the

pickup sped around a corner onto a dirt road, a cloud of dust left in their wake. They were now heading deeper into the jungle again but not uphill this time. Evie looked out to her side. They were passing several single-story houses and even some camping trailers, all brightly painted, with colorful messy front yards. Suddenly Ruby slammed her foot on the brake, and Evie flew forward, saved by her seat belt, and landed back in her seat again with a thud.

"We're here," said Ruby.

All three of them stared out the side of the truck at a bright blue single-story house, small but cozy-looking. Stuck into the ground were decorative pieces of metal art, all shaped like various kinds of fish. On the side of the blue house there was even a giant painting of an angelfish.

"Okay, so evidently Erik really likes fish," said Ruby, stepping out of the car. "I'm not sure how I missed that."

"Sometimes we miss the things right in front of us," replied Evie, jumping out of the truck and staring at the house.

"I guess," replied Ruby. She pushed open the little white gate at the front of the property, and the three of them made their way up the path to the front door.

"Wait," said Evie as Ruby approached it.

"What?" asked Ruby.

"If Erik moved the little shark because he saw me, then I think we can assume he's a little nervous. I'm not sure that going up to his front door and just asking him is the way to do this," said Evie quietly, worried that Erik might be watching her right now.

"So what do you suggest?" asked Catherine.

"I think we need to be . . . sneaky."

Evie walked away from the front door and, as quietly as she could, made her way along the front of the house and then around the corner into the shade along its side. She looked over her shoulder. Catherine and Ruby were following behind. Suddenly Evie heard a noise and she stopped, holding up her hand to let the others know to do likewise. Evie crouched down. She crawled the last couple of feet and flattened herself against the wall. Then she carefully looked around the corner.

"Oh, oh my," said Ruby from behind.

"Oh, oh my" was right.

Before them in Erik's backyard, all manner of large plastic buckets and tools were strewn over the long grass. Massive bags of fish food sat open in the hot sun, and hoses snaked across the yard, making quite the obstacle course. But that wasn't the "oh, oh my" of it all. No, the "oh, oh my" was what looked to be a homemade aboveground swimming pool standing in the middle of everything, around which was a kind of makeshift deck. But not just that. Two teetering bridges crossed it. And standing at the intersection of the two bridges, right over the center of the pool, was Erik.

From where they were watching, he seemed to be shaking.

"Erik?" said Ruby, standing up and walking slowly into the backyard.

Erik looked at her with wide eyes and held his hand out toward her. "Ruby, stop. It's too dangerous."

"What's going on?"

Erik looked at them and bit his lower lip. Then he looked down into the water, then back at them.

"Come on, Erik," said Ruby gently, taking another step closer, "you can tell us."

"Ruby, stop!" he cried out again.

She stopped.

"I . . . I'm trapped. It won't let me down." And just as he said it, there was a sudden flash of gray and white and then a giant splash, sending water pouring over the side of the pool. Erik cowered, balancing precariously on the bridge.

"Is that the little shark?" asked Evie.

Erik nodded but was too terrified to say anything.

"And it keeps jumping up out of the water at you whenever you try to run away?"

Erik nodded.

"It's trapped you in the middle of those two bridges, hasn't it?" added Evie.

Erik nodded again.

Evie turned to look at Catherine, who was staring intently at the pool. "Catherine?" said Evie.

"I understand now," she said, more to herself than to them. "Look how little it is. Can't be more than four feet. Look how thin. It's malnourished."

"I found it a week ago. It was trapped in a small lagoon a few miles north. I saved it," said Erik, a quaver to his voice.

"I wouldn't go as far as 'saved,'" replied Catherine, taking a step closer to the pool. Her movement inspired more thrashing within, and water splashed over the sides. She stopped. "That's why it keeps trying to attack you. It's starving."

"What do we do?" asked Evie.

"Okay," said Catherine slowly, "okay." She removed her shoes and walked over past Evie and past Ruby, right for the pool.

"No, don't!" said Erik. But Catherine wasn't paying attention. She continued to walk, slowly but with purpose, smoothly, with a calm kind of grace, almost like she was gliding. She carefully climbed the ladder and stepped onto the deck. Finally she made it to the edge of the pool. Then in one swift motion she ducked down as the flash of gray and white leapt out of the water right for her. It fell back down, a large splash coming up over the edge and even hitting Evie where she stood.

Catherine slowly got onto all fours, crawled over to the edge, and looked into the water. "It's terrified," she said softly, her voice almost like a low hum.

"Don't go in there," said Erik. "It ate everything. All my beautiful fish I collected. And I'd already fed it. It's an eating machine."

"I sometimes eat when I'm stressed too," said Evie. From her vantage point she could only see the fin of the little shark at moments. She wanted to go closer and see what Catherine was doing, but she was also scared. Besides, only Catherine could possibly do what Catherine was doing. It made the most sense for Evie to stay back.

In one quick movement Catherine slipped into the water. She did it so delicately, it was almost like she didn't break the surface at all; hardly a ripple formed. The fin of the little shark was at the other end of the pool, facing her. From where Evie stood, it looked to her like the two were staring at each other.

Then the little shark charged. It was so fast that Evie hardly registered what was happening. But what she saw was astonishing. Instead of turning and running away, Catherine stayed firmly in place, and as the shark came at her, she bopped it. Downward. Tapped it right on the nose. The shark swam away quickly after that and then turned back to face her again, swimming back and forth and back and forth on the other side of the pool.

"Did you just bop a shark?" asked Evie.

Catherine didn't respond. She was a little preoccupied. Sure enough, only moments later the shark charged again, and again Catherine bopped it on the nose. The movement seemed almost playful, as if Catherine was playing a game, but the little shark was quite clearly rather confused by the action.

And it happened for a third time.

Evie was starting to wonder if there was anything more to this plan.

But almost exactly as Evie generally started to wonder about things, that was when the wonderings were answered. Instead of staying in her spot this time, Catherine took a slow step forward. Her hand was outstretched under the water, almost like one would extend a hand to a dog to sniff. The shark slowly circled around her, and Catherine turned to watch it, never leaving her back exposed. Once again it lunged at her, and once again she bopped it. And then it went back to circling.

No one said anything, no one moved. It seemed also that no one was breathing. Even a couple of birds in a nearby tree were holding their breath. It felt like time was standing still as the little shark circled and circled. And then, slowly, tentatively, it tightened the circle. It was hard to see from where Evie was standing, but it looked like the shark got so close that it brushed against Catherine's leg. Catherine made a small smile then. Her hand was still in the water, and she reached out at the next pass. But instead of bopping, she gave the shark a little stroke as it swam past.

Then Catherine crouched down so her shoulders were covered in water. She was tall enough that Evie guessed she was likely resting on her knees. "It's okay," said Catherine in that low hum of a voice, and at first Evie thought she was talking to the shark. And maybe she was. But Evie realized when Catherine looked up at her with a smile that Catherine was also talking to her.

Evie swallowed her fear and climbed up the ladder, followed by Ruby. They stood toward the back of the deck, looking down into the water, marveling at the scene before them. The shark was swimming calmly around Catherine as she occasionally gave it a light touch. The shark actually seemed to like those touches, like a cat wanting to be scratched in certain places, but only for a moment and then darting away. Looking down at it now with Catherine by its side, Evie realized that the shark might be much littler than Steve, might be malnourished, but it still was very sharklike. Still made of pure muscle and sharp pointy teeth.

Catherine looked up. Erik was still shaking on the high platform above her. "You can come down now," she said. But the man shook his head and stayed clinging to the railing, his sunburned knuckles white from the effort.

Ruby carefully walked over to the foot of the bridge and climbed up onto it. "Come on, Erik. It's safe now," she said, though she glanced down fearfully as she crossed over the pool. The little shark didn't even seem to register her, just continued to brush up against Catherine, occasionally now bopping *her* with its head in a playful manner. Catherine only smiled more broadly at that.

Ruby reached Erik and slowly helped him to release his grip. Then she walked with him bit by bit along the bridge and down the short ladder. When he arrived beside Evie, he collapsed onto the deck in a heap. Evie leaned down next to him to make sure he was okay.

"You all right?" she asked.

Erik nodded. He was pale beneath his sunburn, and still shaking a bit.

"What on earth were you thinking, Erik?" asked Ruby, but not meanly. She sounded more astonished than anything else.

"I wanted to make my own aquarium. I wanted to show people how amazing fish are," he said, his voice quivering.

"But you can't just make an aquarium out of a backyard pool. There are rules and regulations, and that's not enough space anyway for a full-grown shark," said Evie, astonished.

Erik nodded. "It was all temporary. I had a plan to build a big one, once I had earned a bit more money. But then all the tourists left and my shifts were cut . . ."

"The tourists left because of Steve, because he's been looking for the little shark. You're the reason your shifts were cut," said Evie.

"Oh. You think that's why Steve's here?" asked Erik, looking up at Evie with wide eyes.

"Yes, of course I do. You didn't think . . ." Evie stopped. It almost seemed pointless to ask him how he couldn't have realized that. "How did you get this shark out of the water and into your tank in the first place?"

"I spotted him in the lagoon when I was looking for other fish. He couldn't find a way out. He was in trouble. So I helped him and then saw that he was so skinny and hungry. So I figured he would fit in my old exotic fish tank. It was big enough that he could swim a little bit in circles in it, and I thought I could help him get better. I read all about it, and he's definitely healthier than when I first found him." Erik shuddered at the words. Evie understood: a healthy shark was a scary shark.

"But he's still too small and too underweight," said Catherine quietly from the pool. "He's also a she. And probably about just over a month old, by the looks of her."

"Oh? Okay," said Erik. "A she."

"So how are we going to get her back to Steve?" asked Ruby.

"No! No, you can't do that," said Erik, desperation in his voice. "She's my star attraction." He tried to push himself to his feet and failed, flopping back down.

"Erik, you can't be serious," said Ruby with a laugh.

"I am!"

"Okay," Ruby replied, "let me try to explain this to you one more time: You can't afford to build a proper aquarium because you aren't earning enough money. You aren't earning enough money because Steve is driving the tourists away. The only way to get rid of Steve is to give him the little shark, and then you can start earning money again once the tourists get back." Erik nodded along as Ruby explained all this. Then his face fell.

"But—but—" he stuttered.

"Besides," added Catherine, "a great white has never survived in an aquarium, in captivity. Keeping this shark would be its death sentence."

"Well, I mean, that wouldn't be good," he said quietly.

"Why don't you start smaller?" said Evie, jumping into the conversation. "Why not a nice little tank at the inn? With small fish. Pretty fish. Like the one you showed me yesterday? You could tell guests all about the fish, educate them. You can take your time with it. You don't need a full-sized aquarium right this minute."

Erik looked at her, thinking hard. He seemed unable to make up his mind. Fine. Another tactic, then.

"Or, I mean, Ruby might have to report you to the authorities. I'm sure what you did was illegal," said Evie.

"Right, okay, yeah, I like that small-tank-at-the-inn idea," said Erik immediately.

"Good!" said Ruby, brushing her hands together, as she tended to do when a decision was made. "Now, okay. Here's the thing. How do we get the little shark back to Steve?"

It was a good question. It wasn't as if they could call anyone official, not if they wanted to keep Erik out of trouble. "Where's the tank from the basement?" Ruby asked.

Erik pointed slowly over to the other side of the pool. Lying on the far side was a pile of twisted metal and broken glass. Above it was a piece of dangling chain attached to a broken pipe leaning to the side.

"What's that?" asked Evie.

"I made a makeshift crane, used it back in the basement and then brought it here. The shark got angry. Thrashed about. Everything was destroyed." Erik's expression flinched at the memory.

"Oh," said Evie. No tank, then. No crane either, evidently. Not that she'd even thought they'd need one, but of course a crane to lift a heavy shark tank did make sense. "Catherine, do you have any suggestions?"

"Sorry, what?" Catherine was now swimming around with the shark, ducking underwater and playing with it. Playing tag with it, it almost looked like.

"Any suggestions about how to get the little shark back to the cove?" asked Ruby.

Catherine stopped playing to think, which meant the shark bumped into her in frustration, trying to get her to start up again. She laughed and gave it a pat but kept thinking. "Erik, do you have any leftover pool liner?" she asked after a moment.

"Yeah, I think so," he replied.

She turned and looked at Ruby. "How fond are you of your truck?"

➤ CHAPTER 21 ◄

In which Sebastian experiences the experience that is the Lost Boys.

Sebastian truly hadn't thought it was possible for the audience to get any louder than it had been, but the sound in the pitch darkness was so intense, so loud, that Sebastian had the sincere fear that his head might explode. Or at the very least his eardrums.

But then, almost like pressing a switch, at the first chord of music, the audience fell silent. It was an eerie moment, and didn't last long. At the second chord the silence was punctuated by a couple of individual whoops. But the third chord sent the audience into fits. It wasn't the music that had done it. A shaft of white light had turned on, and it was focused down on the stage, near the left of the stage.

Sebastian squinted to see what was happening, but when he saw the top of a head materialize from the floor, he instantly understood. Ujin was being raised onto the stage by an elevator under it. The audience was getting its first glimpse of the actual real-life Lost Boys, and it quite simply didn't know what to do with itself. Ujin's name flashed across the screen, accompanied by a picture of him grinning at the audience. This only made the screaming louder, and Sebastian really wanted to go out onto the stage and ask them to quiet down because they were drowning out Ujin's singing. And Sebastian knew from watching rehearsal how great Ujin sounded. But the audience mercifully quieted down on its own, listening as Ujin sang the opening line of the song. The moment was short-lived, however, as another bright shaft of light hit the stage, close to where Sebastian was standing on the right side backstage. And Yejun's head appeared, rising from the floor of the stage. He joined in the singing, and then the process was repeated twice more with Cheese and Toy. The four of them sang in perfect harmony for a moment. Then they stopped where there was a pause in the song. The audience members tried desperately to keep quiet, but they knew what was coming. Or rather, who was coming.

Kwan's voice did not materialize from the floor of

the stage like the others. Nor did it come from anywhere on the stage. It actually sounded as if it was coming from somewhere up in the audience. Somewhere up farther, higher, in the roof. Sebastian broke free from Suwon's grasp and moved back toward the rear right side of the stage and looked out at the audience, getting his first full view of it. He staggered a bit when he saw them. His brain couldn't process the number of people all standing together. A white shaft of light shot through the air toward the ceiling of the stadium, and that's when both Sebastian and the audience got their first glimpse of Kwan.

He was standing high above them on a catwalk, holding on to something above his head. If the crowd had been excited by the idea of elevators bringing people onto a stage, this concept that Kwan, the lead singer of the Lost Boys, was right there high above them was too much for them to process. In fact, instead of screaming at his appearance as they had with all the others, they just stood there, silent, looking up. Kwan definitely had the most powerful voice of all the band members, and even Sebastian shared in the audience's awe as he sang the final line of the slow intro that would launch them into the fast-paced rest of the song. Kwan seemed to savor the moment. In fact he went even more slowly than in rehearsal, and the musicians had to compensate for that. When he hit the last note, he held it high up with him in the air. It floated above the audience and lingered. Only when the first crash of cymbals and synthesized beats started did the audience break from its spell.

So too, it seemed, did the band. Brightly colored lights flashed across the stage as the boys got into formation, Toy doing one of his trademark flips. And meanwhile Kwan held fast to whatever it was above his head and suddenly came flying down to join the rest of the band. A zip line! He was using a zip line. Sebastian was seriously impressed.

Kwan landed effortlessly and high-fived a couple of girls right at the lip of the stage, before going off and joining the others standing front and center. They launched into one of their choreographed routines, one that was far more complicated than the one they'd taught Sebastian in their dining room. They were perfectly in sync with each other, dancing without missing a beat, and all the while singing in harmony.

Sebastian sang along quietly to himself. He'd heard the song now numerous times, and even though he didn't know the language or the words (he was certain he was butchering them), he didn't feel embarrassed. Instead he felt elated, and for the first time he felt truly honored to have spent time with not only such a popular group but a talented one as well.

The song ended, there was another roar from the audience, and the band stood together and grinned and waved. Then Kwan stepped forward and spoke to the audience. It seemed pretty clear that he was thanking them and generally hyping them up, because the audience would cheer after he finished certain phrases. Then he turned back to the band. Another song started, and they were right back to dancing.

It made so much sense now to Sebastian that they stuck to such a rigorous schedule, and that they worked out so hard. They just went from song to song, dancing the whole time, sometimes doing acrobatic feats. It never looked like they were going to take a break.

Until they took a break.

Kwan said something to the audience, and they cheered. Toy and Ujin came up beside Kwan and smiled and waved. Then Kwan, Yejun, and Cheese dashed off the stage, running right for Sebastian, and he had to leap to the side to get out of the way.

Kwan grabbed a towel from a member of the stage crew and came up beside Sebastian. "Well?" he asked as they watched Toy and Ujin begin a complicated acrobatic routine.

"That was amazing! You have such a great voice, and the zip line was so cool!" Sebastian felt like he'd been onstage as well, he was so out of breath.

Kwan smiled sheepishly. "Thanks." They stood side by side watching as Toy climbed up onto Ujin's shoulders. "They make us unique. It's not me. It's them," said Kwan with pride. "Not many K-pop groups have members who can do that."

"Yeah," said Sebastian.

"You ready?" asked Kwan breathlessly.

"Ready for what?" Truly, in that moment Sebastian had no idea what Kwan was talking about.

Kwan laughed. "Your big moment!"

"Oh. Right." His big moment. Right. He'd forgotten about that in all the excitement. Well, in that case the answer was no. An absolute no.

"After this routine, we'll set up the drums in the middle of the stage. It's going to be thrilling!" Kwan was practically bouncing on the spot as Yejun came over to them.

"You excited?" asked Yejun.

Okay, they had to stop asking these terrifying questions of him. Sebastian could barely speak now, let alone pretend to be enthusiastic. He was hoping Toy and Ujin would just keep flipping and jumping, lose track of time, and bask in the glow of the audience's love. That they would never stop flipping. Ever. Eternal flips.

But no, they stopped. The audience cheered. Toy and Ujin ran offstage. And the tech crew, much to Sebastian's utter horror, brought Kwan's drum kit onto the stage in the low blue lighting of the set change.

I will not panic. I will not panic. This isn't life-and-death. This is just public humiliation.

"Just wait for your cue!" said Kwan as the bright lights came up on the stage again and all five boys rushed back in front of the roaring crowd. Kwan started speaking to them once more in Korean.

Sebastian turned around and looked back into the emptiness of backstage. Maybe this was his moment to run for it. Of course, he had no idea how to get out of the stadium. And of course there was the sudden reappearance of a familiar hand on his shoulder.

"Kwan likes you," said Suwon.

"Yes."

"He's never wanted another band member before now."

"Well, he's never wanted to—" Sebastian stopped short. What was he doing? He'd almost said, "never wanted to leave before." That was not for him to tell.

Suwon looked down at Sebastian with a puzzled expression on his face. "Wanted to what?"

"Opera Boy!" Kwan called out from the stage. Sebastian looked out at him to see Kwan's arm extended and pointing in his direction.

"That nickname makes no sense anymore," said Sebastian.

"Go, they're calling you!" said Suwon, and he gave Sebastian a gentle shove toward the stage.

Okay, okay. He had to do it. He had to just jump in. Like jumping into a cold swimming pool. Except he never did that. He always took the ladder, step-by-step, and acclimatized slowly to the temperature.

Kwan was staring at him intently. Then he yelled out again, "Opera Boy!"

"Go on, Sebastian. This is what you wanted," said Suwon. He wasn't mean or insistent. There was warmth in his voice. Support.

But also . . . this so wasn't what Sebastian wanted.

Sebastian nodded, and then he just did it. He just walked out onto the stage. It wasn't really that hard, as it was the same floor as the wings, but somehow it felt like walking into a whole other world. The audience cheered as he joined Kwan. And as Sebastian stood in the blinding light, he felt all his senses obliterated under the brightness and the loudness around him. How did the band manage to dance and sing in front of all of this? How was he going to be able to play?

Fortunately, he was still gripping his drumsticks tightly, so at least he had a means of playing. Even if he didn't have the ability.

"Wave!" encouraged Kwan, and Sebastian waved. The slight act of raising his hand up to shoulder height and moving it back and forth a few times produced such a response from the crowd that Sebastian immediately shoved his hand into his pocket.

Kwan said something enthusiastically in Korean, the audience cheered some more, and the lights suddenly went all blinky and colorful. Then he looked at Sebastian and made a gesture with his head toward the drum kit.

Okay, okay, it was time.

Sebastian turned kind of robot-like and walked to the drum kit. Sitting down behind it helped block his view of the audience a bit, and he felt better for it. He glanced at the Lost Boys, who had all taken their positions around him. They were poised, ready to start. So. They should start. He tried to take a deep breath, but it was more like a shaky, shallow one. Then Sebastian raised the drumsticks over his head: "One, two, three . . . Shoot." The sound of one of the sticks falling to the floor echoed through the suddenly silent stadium. One of those convenient silences like when you're about to tell someone a really private secret at a party and suddenly everyone decides to take that moment to sip their drink.

Sebastian got up and chased the stick across the stage until it stopped rolling, gave Cheese a forced smile, and then rushed back to the kit. His face was flushed and burning.

This time he'd do it. This time. "One, two, three, four!"

And he started playing.

He started playing in front of thousands of people. He started playing with bandages wrapped around his fingers and fear wrapped around his heart. He started playing.

He wasn't great.

He wasn't terrible.

And.

He liked it.

➤ CHAPTER 22 ◄

In which we attempt a shark
rescue. Which is a perfectly
normal thing that happens
all the time.

Lining the bed of the pickup truck had been difficult, to be sure. Especially making sure the water
wouldn't splash up and over the sides. And filling it
with just the right amount of water—water for a shark
to swim in and thus breathe and water for a human to
sit in without displacing it—was also a bit of a trick.
But the hardest part of the whole experience was yet to
come. The hardest part was transferring a scared little
shark that wasn't so little compared to average-sized
things into the back of a truck without losing a limb
and without it losing its life.

The truck had been backed up as close to the edge
of the pool deck as it could be, the water inside the

back sloshing around. Meanwhile, Evie, Erik, and Catherine had set to work fashioning a kind of shark stretcher. They used two long metal poles, one from what remained of the crane, the other from the front yard (it had had a metal fish hanging off it at one point), and fastened the remaining pool liner around the poles. It was just under five feet long and looked fairly durable. Still, Evie was concerned that once they tried to hoist the little shark out of the water with it, the whole thing would fall apart.

"It doesn't hurt to try," Catherine had said. She was sitting on the deck now, right next to the pool, where the shark kept jumping up to get her attention. Catherine was so comfortable with the shark now that she dangled her hand in the water so that it had something to rub up against.

"Okay," said Catherine, standing up and examining their work. "It looks good. Looks very good." She looked at Erik and Evie and put her hands on her hips. "Well, now we need two people in the pool and two people out of it."

"What?" said Evie and Erik at the same time.

"We need two people in the water to trap the shark in the stretcher and two people to grab it from the outside. Evie, I think you should come into the pool with me," said Catherine in that very practical way of hers.

"What?" squeaked Evie again.

"You're the smallest, and trying to lift the stretcher out of the water will require a fair bit of strength. In the water, thanks to buoyancy, the shark will be much lighter to lift. Since all four of us need to participate in this, it makes the most sense for you to . . . Yes, I think you should come into the water, and Erik and Ruby should carry the shark out and into the truck." It was just a suggestion. Anyone could have said no. But it didn't exactly feel like a suggestion the way Catherine said it. It felt more like all their fates had been sealed.[15]

"Ruby, are we ready?" asked Catherine as Ruby climbed out of the truck. The back with the water sloshing around inside was right below the deck level. In theory, Evie supposed, they could have thrown the shark inside. Not that anyone was capable of doing that, of course.

"Ready? Not sure. But I don't think that's something I'll ever be sure of," Ruby replied.

"Right. So you and Erik prepare yourselves on the deck. When you get the stretcher, carry it over and lay it right inside the bed of the truck. I'll get in with it as quickly as I can. Ruby, you're driving. Erik, take the passenger seat, and, Evie, I'm afraid you get the

---

[15] Or "sharked," as the case may be.

backseat again." Everyone nodded, including Evie. She was used to sitting in small backseats and didn't mind being a little squished. What she did mind was getting into shark-infested waters.

"I guess it's time to do this!" said Catherine, and she easily slipped back into the water. The little shark was so thrilled she was there that it started to swim around much more quickly, bopping into her and jumping up out of the water at moments. "Come on, Evie," said Catherine, smiling at her.

The way the shark was thrashing about now reminded Evie of being in the basement. Of the sheer terror she had felt. She knew the shark was happy; at least, she hoped the shark was happy. But a happy shark and an angry shark looked pretty much the same. Why couldn't sharks smile?

Or would a smile be more horrifying?

"Evie, come on," said Catherine with an edge to her voice.

Oh, sure, easy for you to say, every-animal-on-the-planet-whisperer. Totally easy for you to say. Besides, Catherine looked formidable, like a proper opponent you could respect. She was tall and strong and had bright red hair. Evie was small and pale. She looked like a nice, tasty appetizer.

"Okay," said Evie, more to herself than to Catherine. She took off her shoes and inched her way to the edge of the pool and stared down. The shark swam by just then, causing her to flinch. She took in a deep breath and sat on the edge, dangling her feet in the water. Normally she'd stay like this for a bit until she got used to the cooler temperature, but all she could think was that her dangling feet might resemble a yummy treat. So she jumped in quickly. The water was cold, but that didn't shock her. If she hadn't been scared for her life, she might have noticed how refreshing it was. The one thing she did notice was how much higher the water was on her than on Catherine. She felt extremely small and extremely vulnerable.

"Good," said Catherine just as the shark swam over to Evie to appraise her. "Stay calm."

Oh great, the one instruction that was the least effective.

"Stay still," added Catherine, and *that* Evie could easily follow. She was paralyzed with fear. The shark swam up to her and seemed to be sizing her up. Then it swam around her once, brushing against her as it did. She stumbled, astounded at how strong the creature was. Its body appeared to be made of pure muscle.

The shark didn't like the stumble and lashed its tail as it swam back over to Catherine. "I'm sorry," said Evie quietly.

Catherine laughed at the shark, giving it a little tickle. "It's okay. You're doing an excellent job."

Evie wasn't so sure, but she was determined now. The shark swam close past her once more.

"Oh hey," said Evie.

"What was that?" asked Catherine.

"Oh, it's nothing. It's just . . . yeah, it does have blue eyes." She gave Catherine a small smile, which the explorer returned. Then it was back to business.

"Okay, let's go get the stretcher." Catherine came over to the side of the deck next to Evie, the shark in her wake. Ruby and Erik folded the stretcher so that the metal poles touched each other lengthwise and the pool liner dangled below it. They carefully passed it down, and Evie took an end in her small hands. "Evie, I want you to take a side, not an end," instructed Catherine.

Evie nodded and chose the side closer to the deck. Catherine took the other side, and now they each held on to one pole. Catherine stepped back, and the stretcher opened up underwater. The shark swam past it, curious, but then darted away.

"Once we trap her in it, she's going to panic, so we're going to have to be fast. We'll come back close together so she's squeezed inside the pool liner and can't escape. And then we'll walk as fast as we can back to Ruby and Erik. You two choose a front or back end and get ready to grab it." Catherine was so clear in her instructions and so calm, she obviously had a lot of experience with this kind of thing. Well, maybe not with moving sharks out of swimming pools, but with telling other people what to do.

"Is everyone ready?" asked Catherine.

"Ready!"

"Evie, here we go," said Catherine, and they made their way slowly over to the little shark. It darted out of the way, and they had to follow it to the other side of the pool. It did it again. And again.

Evie was starting to feel less scared and more annoyed. "Let's try to corner it," she suggested.

"There aren't any corners," replied Catherine.

"I mean, let's try to get her up against one of the walls."

Catherine nodded. "Good idea. Follow me."

Evie didn't love the idea of trapping a shark, mostly because she assumed the shark wouldn't love the idea of being trapped. But she knew it was the best idea they had at the moment, so she followed Catherine obediently, and they managed to get the shark up against a wall. "Stay put. I'm going to walk here." Catherine slowly walked so that the end of the stretcher was now next to the shark's head. "Any moment . . . ," she said.

And suddenly the shark burst forward.

"Now!"

Evie leapt toward Catherine just as Catherine leapt toward her, and they held the two poles flush against each other. The shark was thrashing about in the pool liner below them, trapped. It was very strong, and Evie wasn't sure she would be able to hold it.

"Let's just carefully cross the pool," said Catherine calmly.

Evie nodded, and they began to drag the stretcher through the water as the shark thrashed about, desperate to escape. It took some time to make it to the other side where Ruby and Erik were waiting, but eventually they got there, and Evie and Catherine maneuvered themselves so that Catherine was standing parallel to the deck and Evie was closer to the middle of the pool.

Erik leaned over and grabbed the two poles on one end, and Ruby grabbed the two poles on the opposite end. Now all four of them were holding on to the stretcher: Evie and Catherine on the sides, Ruby and Erik on the ends.

"On the count of three," said Catherine.

Evie flinched as the tail of the shark hit her leg in its thrashing about. But she didn't drop the stretcher.

One.

She could do this.

Two.

This was totally a thing people could do.

Three.

She was doing it!

They hoisted the stretcher up, the shark clearly unhappy about the whole thing. Suddenly Evie was free of it, and all she could do was watch as Ruby and Erik ran across the deck and dumped the stretcher and shark into the back of the truck. It was odd. Just a moment before she'd been terrified, having to help wrangle a shark, but now, unable to help or really do anything but watch, she felt antsy, wishing there was something she could do. Evie turned to look at Catherine, but the explorer had already bolted from the pool and was making her way over to the truck to join the shark. So Evie followed her example and quickly climbed out of the water. There was just enough room for both explorer and shark in the back. And without being trapped in the stretcher, the little shark started to swim frantically around and around in a tiny circle in the back of the truck. It calmed down substantially when Catherine joined it, slowing its circle, but it still kept swimming.

"Let's go quickly. Great whites need to keep swimming to stay alive, and this little lady doesn't have much room to do that. Plus I fear she was seriously traumatized in that tank in the basement, and this is bringing all that back to her now," said Catherine. Evie grabbed her shoes off the deck and quickly jumped into the backseat of the truck so that Erik could climb into the passenger side.

Ruby took off as fast as she could, which really wasn't that fast. They couldn't risk losing water over the side; and the water itself made maneuvering the truck difficult. "You sometimes forget how heavy water is," said Ruby, carefully taking the turn out of Erik's driveway and onto the street.

"I don't," said Erik. Evie could only see the back of his head and had an excellent view of his bright red ears, the skin on them peeling a bit from the sunburn, so she couldn't see his expression. But she assumed he was referring to the time when he had to cart the shark to his place all by himself.

"Say, how did you get the shark to your place? I know you had a big tank and a crane, but the rest of it . . . how did you do it?" asked Evie.

"It's a long story. Let's just say it's good the loading doors go directly into the basement," replied Erik. Evie gave him a moment to explain further, but evidently he didn't feel much like sharing.

"I have one question, though," she said, changing the subject slightly. "Was that you outside my window the other night? With the wagon?"

At that, Erik turned and looked at her. Then he nodded and faced forward. "Yeah, I was getting it some fish."

Evie felt victorious in her correct conclusion and turned to look out the back window into the bed of the truck. Catherine was holding on to the sides, trying not to flop about in the water. The shark was swimming in a slow circle over and over. It didn't look happy at all.

Not that Evie blamed it.

To be perfectly honest, she was feeling pretty darn stressed herself.

➤ CHAPTER 23 ◄

In which there is
a confrontation.

"That was amazing!" said Kwan as they all rushed back into the wings, the applause from the audience still echoing in Sebastian's ears.

"You did it!" said Ujin, grabbing Sebastian around the middle and hoisting him up into the air. Considering how nauseous Sebastian was still feeling, having done what he'd just done, the action was definitely not appreciated even if the sentiment was.

He was returned to earth just as Suwon approached with a smile. "Well done. The audience loved you. I never thought it possible, but evidently changing the band can be a good thing." He stuck out his hand to shake, and Sebastian did not know what to do.

"What is it?" asked Suwon.

"I can't. I can't do this anymore," said Sebastian. The adrenaline was wearing off quickly. He looked at Kwan. "You have to tell him, or I will have to tell him." Lying was hard. More than that, it was just so exhausting.

"Go," said Kwan to the other Lost Boys. "I'll join you soon." The Lost Boys looked concerned but agreed and returned to the spotlight and the roaring fans. Kwan looked back at Suwon now with a sad expression. All the joy and light from the recent success onstage was extinguished from his eyes.

"Kwan, what's going on?" asked Suwon.

"Sebastian doesn't want to be a Lost Boy. We did this to prove a point," said Kwan very quietly. Sebastian had never seen him so nervous before.

"A point?"

"You always say we are irreplaceable, but . . . I want to be replaced. I need to be." Listening to the feeling in his voice, it was only then that Sebastian realized they were talking in English still. Kwan needed Sebastian to understand because Kwan needed his support.

"I'm confused," said Suwon.

Kwan stood there silently, looking at his feet.

"He wants to see what else is out there. He wants to leave the band," said Sebastian, placing a hand on Kwan's shoulder.

"Oh," said Suwon.

"And we thought if we showed you that the fans would accept a new member, you'd see that he could be replaced, that the band wasn't doomed." Sebastian looked out at the Lost Boys onstage singing and dancing their hearts out.

"It's true," said Kwan.

Suwon thought for a moment. For longer than that. And then, finally: "Why didn't you just come talk to me?"

"Because—" started Sebastian.

"Because I didn't want to let you down," interrupted Kwan. "Because I thought that if you knew I wanted to leave, you'd throw me out. Out of the compound. Out of . . . my family." Kwan lowered his head so that Sebastian couldn't read his expression.

Suwon placed his hand on Kwan's shoulder and sighed. "Oh, dear boy, I'm sorry. I'm sorry you feel this way. I would never have done that, I promise you. I would not desert you. Not like . . . not like . . ." He stopped. "I am very proud of you. I'll always be proud of you." He smiled then, and Kwan looked up. Only then did Sebastian see a tear shining on the boy's cheek.

Kwan nodded slowly and wiped away the tear.

"So you will tell me the truth from now on?" asked Suwon.

Kwan nodded. "Yes."

"And you always have a home with me, a family, no matter what you decide," added Suwon. Kwan smiled brightly then. They smiled at each other.

And then: "Um, Suwon hyung?"

"Yes, my boy?"

"Could we maybe get phones?" asked Kwan almost shyly. "And maybe a little bit more freedom? I think that you think we need to be protected at all times, but we're older now. And we need to learn how to take care of ourselves."

Suwon thought carefully about this. "You are right. Let's have a meeting tonight. After all, we have a new family member to integrate into the group as well." He turned and smiled at Sebastian.

Sebastian took in a deep breath. "Suwon, I'm not interested in being in the band. This was all to prove a point. I want to go home. To my family."

Suwon smiled that knowing smile. "But we are your family."

Sebastian sighed hard. "Okay, so you really, really need to believe me that I'm not a runaway and that I was kidnapped."

Suwon shook his head sadly. "Still in denial, I see."

"No, Hyung. He *really* was kidnapped," said Kwan.

"You had better go back onstage. We'll talk about this later."

Kwan gave Sebastian an apologetic look, and then he joined his band members, who were stalling for time, doing more acrobatics. Once he joined them, the Lost Boys returned to their routine as if nothing had happened. But so much had. So much on and off the stage. There was extra life in Kwan's performance, an extra bounce to his step. And when it came time for his flip, for the first time ever he was able to do a double. This, of course, caused the audience to roar with appreciation, as did the other band members.

Sebastian was happy to see it, but he couldn't enjoy the moment. The knots in his stomach reminded him yet again of their presence.

Right. Escaping.

It felt wrong, just leaving like that, no goodbye, nothing. But with Suwon's fierce determination to prove everyone, including Sebastian, wrong about Sebastian's family situation, and with Suwon standing close to where the stage began in the wings, and the boys performing, there was no better time than this.

"Goodbye," Sebastian muttered under his breath.

Then he turned around and walked right into Mr. I.

➤ CHAPTER 24 ◄

In which we drive
a shark along a highway.
Again, totally normal.

It took twice as long to get back to the cove as it had taken to get to Erik's, as they were driving half the speed, but eventually they were out of the thick brush and moving along the wide sunny highway. It was actually a small saving grace that so few cars were coming to the cove these days. Otherwise, Evie envisioned a huge frustrated line of them behind their truck, beeping their horns, angry that they were going so slowly.

Eventually the Outlook Inn came into view, and on their right, the beach. Ruby slowed to a stop. "Evie, open the back window," she said.

Evie did, and Catherine swam up to it. "Yes?" she asked.

"What do we do now?" asked Ruby.

"We get her back into the stretcher," said Catherine.

Ruby sat for another moment, thinking hard. Then she said, "Forget that. I'm backing into the sea."

"But your truck!" said Erik.

"She's pretty tall. I figure if we just get the rear tires in and open the back, that should be good enough. You two get out, though, just in case," Ruby added.

Catherine shook her head. "I'm staying with her till the last moment, to help keep her calm."

There was no arguing with Catherine, though. Erik made a few squeaks of protest. But he slipped out of the truck, and Evie clambered over the seat to join him. They walked along the beach away from the truck and watched as Ruby slowly brought her vehicle around and started to back down over the boardwalk and onto the sand.

Evie turned and looked out at the sea, and in that moment made a very loud gasp. Right there, in the shallows, was Steve. He was huge. Well, he'd always been huge, but to see him so close now was to get a true sense of just how huge he was. He wasn't anything like the little shark, who was lean and sleek. He was broad and heavy, thick and leathery. Clearly somehow he had known that the little shark was nearby, and he was coming to find her. If it hadn't been so scary, Evie would have compared it to a dad picking up his daughter at school, waiting in the parking lot for her to arrive.

And maybe it was. If the dad had plans to eat the principal too.

Though now that Evie thought about it, maybe that was a bit unfair. After all, the little shark had actually been quite nice to Catherine and even to Evie as well. Sure it had tried to attack, but it was scared, it was in a pool, it was hungry, and it had no idea what was going on. Heck, Evie herself could picture maybe having a similar reaction in a similar circumstance. She remembered her fight-or-flight response kicking in when the scary men had been coming after her.

Evie felt a little guilty for judging the sharks so harshly.

Ruby was slowly backing the truck over the sand and reached the water's edge. The waves were much choppier now, crashing with some violence against the shore. She stopped the truck for a moment, and then backed up farther into the surf. It had looked almost like the vehicle had stopped to take a deep breath before diving into the water.

The sea rose up around the back tires of the truck.

The front tires were up on the sand so the whole truck was on a slight declined angle now. Then Ruby turned off the engine, stepped out of the vehicle, and quickly made her way over to where Evie and Erik were standing.

"I can't believe Catherine's about to do this with Steve right there," said Ruby, slightly out of breath.

Evie couldn't believe it either, and yet also she totally could. This was an extremely Catherine thing to do, really.

There was a moment of quiet as they watched Catherine move toward the back of the truck, her bright red hair highlighting her movements. Then there was a pause. A pause that seemed to last a little too long. And then Catherine pushed down the tailgate of the truck.

➤ CHAPTER 25 ◄

In which we . . .
Seriously?
Another chase sequence??

Maybe it was the two days of working out he'd done with the band, maybe it was the limited dance training, but whatever it was, Sebastian's reaction time didn't lag for one moment. He turned on his heel and darted away from Mr. I. Which happened to be toward the stage. A cheer greeted Sebastian's return, which for a brief moment he did find kind of flattering, and the boys turned to see him standing in their midst. They grinned widely, and Kwan shouted out, "It's Opera Boy!" There was another loud cheer, and Sebastian gave an awkward wave at his "fans."

Then he remembered. He looked to his right. Mr. I was being oddly polite, not coming onto the stage.

Sebastian made a beeline toward the left side of the stage instead. But standing there was Mr. K.

Kwan danced over to him and, covering his headset, asked, "What's going on?"

"My kidnappers, they're back!" Sebastian pointed at them both, and Kwan stared in surprise.

"The scary dudes!"

"Yes!"

The rest of the band gathered around just as Mr. I and Mr. K decided to break the threshold between the darkness and the light and step onto the stage. The audience made an "Ooh" sound at their arrival, anticipating some kind of theatrics. And, knowing these men, theatrics were not out of the question, thought Sebastian.

Kwan shouted an order in Korean, his voice resonating around the stadium. Ujin and Toy darted over to Mr. I, flipping and leaping as they did. Yejun and Cheese meanwhile danced their way to Mr. K, drawing him into their routine most unwillingly. Sebastian, feeling very out of place just standing there, performed the short routine the boys had taught him two nights ago.

What was he doing? He needed to run for it. He'd seen crowd surfers before in videos, and though this didn't seem like the kind of concert where people did such a thing, maybe they'd be inspired to try it? The crowd was certainly thick enough. He darted to the edge of the stage and was about to take a leap, when he saw Mr. M standing there, front and center. Sebastian faltered and tripped over his own feet, lunging toward members of the audience, and they caught him.

"Push me back!" he shouted. He also gestured toward the stage in case they didn't understand. They helpfully pushed him back. His feet slid around underneath him, but he got his footing again on the stage and ran back to its center. He looked around. Mr. I and Mr. K were still being blocked by crazy acrobatics and dance moves, but Mr. M had pulled himself up onto the stage at the front and was coming right for him.

"Stand on the X," ordered Kwan as he leapt in front of Sebastian.

"The what?" Sebastian called as Kwan lunged at Mr. M, shoving the man with the eye patch backward into the crowd. The crowd caught him and, thinking that he too wanted to be back onstage, placed him there politely, just as they had with Sebastian.

Sebastian looked down and saw a large yellow X on the stage floor. He didn't know what it meant, but he ran over to it and stood there.

Nothing happened.

Mr. M came charging at him, and Kwan tried to

restrain him. But the teenager was much smaller, and despite his wiry strength, he was no match for the brute force of Mr. M.

Standing there, literally on a target, just felt really wrong. But Sebastian at this point had no idea what else to do.

Suddenly it seemed he was getting shorter. Weird. Sebastian looked down. The lift! Of course! The lift! He was being lowered under the stage, thanks to some very helpful technician, but, man, oh, man, was his escape taking forever.

World's slowest escape, that was what it was.[16] Kwan was now holding fast to Mr. M's legs and was being dragged. Eventually Mr. M pried the lead singer off and threw him toward Sebastian. The last thing Sebastian saw before he was completely under the stage was Mr. M making one final desperate lunge toward him, and Kwan flying down into the hole with Sebastian, landing right on top of him. Once they were totally underground, the lift stopped and Sebastian and Kwan rolled to the side to allow the lift to return to place, much faster than it had gone down, and almost

---

[16] Technically it wasn't the world's slowest escape. That honor goes to Sir Archibald Buffle, who attempted to escape the Tower of London by hitching a makeshift wagon to a team of turtles.

taking off Mr. M's right arm, which he'd stuck down into the hole, reaching after them. Luckily for him, he snatched it out just in time. Sebastian was grateful. He'd seen a lot in the last few weeks, but he wasn't sure he was ready to see a severed arm up close. And Mr. M really didn't need to lose another body part. That wasn't fair.

Sebastian and Kwan untangled themselves from each other and stood.

A firm hand was suddenly on Sebastian's shoulder. He whipped around, prepared for a fight, but it was Suwon.

"Come with me," he said. And Sebastian, at this

point thinking him very much the lesser of two evils, followed quickly, Kwan at his side.

They ran through a maze of ropes and wires, and it was a miracle that nobody tripped and fell on their face. Then they were back in the cement corridor under the stadium. They raced along, even though no one was chasing them, all of them understanding that this was not the time to be complacent. They made it back to the parked bus, but Suwon ran right past it, leading them farther up the long wide ramp until they were out in the cold night air. A large crowd had gathered behind tall fences by the exit and was a little confused by their appearance. Then they noticed Kwan, and the cheer once again was deafening.

Kwan ordered something loudly, and in one swift move the crowd parted. He thanked them and quickly took a selfie with a pair of girls as he, Sebastian, and Suwon made their way through the crowd and onto a main street, city lights bright everywhere.

It was only then that they stopped. Suwon hailed a cab. Almost as if it had been waiting for them, one screeched to a halt right beside them.

"Take him to the airport," he said to the driver in English so that Sebastian would understand. Sebastian looked at Suwon gratefully as he opened the door and slid inside.

"I'm sorry I didn't believe you," said Suwon.

"I'm sorry I thought you were evil," replied Sebastian.

"You did?"

"My mistake. But seriously, I think you need to start trusting your boys more." Sebastian didn't think he had time for this moment of advice-giving, but still, he felt obligated to do it. For Kwan's sake. Kwan grinned gratefully, so Sebastian knew he'd done the right thing.

"I think you're right. Being protective, I suppose, doesn't always protect," said Suwon, smiling. For the first time Sebastian wasn't suspicious of Suwon's smile. Sebastian closed the door, but Kwan knocked on the window, so he rolled it down.

"If you ever need anything, if you ever need the Lost Boys, just let us know. You'll always be a member! And we take care of each other."

Sebastian really wasn't sure when that time would be, but it was a gallant offer and he appreciated it. "Thank you!" he called back. Then there was a moment when he realized he was likely never going to see Kwan again, unless of course he pulled up some of the Lost Boys music videos or something on his computer. "Goodbye," he said awkwardly.

Sebastian hadn't really ever said that kind of a

goodbye before. The kind where he really meant it. Such a finite word. Not "au revoir," which in English meant "until the next time we see each other." Not "see you later." But "goodbye."

Kwan seemed to be thinking the same thing. He gave Sebastian a sad smile.

"Goodbye."

And with that, the cab drove off, leaving Sebastian very much on his own.

># CHAPTER 26 ≺

In which we witness
a reunion.

A great whoosh happened then. It was watery. It was shark-y. And it was explorer-y. All three tumbled into the cove in a wave, and it was hard to observe what happened next. It was all swirls of water and waves of foam. Finally things got less messy. A little fin could be seen swimming toward a larger fin as the larger fin swam toward the smaller. But more than that, a moment later a redhead could be seen being pulled under the surf.

"It's got her!" said Evie in terror, and she ran toward the water.

"Evie, no!" Ruby cried out.

But Evie didn't listen. She knew somewhere deep

down that there was pretty much nothing she could do to fight off a shark, but she couldn't believe that there was nothing she could do to help. Just as she arrived at the shoreline, the redhead bobbed up above the water again, this time much farther out. Catherine waved her arms for a moment above the waves, and then she went under again. Evie felt an uncontrollable urge to dive into the water.

Ruby's firm hand restrained her.

Evie turned and looked at her. "We have to help!"

"There's nothing we can do," said Ruby. She was staring hard out into the water. "And besides, look!" Evie turned and watched as Catherine's head reappeared above the waves even farther out now. She was still flailing, but it didn't quite look like she was being eaten by a giant beast in the sea, really. Maybe she wasn't injured. Maybe it was simply the waves being too strong.

That was it!

Catherine hadn't been pulled out by the shark; she'd been pulled out by the strong undertow of the waves.

"We should swim out, save her," said Evie.

Ruby nodded. "Not we. I'll do it." She quickly removed her shoes, but as she did, Evie noticed something out in the water. Something horrifying.

A large dark gray fin.

Heading directly toward the red bobbing head.

"Ruby, look!" cried Evie.

Steve was making a beeline right for Catherine. He was coming so fast, he was almost there. Evie wanted to look away, but something rooted her to the spot. She stared, too shocked to move, too shocked to close her eyes, too shocked to do anything but watch the demise of Catherine Lind. One of the greatest animal experts in the history of the world.

The shark attacked and pushed Catherine's body up out of the water. It continued to push so hard that Catherine fell over the top of it and landed on the shark's back. That was kind of weird. Why hadn't it taken a bite out of her? They watched as the shark dipped back underwater and Catherine turned around to hold on to its fin. Then it swam. It swam . . . right . . . for them.

"Move, move, move!" said Ruby, grabbing Evie by her shirtsleeve and dragging her up the beach.

The shark approached as fast as their truck, and it looked like it was going to barrel right into them, up the beach and everything. Suddenly it turned sharply in the shallows, Catherine rolling off its back abruptly into the water. And then it swam back into the deep. Evie noticed a little fin making small circles off in the distance waiting for Steve's return.

This time Ruby and Evie ran toward the water and into it. They each grabbed an arm and helped Catherine as she crawled onto the sand, coughing and breathing hard.

When they were safely out of the water, Catherine rolled over onto her back.

"What was *that*?" asked Evie, collapsing into the sand beside her.

Catherine lay still, catching her breath. Everything seemed to calm down. Even the waves seemed less violent in that moment.

"That," wheezed Catherine, "was a thank-you." She propped herself up onto her elbows and looked out into the water. Evie did likewise, and they watched as a big fin approached a little fin, and then both sharks swam out toward the edge of the cove until they seemed to disappear over the horizon, heading off—well, who knew where—but heading off that way. Together.

➤ CHAPTER 27 ◄

In which we head back to the airport. Finally.

The journey to the airport felt longer than the journey from it. Of course, that might have had something to do with the chase sequence that had been quite a distraction from the passing of time. Still, all the day's events weighed heavily on Sebastian's shoulders, and he didn't mind the slightly longer ride, just to rest his eyes for a moment. But eventually he was passing under the inverted Y towers of the Incheon Bridge and saw the spaceship-looking airport in the distance, that brightly lit beacon unchanged from two days ago. It was a most welcome sight. Now all he had to do was get inside, call his parents, get them to buy him a ticket on the next flight out, overnight his passport or something, and then he'd be home. He'd be home. Safe. With his family.

And then, of course, he'd have to decide whether he really wanted to go in search of Alistair Drake after all this. It seemed an exhausting prospect, but it wasn't entirely unwelcome. After all, as weird and scary as his two days in South Korea had been, at times he had also had some amazing experiences. And met some pretty amazing people as well.

"Just drop me off at departures," said Sebastian.

The cabbie didn't reply, but that was okay. Even if he dropped Sebastian off at arrivals, Sebastian would find his way.

Except the cabbie didn't actually seem to be heading toward departures *or* arrivals. He seemed, in fact, to be taking a different route entirely into the airport complex.

"Um, sir?" asked Sebastian. He leaned forward and noticed that his cabdriver wasn't a man after all. She also wasn't Korean. "Oh, sorry. Um, ma'am, I guess. Um, where are we going?"

But the cabbie still said nothing.

And at this point Sebastian began to feel his breath get short again. And the knots in his stomach that had just untied themselves glanced up and said, *Again?* before retying themselves even tighter.

Even though they were moving fast, Sebastian tried the door handle. He feared it wasn't a risk to do so, and he was right: the door was locked. He sat there, helpless, panic rising up from his toes and filling his body. Soon the cab turned a corner, and Sebastian found himself on the tarmac. But not just any tarmac, no, the tarmac where the private planes loaded and unloaded. The cab pulled up in front of a plane. But even worse than that, the cab pulled up in front of three men standing sentinel: one whose jaw was wired shut, one whose face was half-melted, and one wearing an eye patch.

They surrounded the car, and Sebastian felt completely helpless. The woman in the front seat turned around. "This is your captain speaking. We hope you've enjoyed your time sightseeing in Seoul. We'll be taking off shortly. Please sit back, relax, and enjoy your flight."

And with that, his door was yanked open by a grinning Mr. M, and Sebastian was pulled rather unceremoniously out of the cab.

➤ CHAPTER 28 ◄

In which Evie and Catherine are rewarded.

It was a very quiet dinner. The sky was turning a rich blue over the cove, and the trees were falling into shadow. The air hummed with the sound of a thousand cicadas. It sounded like the insects were singing a song of victory in Evie and Catherine's honor. Evie thought it was one of the most beautiful things she'd ever heard. A cool breeze picked up, and she wrapped the thin blanket around her shoulders tightly as she bent over and helped herself to a second helping of stew.

"My favorite dinner," said Thom when she did.

"But two nights in a row, Dad?" said Ruby, leaning back in her seat and bringing her legs up under her.

"Hey, you don't know. It could even be more than

that." Thom smiled, and Evie could see then the family resemblance between father and daughter. "So," he said, "what time do you want to leave tomorrow?"

"Well, the flight's at noon, and it'll take a couple of hours to get to Cairns . . . ," said Catherine.

"Let's say we'll leave at eight, just to be on the safe side," concluded Thom.

Catherine nodded. "Thank you again for this," she said.

"It's the least I can do," Thom said. "You saved the town. More important, you saved my little girl's business. And if there's one thing that Steve taught us, it's that family is the most important thing."

"Though, you did say no more exceptions," said Evie.

"Well, I guess this is an exceptional exception, then," said Thom, smiling again.

Evie smiled back. It seemed like the end of something even though it was only just the beginning. But it felt good, it felt hopeful and right. Tomorrow they would be off to Newish Isle. Tomorrow they would find the town and the volcano. Tomorrow they would find Benedict. And if they had been right in their educated guess, most important of all, they would find Sebastian. Help him. Save him.

And everything would be as it was supposed to be.

And then they could finally, after all this time, begin their hunt for her grandfather.

It was all coming together.

And even though it was hardly the polite thing to do while still with company, Evie closed her eyes. And fell into a deep and restful sleep.

➤CHAPTER 29◄

In which Sebastian and Evie
each in their own unique
fashion make their way toward
Newish Isle and the Vertiginous
Volcano, using various modes
of transport. You know, taking
planes and buses and other
things too and stuff.

Point is, they both traveled.
Evie got there first. You know,
I feel like I've really told you
everything you need to know
in this chapter subheading. So
how about we carry on to . . .

➤ CHAPTER 30 ◄

In which Evie sees
a silly house.

"This is our stop," said Thom, rising and slowly maneuvering his way into the aisle of the bus.

"It is?" asked Evie. She looked out the window. They were on a narrow two-lane highway, with jungle stretching out on either side of them. It really didn't look like they had arrived anywhere. Though, of course, technically, everywhere was an anywhere. Still. It confused her.

"Come on, Evie," said Catherine. She was already following Thom to the front of the bus, and so Evie quickly jumped up and slipped out into the aisle herself.

The bus they were on was much smaller than the

one they'd taken to Creaky Cove in Australia. This was more like an overly large van. And also unlike the bus to the cove, which had been practically empty, this one was full of passengers, some talking happily with each other, others getting a few extra moments of sleep. It was tricky getting to the front of the bus without bumping into someone or something. Evie apologized when she accidentally fell against a woman's shoulder as the bus came to a sudden stop, but the woman just smiled back at her and shook her head.

Evie made her way to the exit and stepped out into the thick, humid air.

The bus charged off the moment Evie's foot had left the last step but before it had even made it to the ground to join the other one. She stumbled forward and turned in surprise, and watched as the bus vanished quickly around a bend.

"No time to waste, I guess," said Thom.

Evie joined him and Catherine standing at the edge of the jungle. They had already journeyed quite a distance since landing on Newish Isle. This was their third bus and, Evie fervently hoped, their last. Though, looking around, she feared it wasn't.

"Are we waiting for another bus now?" she asked, feeling quite dejected.

Thom shook his head and smiled brightly. "No! We're almost there."

"We are?"

"How skeptical you look! And yet you worked so hard to get me to take you all this way. Remember, you could be back in Cairns trying to find someone else," said Thom.

"Oh! I don't mean to sound ungrateful! I'm sorry." That was the last thing Evie had intended.

Thom laughed. "No, of course. You're tired. It's been a very long journey. But we are, in fact, here."

Thom turned and then walked straight into the thick brush, vanishing almost instantly in the dense, dark foliage.

Evie looked at Catherine for a moment, and then, shrugging in unison, they followed him.

The temperature dropped a full ten degrees in the shade of the dripping jungle, and it was so dark that Evie almost longed for a flashlight. She also could really have used a towel. She was seriously not used to all this humidity.

What she also wanted to do was ask Thom just how much farther they had to go and what came next, but the man was so determined to keep everything secret that she had stopped bothering to ask after bus number two. She supposed she should be grateful. He could have decided to blindfold them or something.

She followed behind Catherine, nervously, worried some beast might suddenly jump out at her, but then she realized that Catherine was a marvelous shield to travel behind. The explorer had clearly spent a lot of time in the jungle, and she knew exactly where to place a foot, when to duck, what to climb over. Evie copied her footsteps precisely. And of course if any beast did come and jump out at them, Evie was pretty sure she'd just have to cry out and Catherine would be able to save her. And then maybe adopt the beast as a pet or something.

They kept going and going, trudging along in what was—there was no other word for it—a tedious fashion. Evie's feet were completely drenched, her shoes soaked through, and just when she could resist it no longer, when she felt the bubbling and rising of an "Are we there yet?" in her throat, they stopped.

"We're here!" said Thom, grinning at them both, and then he pulled back a large palm frond, revealing . . . a small house.

That was it.

A small house sitting in a clearing maybe a hundred

yards away, situated behind a little manicured garden. It sat on its own, with brush growing tall and thick beyond it.

"This . . . isn't a town," said Catherine, and Evie was grateful that Catherine was just as confused as she was.

Thom laughed as if she'd said the silliest thing that could have been said, and he walked up to the front of the low wooden bungalow. A chicken ran by as if to warn the owners of the arrival of strangers. Then Thom turned abruptly and walked to the far left-hand side of the house, its very edge, as it were, completely avoiding the front door. Evie now wondered if he planned on going around to the back, as she and Catherine had done at Erik's.

No. No, that wasn't his plan, it turned out.

His plan was . . . Well, his plan was to grab the side of the house and push, heaving the entire house to the side as if it was a sliding closet door or something, until a large gap in the foliage behind was revealed. Not just a gap but what looked to be an alley, at the end of which were houses and a dirt street, even, and, my goodness, the possibility of an entire town.

Cautiously Evie approached the gap, and even though she was dying to get a closer look at the town, she turned to have a closer look at the house. From her new angle she could see that it wasn't a house at all. It was a "flat," like a set piece for a play or film. It was two-dimensional but painted to appear three-dimensional from afar. She looked down and saw beneath her feet a deep groove out of which the "house" was protruding upward. How far into the earth it went, she had no idea, but it was deep enough so that the "house" could slide along inside the track and not be top heavy and fall over.

It was the strangest secret entrance she'd ever seen.

Then again, she hadn't seen all that many secret entrances, so who was she to judge?

She turned and looked into the jungle on the right, examining it, and took a step in its direction.

"Careful," said Thom. Evie looked at him, confused. "The house is on a natural bridge into the town. There's a deep trench that encircles the rest of town and its surrounds, just hidden beyond those trees."

"Oh!" said Evie, quickly taking a step back as if the earth below her might give way at any moment.

"Step on through, Evie," said Thom with a smile. "I have to close the house behind you."

Evie looked up and saw that Catherine had already passed through the opening and was now standing, her back to the town, waiting for Evie to follow.

"Oh, okay," Evie said, and took a large exaggerated step over the groove. Then she turned back to Thom. He was standing behind her, on the front side of the house, and with one of his classic smiles, he began to slide the house back into place. "Wait!" cried Evie.

He stopped short. "Yes?"

"You're not coming with us?"

"No. No, I need to get back home." He looked quite comfortable with the idea.

"But . . ." Evie was quiet for a moment.

Thom let go of the side of the building and walked up to her. Crouching down, he said, "But what?"

"But . . ." She didn't know what to say. She felt nervous, even though she was with Catherine. When Thom left, the two of them would be alone for really the first time in a strange country, in a very strange town. Maybe she'd gotten too used to Ruby's and Thom's helpfulness.

"We'll be fine, Evie," said Catherine, coming up from behind. "We've got each other." Evie was feeling a little frustrated with herself now. She hated when she sounded like a kid, and here she was, framed by two adults reassuring her that someone would take care of her. She'd been taking care of herself just fine for the last two years, thank you very much. And she'd more than held her own with Sebastian and their adventures around the city.

She gave a sharp nod and smiled. "Of course! I'm just being silly. Thank you, Thom!" She stuck out her hand. Thom stood up straight and took her hand in his, shaking it warmly.

"Yes, thank you," said Catherine.

"My pleasure. I owed you. But I swear, you are the very last. That's it! No more exceptions. Not even exceptional exceptions." He held his finger up in the air as if making a grand proclamation. Which he kind of was.

Evie laughed.

And then Thom went back to his position at the edge of the house, and heaved it closed along the track. And soon he was out of sight, hidden behind the façade of a fake house. Or they were. Or all three were.

The house was painted on Evie's side also, but it looked fresher, a little happier. Almost more three-dimensional, in a way. It was an impressive work of art, that was for sure.

"Come on, Evie," said Catherine with a rare small smile, and Evie turned to follow her down the narrow alley. She glanced back over her shoulder and marveled at how the fake house was barely noticeable. Why the entrance needed to be concealed on this side, Evie had no idea, but it likely was as simple as someone wanting it to blend in with the surroundings.

Evie followed Catherine until they stepped out into a happy little town square. A few kids were playing soccer on one side, and a fountain gurgled in the middle. An older man sat on a chair watching from his front porch, and two teenagers were lounging at the base of the fountain, sunbathing. But the moment Catherine and Evie appeared, everything stopped. Everyone looked at them closely, though it felt like they were more curious than scared or suspicious. And that was when Evie realized that by finding their way to the town, they'd passed a kind of test. These people trusted them.

Catherine approached one of the teenagers and spoke to him. He looked at her for a moment and then turned to the girl next to him. They chatted in another language, and then he told Catherine in English, "Peter knows. He lives over there." The boy pointed toward a small path leading toward another on the edge of town.

"Thank you," said Catherine, and she returned to Evie. "Peter knows where Benedict is."

"Who's Peter?" asked Evie, grateful that the teens at least knew who they were talking about.

"No idea. Shall we?" Catherine pointed toward the path, and they started down a thin dirt trail bordered by short grass that led out of the tiny town toward a little house on top of a small hill. The house was quite pretty—picturesque, even. It stood on stilts, though only a few feet off the ground, not nearly the same kind of height as Thom's home in the trees. It had a low, sloping grass roof that met up with slightly faded but colorfully painted walls in a lively yellow. And as Catherine and Evie approached, they noticed a young man sitting on the narrow staircase that led up to the door. He was so engrossed in a thick book on his lap that he didn't even notice them until they said hello.

"Are you Peter?" asked Catherine.

The young man stared at her for a moment. Evie couldn't tell if he was scared or confused. His brown eyes were huge, the whites impressively so.

"Catherine Lind," said the young man with a slight accent.

Evie looked at Catherine, and she couldn't tell if the explorer was scared or confused.

"Yes," said the explorer carefully.

"You are the famous Catherine Lind." The young man's eyes grew even wider, if that was possible, which, it turned out, it was.

"Well . . . I don't know about famous," said Catherine, looking uncomfortable.

The young man stood up and held the book under his arm. He stuck out his hand. "I'm Peter Booth. I'm Benedict Barnes's apprentice. Well, that's what I call it." He smiled a little at that.

"What does he call it?" asked Evie.

Peter shrugged. "He doesn't call it anything. He doesn't like me tagging along all the time. He lets me, though. He sees I care about photography. He loaned me this!" He held up the book, a worn copy of *Photographing Everything: By Which We Mean Everything*. "You must be looking for him. I'll take you to him. He will not be happy to see you, but I'm so happy to see you. To meet you. And you, too, little girl." He smiled at Evie.

"Evie Drake." She extended her hand. Peter's eyes grew so wide that Evie was certain this surely had to be the farthest extent that his eyes could reach. It took her a moment to understand his reaction. "Uh . . . yeah. Oh. Yeah." Her last name. Of course, her last name.

"Drake?" asked Peter, his jaw practically on the ground.

"Yup, that's my last name." How awkward. And

yet, how kind of wonderful, too. To have someone who had some sense of who she was because of family.

"Oh my. Oh my, my. It's so lovely to meet you. So lovely to meet you both. Come with me. I'll take you up the mountain. It's a long walk but pleasant. He won't be happy to see either of you at all. Oh, it's just so fantastic to meet you both!"

And with that, Evie and Catherine, after a glance at each other, followed Peter back through the town and out the other side and began their long and evidently most unwelcome journey to the top of a volcano.

➤ CHAPTER 31 ◄

In which Sebastian wakes up.

Sebastian was getting seriously tired of waking up with a start. In fact, he was getting so tired of it, he could likely have fallen asleep from it, but he didn't because he just knew he'd end up, of course, waking up with a start afterward.

He sat there, bleary-eyed, heavy-bodied, like he was balancing a massive weight on his head. For a moment he actually thought he was, until he realized someone had put those sound-canceling headphones on him to protect his ears. In any event, he was altogether and completely disoriented and generally unhappy. It took him a full five minutes to figure out he wasn't in the private plane, as he'd assumed, but back in the helicopter. Or in *a* helicopter. How had that happened? When had that happened? How had he slept through all that? He thought back to the plane and remembered being given some water to drink. Had they given him something to make him sleepy so that he wouldn't try to escape again? In his fuzzy state, Sebastian's logical brain still was able to answer: *Most likely yes.* It was tough to gather his bearings, feeling like this, and he was pretty resentful that they'd done that to him. Though, he did have to confess, he probably would have tried to escape again had they not.

He looked around the helicopter. This one looked different from the one he'd flown away from the Explorers Society in. Roomier on the inside, large enough that he was sitting only opposite the frowning Mr. K, while the other two were sitting somewhere behind him. It was also daylight. It was also distinctly not Seoul.

Seoul. The Lost Boys. Kwan. Suwon. They all seemed part of a dream, and maybe they were. Maybe, now that he thought about it, he'd been flying all this time, and when he'd gotten mouthy in the private plane someone had drugged him and the rest had not happened at all, had just been a fever dream. The more he thought about it, the more sense it made. He hadn't really joined a K-pop group. That was too absurd for words.

Then he looked down at himself.

He was still wearing the shiny jeans and the shiny sports jacket over the artfully ripped white shirt.

Okay. So he'd really joined a K-pop group.

How he missed his K-pop group.

The grogginess was slowly leaving him, and finally he was able to feel a bit less resigned and nostalgic, and more scared and frustrated. No, not frustrated, angry. Angry with himself and with these men and with the pilot of the plane and now helicopter. He'd been so close. So close to getting away. Getting to Evie. Getting home. And to have that all ripped away at the last moment just like that—in, admittedly, a very clever fashion—well, it was really all too much for him to bear.

"I hate this," he said, the anger bubbling forth and spewing out bitterly. He crossed his arms and seethed.

"I'd be surprised if you didn't," buzzed an annoyingly jovial familiar voice in his earphones. "But think of it this way: you had a once-in-a-lifetime experience." Mr. M paused as he always did when he thought about what he'd just said. "Well, I suppose all your experiences from this point on will be once-in-a-lifetime. Seeing as there isn't much of it left." He said it as fact and as a fascinating realization, not as a threat. But of course, it made Sebastian's blood run cold. He turned around to look at Mr. M sitting in the seat behind him.

"I think I'll have as many experiences as I want to, thank you very much. Because I'm never telling you anything," spat Sebastian at Mr. M.

"Well. We'll see about that," replied Mr. M with a smile.

Sebastian hated that smug smile so much. He hated it! He was this close to getting up and smacking Mr. M in the face, and that was crazy-weird because Sebastian had never had a violent tendency in his life. Even his temper tantrums as a small child had always been measured and polite. No kicking or screaming, just an "I would still rather like to do this thing, please."

But he was angry, and he was scared, and he also was still a little fuzzy, and he hated Mr. M so much and hated all of them so much.

Still, of course he wouldn't hit him.

He just smiled back instead.

Which appeared to strike Mr. M just as well as any physical blow would have, because he frowned and turned away in a huff.

Sebastian, too, turned away, with a small feeling of triumph, and looked out the window. They were flying over a brilliant blue body of water, and even though it was the last place he wanted to be, he was still quite impressed by the sight. There was no land around for miles, and he wondered why they were in a helicopter in the first place. Why not still in the plane?

There was something ominous in that question, and Sebastian wrapped his arms more tightly around himself and sank lower in his seat.

What did the helicopter mean?

➤ CHAPTER 32 ➤

In which we meet Benedict Barnes. Properly. Not like back in the intro.

"He's up ahead, just beyond that ridge," said Peter, pulling back a large branch and pointing.

Evie was impressed by how not-winded he was. He had taken them halfway up the mountain at quite a clip, but since Catherine hadn't said anything and since it did make the most sense to get to Benedict as fast as possible, Evie had kept quiet. A good thing too, because now she could hardly speak for lack of breath. The journey through the jungle up the mountain had taken them an hour, and they hadn't packed any water or food, and neither had Peter. And yet he seemed perfectly content and fresh.

"I'll leave you now. Let you speak with him alone.

He's not going to be happy to see you. It'd be best if I wasn't there," said Peter cheerfully, and he turned around and started to head back down the mountain, just like that.

"Why do you keep saying that?" Evie called after him.

He stopped and looked at her. "Saying what?"

"That he won't be happy to see us?"

"Oh! Well. He refuses to talk about the team and won't read that letter Alistair Drake sent him. It seems quite clear to me. Is it not to you?" he asked sincerely.

"If he refuses to talk about us, how do you know so much about us?" asked Catherine.

"I did research. And I don't hate you." Peter smiled at that, and then with a wave turned around and disappeared into the foliage.

"Ever feel really not wanted?" asked Evie.

"Well, right now, as a matter of fact," replied Catherine. They looked at each other for a moment. "Oh. That was you being sarcastic again, wasn't it?"

"It was!" said Evie with a smile. Catherine smiled too, and then they started up the mountain again.

By the time they reached the end of the jungle, their clothes, which had just begun to dry off, were now fully drenched with sweat once more. Evie's hair stuck uncomfortably to the back of her neck, and what she wanted more than anything was just to jump into a lake. Preferably a very cool one. Though, as they stepped into the sunshine, Evie realized that that wasn't likely to happen anytime soon.

Before them the landscape had changed drastically. An incline of grass and dirt presented itself to them and then vanished over a small ridge. Beyond it the top of the volcano grew tall and dark, covered in black volcanic rock and looking not just a little ominous. The peak wasn't far away. Evie was tempted to run for it, to go right up its side and look over the edge. But that wasn't what they were there for. This wasn't an exploration; this was a meeting. She did have to confess, though, that a meeting on the side of a volcano was way better than one in a dank, dark boardroom underground.

They made their way along the slight incline of dust and dirt and short grass, enjoying the breeze that now cooled their bodies, until they climbed over the ridge. The temperature was dropping, which was a massive relief, and the breeze was turning into a proper wind. However, they now faced a new problem: walking against the wind was very challenging, slowing their progress and bringing tears to their eyes from the exposure. Finally, her cheeks wet from her watering eyes and her legs approaching the end of their usefulness,

Evie felt the texture of the ground change beneath her feet. She had made it to where the dirt turned to basalt at the very base of the volcano's tip. Yes, they had arrived, in the shadow of the mountain peak, at a small campsite with a little beige tent and an extinguished fire pit. And sitting on a promontory, not much farther away, looking in the opposite direction, was Benedict Barnes.

He sat cross-legged, in khaki trousers and a dark green jacket, the collar pulled up around his throat. He was perfectly still, his camera dangling from his neck. He was staring through his black-framed glasses at something. Or nothing. Or everything.

They approached the campsite, and the sound of their feet crunching on the stone should have signaled their presence to him. But he didn't turn around. They were tentative in approaching where he sat. It seemed one of them really ought to have called out to him. It was almost as if they were being sneaky, almost like when someone tiptoes up to you and then says "Boo!" to startle you. Now that Evie was thinking about it, she found she was actually kind of tempted to do it.

But she refrained.

"I don't know why you came here," said Benedict. His voice was soft and calm and warm. "I don't want anything to do with you, Alistair. You know that."

Alistair? Evie looked at Catherine in confusion. That was a bit unexpected.

"It's me, Benedict," said Catherine. Her voice too was soft. Almost as soft as when she spoke with animals.

Benedict turned and stared at her. Many people had stared at them in the last few days but none of them quite like this. There were so many emotions on his face, and yet Evie couldn't pinpoint exactly which ones. The emotions swarmed around like leaves dancing in the wind, never really landing anywhere. And just when she thought she'd figured them out, they would fly off again. Finally: "Catherine."

"Hi," Catherine said.

"What are you doing here?" he asked, rising carefully, his right hand lingering, still touching the earth for a moment as he rose.

"We need to talk," she said.

He walked over to her, still staring. "We couldn't have talked back in the city?"

"No."

Evie felt squirmy. She was bursting at the seams to say something. To be a bit clearer than Catherine was being at the moment. But sometimes directness, she knew, wasn't the point. Right now other things were going on. What they were, she was less sure of.

"If this is about Alistair, I don't want to hear it," said Benedict. Again, he didn't sound mean when he said it. He just said it.

"Well, you're going to have to," said Catherine.

"And why's that?"

"Because this is his granddaughter." Catherine pointed to Evie, though she really hadn't needed to. Evie was standing right there. The only other person on the volcano with them.

Benedict directed his attention to her now. Again his expression was unreadable.

"Hi," said Evie. Yup, just like Catherine, that was pretty much all she could say in the moment.

He kept looking at her closely, and for a second Evie got a sense that it was with amazement. But the expression was fleeting, and, finally, after a moment longer he said, "All right, I'll listen. But that's all. Let's sit." Benedict directed them back toward the promontory. It jutted out over the far side of the mountain, which dropped steeply off and down, to far, far below, where it crashed into the sea. She understood now why the volcano could only be climbed up on one side.

The promontory was large enough for half a dozen people. And they sat, all facing outward toward the view. From where they were sitting, it almost felt like they were floating on air. It might have seemed silly, but it was the first time Evie had even realized there would be a view. She hadn't once in their climb thought to look up or out, so focused had she been on the journey ahead. Hmm. That felt like a metaphor for something. Well, no matter.

Evie gazed out at what lay before her. Even though she had been spoiled with views of late, this one certainly did not disappointment. It was vast, sweeping, spectacular. The island fell away all around them, and the sea could be seen on three sides. Everything was green jungle and blue sea and, if she turned around, black basalt. The town wasn't visible at all. It was as if they three were the only humans anywhere.

"Wow," she said, feeling instantly kind of ridiculous after she said it.

"Tell me what you came here to say," said Benedict. He raised his camera and looked through the small viewfinder. Evie hadn't seen anyone take a picture that way in a long time. It was old-fashioned.

But also kind of cool. She waited to hear the shutter click, but it didn't. Benedict lowered the camera instead.

"Why didn't you take a picture?" asked Evie.

"I don't know," replied Benedict in that same calm manner, but there was a note to his voice now that sounded a little puzzled. As if he both didn't know and also didn't know why he didn't know.

"Benedict," said Catherine, "Alistair is in trouble." Benedict picked up the camera again. "He's in danger. We don't know where or why, but we think he's sent letters to all of us to use together to find him. To help him. Were you sent a letter? Peter said something about that."

"I told you I don't have any interest in him," said Benedict, still staring through the viewfinder, not answering the question.

"But he could be killed," said Evie, not able to contain herself anymore and not exactly sure why she had held back in the first place. There was just something about Benedict that made her want to behave respectfully.

"I doubt that very much," replied Benedict.

"Why?" asked Evie. She certainly didn't doubt it.

"Alistair is too smart to get himself killed." He put the camera down and looked at her. "He's fine. You needn't worry." He gave her a smile intended, Evie was sure, to comfort her. It didn't.

"I don't know how you can just say that," she said. "I mean, he sent a letter to your bankers, the Andersons, saying he needed help. I saw it. They gave it to me when I was at their home for one of my weekly dinners with them. My grandfather wouldn't be lying about that. Maybe he has always been smart enough to get out of things in the past, but surely him asking you for help now demonstrates just what kind of a horrible situation he's in!" She was up on her knees facing him now, looking away from the view. What did a view matter really, in the larger scheme of things? Besides, she'd seen so many of them in the past few days. They weren't nearly as important as important things.

"I suppose that's a fair point," said Benedict after a moment. He thought a bit longer and then turned back to look outward. "I'm still not interested in helping him."

"W-well . . . ," sputtered Evie. "Well . . . Well, what about Sebastian?"

"I don't know who that is," said Benedict.

Right. Of course he didn't.

"Well. Yes, there's more to the story than just Alistair," said Catherine. "There are these men after the map. We aren't positive, but we think they're likely on their way now. To find you. And to get your piece."

That made Benedict look away from the view once again. "And Sebastian is the man in charge?"

Evie scoffed. She couldn't help it. She knew it was inappropriate, but picturing Sebastian as the leader of those men in the black leather jackets just made her laugh. She imagined him dressed the same way trying to look menacing. It was too absurd.

"I take it he's not," said Benedict.

"No. No, Sebastian's my friend. He got himself into all this because of me. It's all my fault. He was helping me try to find my grandfather. Trying to find you. He even went to your class. He had a weird moment with the TA. . . ."

"Derrick is a bit of a ridiculous person. He was assigned to me. I didn't choose him," said Benedict, shaking his head.

"Well, then we found Catherine, and then we found the key to the map, and then Sebastian chose to destroy the key in the fire to protect me. But he didn't actually."

"He didn't?" Benedict seemed quite fascinated by the story, leaning in and listening intently.

"No. He's got a photographic memory. He burned the key to the map because he remembered it. So now he's the key. And these evil men have kidnapped him because they need the key, and we need to rescue him." Evie paused and took a breath. "Too."

Benedict nodded as he processed the story. He looked at Catherine. She nodded to confirm what Evie had said, which Evie found marginally offensive, but not too much. After all, Benedict didn't know Evie, so how was he to trust her, really?

"I can't come with you. I can't do this," said Benedict finally. "I can't."

"You have to!" Evie pleaded.

"No, I don't. But I will do this. I'll give you the letter. I'll give you my piece of the map."

"They'll still come after you. They'll still think you've got it. And they don't need to keep you alive like they have to keep Sebastian alive," said Evie. She didn't know why it wasn't good enough that he give them the map and letter. She wanted more. She wanted him to help them, to look for her grandfather with them. Benedict's refusal just felt so wrong.

"They are back at the house in town. I'll take you there. Then, don't worry, I can take care of myself." Once again it was said kindly, and once again Evie felt low. But she nodded as he stood, and joined him and Catherine as they walked back toward the camp. She lingered a bit behind, dragging her feet along, taking things slowly, putting off the inevitable.

Then she heard it.

She wouldn't have recognized it had she not remembered the sound so distinctly. It was very far off, just a quiver in the air. But she was instantly whisked back in her memory to that fateful day, to the last time she saw Sebastian.

"Helicopter!" she called out.

➤ CHAPTER 33 ◄

In which
the unexpected happens.

The black peak of the volcano rose out of the lush green of the island as the helicopter flew to the southern side, and Sebastian could do very little but stare. The volcano stood starkly against the brilliant blue sky, but the lush vegetation that grew up its side made it less formidable, more elegant, almost. It certainly didn't look dangerous. He knew very little about it. He didn't even know if it was still active.

"Ah. The Vertiginous Volcano," said Mr. M, coming over to him and looking out the window as well. "Still active but hasn't erupted in a thousand years. Wouldn't it be just impeccable timing if it did today?"

Sebastian glanced up at him and then back at the

volcano. It grew and grew as they flew closer and closer to it. He narrowed his focus, trying to see inside it, but they were coming at it from too low an angle.

However, that being said, he could see . . .

"Mr. I!" called out Mr. M. "We have company. How perfect! Get ready!"

Sebastian stared at the small figures close to the top of the mountain. It was hard to make them out, but one had very distinct red hair, one had a brown domed head, and the other was much shorter than the first two, and he had to assume that that one was . . .

Evie. She'd *come* for him. She'd actually kept her promise! He thrilled at that, and then felt guilty for ever thinking that she would do otherwise.

Sebastian turned back and looked at the men. Mr. K was sitting in his seat, glaring at him, but Mr. I was up, fastening a harness around his own body with Mr. M's help.

"What's going on?" asked Sebastian.

"First attempt is to just grab them. Don't want to waste time if we don't have to," said Mr. M.

"You can't be serious," said Sebastian. That was impossible. There were three of them. Mr. I couldn't grab them all. They'd run away, they'd get out of there faster than some person hanging on a cable could catch them. Wait. Why would he discourage this? "You can't use a long rope," he said.

"What?" asked Mr. K.

"The longer the rope, the less control the helicopter will have over its swing. You need something shorter and then bring the helicopter lower," said Sebastian. Helicopter lower. That was smart. In more ways than one.

Sebastian wasn't quite sure why it was, but he was almost giddy with excitement now. It was something about seeing Evie and Catherine and likely Benedict. Seeing that they were trying to help him. It inspired him. It made him happy. And it gave him a renewed sense of purpose.

"He's right," said Mr. M. "Thank you for being so helpful." He grinned in that special way at Sebastian, and Sebastian did his very best to look upset with himself for accidentally helping. Which, of course, he had very much done on purpose.

"I didn't—I didn't mean to," he stammered, hoping he sounded flustered.

"That brain can't stop problem-solving, can it?" said Mr. M with a smile. "Well, it's admirable. It really is. And thank you." He turned toward the pilot. "Did you hear him? We need to get lower." The pilot gave him a thumbs-up and took them downward. They were practically grazing the tops of the trees now.

"Come up from below," said Sebastian, pretending to say it to himself.

"Come at what from below?" asked Mr. K.

"What? Nothing. I didn't say anything." Sebastian looked out the window and did everything he could not to smile.

"Hey! Mr. M, kid says to 'come up from below,'" said Mr. K over the headset.

"Oh yeah. Coming down at them from above, they can run away," said Mr. M, thinking it through. "But we'll take them by surprise if we head down the side of the mountain and come up beside them. They'll hear us, of course, but won't know where we're coming from, and by the time they figure it out . . . it'll be too late. Nice." Mr. M went over to the pilot and had a word in her ear. Sebastian watched the conversation in the reflection of the window. He wasn't exactly sure of his plan. He just knew that the lower they got, the more chance for escape he would be given.

The helicopter went up then, flying right up past Evie and Catherine, and Sebastian stared in wonderment. It seemed like they might even be close enough to see him, but probably not. He felt a small stab of panic as the helicopter kept getting higher and farther away, until he realized that the pilot was taking them up and over the volcano to the other side of the island in order to sneak around it and come up from below, according to his suggestion.

As they soared above the volcano, Sebastian pressed his forehead to the glass, looking down into its depths. It wasn't all that deep, really, not relative to what he'd been expecting. And the hole was covered over with solid magma. It wasn't like the bubbling red innards of volcanoes he'd seen in movies. It was kind of a disappointment. Nonetheless, the view was impressive—the jutting walls of the crater rising from the covered hole, straight and determined and very unnatural-looking.

The helicopter was descending again quickly, and Mr. I and Mr. M together yanked open the door. Mr. M braced himself as Mr. I finished tying the rope to his harness and examined his surroundings. The sound of wind rushing and blades spinning was overwhelming, so loud that it was impossible to hear what Mr. M was saying through the headphones. They watched and waited for their chance, getting lower and lower. It was only then that Sebastian took stock of what a good flier the pilot actually was. She was avoiding rock formations and too-tall trees rather masterfully, he did have to admit.

What she wasn't able to avoid, however, was a soccer ball.

The helicopter veered sharply, tilting to one side. It wasn't that the ball had been particularly hard, but a soccer ball hitting the windshield was an unexpected thing. And even more unexpected when your windshield was connected to a helicopter. So Sebastian was not surprised that it had shocked the pilot. It wasn't like the soccer ball was able to do any damage either, but a sudden tilt to the side, where the tip of one of the helicopter blades catches the side of a tree, could be surprisingly dangerous.

The helicopter tilted wildly, turning almost ninety degrees, and Sebastian went spilling toward the open door. Mr. K still had his seat belt on. Seat belts really were useful, so Mr. K was safe, not that Sebastian had time to care. He did have time to note that he, on the other hand, was not wearing his seat belt. And after that, all he had time for was to flail his arms about wildly and grab the first thing he could as his body fell through the air. Which turned out to be Mr. I's legs. That was fortunate. What was unfortunate was that Mr. I hadn't found anything himself to hang on to, and so he and Sebastian went swinging out through the open door into the air.

Mr. I was attached to the helicopter by the rope,

and once they reached its end, they both went flying wildly underneath the helicopter and up almost level with the other side. And then back down again. The wind whipped around Sebastian's face, his shiny sports jacket flapping violently about, and he felt even more disoriented than when he'd been drugged. *Focus, Sebastian, focus.* He looked down. No, that wasn't doing it. The world was spinning and whirling frantically below him. He looked up at Mr. I instead, toward the open door to the helicopter. Mr. M had managed to stay inside and was holding tightly to the frame, staring at Sebastian in a way that looked like he was actually kind of impressed. Well, yes, Sebastian had been rather impressive just now. But this wasn't helping either. So he turned his gaze in front of him. Toward the trees coming up to greet him. And that was when he realized *I'm not tethered to the helicopter.*

Sebastian let go of Mr. I's legs and leapt. Once again. Without looking.

Because evidently that was his new thing.

➤ CHAPTER 34 ◄

In which things
come crashing down.

They didn't know where the helicopter had gone after it had launched itself up and over the volcano, but they certainly did hear it as it came crashing down, and they did see the smoke rising up from a distance, back toward the jungle.

"Sebastian!" cried Evie, and without thinking, without needing to think, she dashed past the campsite and back through the short stubby grass. She ran faster than she'd ever run before, the easy decline propelling her forward. Faster than when she'd been on top of the university building, being chased by Mr. K, faster than she'd run around the bear pit at the zoo. It was one thing to run for your life, but it was quite something else to run for someone else's life. Catherine and Benedict caught up to her easily, though—they did have much longer legs—and she more than welcomed their company. They all made it to the jungle and broke through into the brush, a branch whipping Evie in the face and causing her a sharp pain that she barely registered.

"Sebastian!" she called again. She didn't know why she was yelling his name so much, but it pushed her forward. She'd save him. She'd find him. Because he was alive. He was alive and he was okay and he was alive.

He had to be alive.

"Evie!"

She almost hadn't heard it over the sound of her own beating heart and frantic breathing. She skidded to a stop, as did the explorers, and looked wildly about her. "Sebastian, where are you?" she shouted.

"Up here!"

Evie retraced her steps toward the voice, looking up into the canopy above her. She caught a glimpse of something shiny in the sun. She didn't remember Sebastian as being particularly shiny, but maybe . . .

"Sebastian!" It was him. He was there. He was whole. He was okay.

"I'm coming down," he announced.

"I think that's a solid plan," replied Evie, grinning ear to ear as she watched him make his way down the tall tree. *Man, trees really are wonderful things,* Evie thought, fondly remembering the tree in the Explorers Society headquarters. *They always seem to be catching people and making them not fall to their deaths and stuff.*

And then, finally, after what felt like way too long and like she couldn't bear the wait anymore, Sebastian was there, on the ground, standing in front of her. A little bruised, a little worse for wear—his shirt thoroughly ripped to shreds—but safe. And alive.

So very much alive.

➤ CHAPTER 35 ◄

In which we change the point of view.

"Sebastian!" Evie cried yet again, and she launched herself at him. He really ought to have expected it, but it still took him by surprise as she drove the air right out of him. He also made a squeak of pain as she squished his aching and bruised body. "You're alive!" She finally released him, and he took in a deep breath.

"Of course I'm alive. They need my brain, after all," he said, patting his hair back into place.

"Of course, but you're all there! You aren't missing any limbs or anything! You aren't all cut up and injured! Except . . . your hands. What happened to your hands?"

Sebastian looked down to remind himself. Oh.

Right. The bandages from drumming. "It's really nothing, I was drumming. A lot. And there was some bleeding after a while."

"Drumming?"

"Can we talk about it later?" asked Sebastian, feeling oddly uncomfortable.

"Sure. But does the drumming have anything to do with the outfit?" asked Evie with a smile.

Oh right. His sparkly ensemble. "Yeah. It's all . . . related."

"It's super shiny."

Sebastian nodded in agreement; that, it was.

"Are you wearing eyeliner?"

"Yup."

"Cool."

They both stared at each other. He wasn't sure how he could express all the gratitude he felt right at that moment, seeing Evie, seeing that she had indeed come to rescue him like she'd promised. It felt like too much, like more than words were capable of expressing. "Hey, uh, thanks for coming for me." *Yeah,* he thought, *words are totally inadequate right now.*

"Well, it's more like you came to us," replied Evie.

"We came to each other," Sebastian said firmly, and Evie smiled at that. He smiled back. It was nice to smile. Sebastian looked around for the first time and saw Catherine staring at him with her usual inscrutable expression. Next to her was a man he recognized from photographs. Just like Catherine, it seemed as if he'd barely aged in the last two decades. He looked formidable—strong and solid. Intimidating.

"Benedict Barnes?" asked Sebastian.

"Yes, and you're Sebastian," replied Benedict in a warm voice that seemed totally incongruous with his appearance.

Yes, I am. "Yes, I am," he answered. There was something about acknowledging the fact that he was who he was that made him feel both sure and unsure. Did he know who he was? He was feeling less so every day.

"What happened? Where are they? We heard a loud crash," said Catherine, stepping forward.

"This is going to sound crazy, but I swear we were hit by a soccer ball," replied Sebastian.

"A soccer ball?" asked Evie, though she seemed less confused and more thoughtful.

It was all quite difficult to relate, as he wasn't entirely certain what had happened himself. He remembered letting go of Mr. I's legs and leaping. He remembered reaching out and feeling hopeful. But then he also remembered blacking out for a moment and waking up in the top of a tree. Probably a good thing he'd blacked out, because his body had gone limp, and as a result he was only scratched and bruised, nothing more.

"You look pretty beat-up," said Evie. He could hear the tinge of emotion in the statement.

"I'm fine. I really am. I double-checked up in the tree. I'm very safety-conscious." He was many-things-conscious, as a matter of fact.

"The others, are they . . . are they . . ." Evie stopped.

"I'm not sure, but knowing them, knowing how they are, I bet they're okay," he reassured her, even though in a strange way it also wasn't a reassurance. Still, he knew she wouldn't wish harm on anyone, not even scary evil men in black. "In fact," he continued, "I think all of us are in quite a bit of danger. Let me tell you, these guys are violent. And ruthless. And quite irrational, too, at times. And mean. Just plain mean. Except I guess maybe the new one. The guy we met for the first time in your room. Who kidnapped me. His name is Mr. M. He sometimes acts weirdly nice. Which is almost scarier, actually. So really, my original point stands." He was rambling now, not a thing he normally did, and something he tended to judge negatively in others when they did it. But he was overwhelmed, and in a bit of pain, and extremely happy to see everyone and yet totally scared at the same time. He wasn't in control of his word-stuffs anymore.

"We need to get out of here," said Evie, turning to the explorers. There was a clear note of panic in her voice.

Yes, that was the point I was driving at, thought Sebastian.

"That might prove difficult," said Benedict thoughtfully.

"Why?" asked Evie, completely indignant.

"That's the only way down," replied Benedict, pointing to where the black smoke could still be seen rising though the trees.

Sebastian's stomach fell, and from the expressions on their faces, he was guessing that the same had just happened to both Evie and Catherine. For some reason Benedict looked quite unruffled about the whole thing. As if it really wasn't such a big deal.

"So we're just trapped, waiting here for them to climb up and find us, like sitting ducks?" asked Evie, her voice getting higher in pitch.

"There is another way, but I wouldn't recommend it," said Benedict.

"Why not?" asked Sebastian.

"Well, it's very physically challenging, and many have died attempting it." There was something in that calm, smooth voice of Benedict's that somehow made whatever he was about to suggest seem not all that challenging to Sebastian.

"Oh," he said.

"I don't think we have much of a choice," said Evie. "Staying here isn't going to keep us any more alive either."

"Fair point," said Catherine.

Benedict looked at Evie for a moment and then at Catherine. "Just like old times." Catherine smiled a sad smile at that. "Well, then, follow me," Benedict instructed.

Follow me.

An easy enough thing to do in normal circumstances. "Where's the restaurant?" "Just around the corner—follow me!" "There's a great statue hidden in the park—follow me!" "I'm a magical cat and have a magical quest for you—follow me!" But a "follow me" that is in essence a "So what we have to do is climb into the volcano itself down the steep face of the cliff and not fall to certain death in order to access a small tunnel through the mountain halfway down, which we'll use to crawl down to another exit in the jungle to our safety" . . . well, that kind of a "follow me" is a lot less straightforward.

And this was, as Benedict explained as they walked

out of the jungle and along the dirt and grass back toward the base of the dark peak, exactly the kind of "follow me" he had in mind.

So "follow me" they did, and walked toward the campsite. They made their way past it and around the beginning of a jutting promontory. On the other side, Sebastian saw a path. It wasn't much of one, and was quite clearly not that often trod along. It wound up around the black peak of the volcano, taking them to the very top, the rim. They followed the path as it rose and curved along the side of the volcano, up and up until they found there was no more up to go. They stopped, standing on what was approximately a twenty-foot-wide edge that ran around the chasm. It was a bit like standing on the lip of a gigantic coffee cup. Looking into the crater from this perspective, Sebastian felt a little silly that he'd been disappointed with the volcano earlier. The crater that dipped away below him was vast, the rock walls tall and daunting. There was no life up there, no vegetation, like a fortress built by nature.

They couldn't stop to marvel at the view or be impressed that they had made it all the way to the top, though. They didn't have the time. For as Sebastian turned and glanced down the mountain back the way they'd come, he noticed three dark figures emerging from the jungle in the distance below them.

"They're coming," he said, and pointed. The others looked. And then Benedict gestured for them to continue following him single file along the edge of the crater, the perimeter of the volcano. Evie went second, Sebastian was behind her, and Catherine brought up the rear. Eventually they came to a stop, and Benedict got down on his hands and knees. They all came up beside him and followed suit, sticking their heads over the edge of the hole and looking down into the blackness. Sebastian knew that the volcano was in no danger of erupting right at this moment, that far more seismic activity would have to be taking place beneath the surface in order for an eruption to occur, but as he stood there, inhaling the sulfurous smell that rose to greet him, it still felt as if an eruption was eminent. It wasn't science. It was more metaphorical. Sebastian resented the heck out of his brain at the moment.

"Well, this is it," said Benedict. "Normally professional climbers do this with ropes and helmets and gear. We don't have such equipment with us."

"To be fair, we're not professional climbers," said Evie.

"I don't understand," said Benedict.

"Uh, well, I mean . . . if professional climbers need equipment, maybe nonprofessional climbers don't."

There was a long pause.

"That doesn't make sense," said Catherine.

"It's a joke. It's an Evie joke," explained Sebastian.

"Hey, what does that mean?" asked Evie, turning around and looking at him.

Oh no, he hadn't meant it in a bad way. It was so

nice to hear one of her jokes again. "It means it's a little inappropriate but quite clever."

Evie stared at him for a moment longer and then smiled. "That's a very nice thing to say. Thank you."

Well, yes, he supposed it was. He'd just meant it as factually accurate, that's all. Still it made him happy that she thought so. "You're welcome."

"Well, regardless, this is not going to be easy," said Benedict, sitting up on his knees. "And it's really every man, woman, and child for themselves, I think. But we can try to help each other out as best we can. I'm going first. Watch what I do."

Sebastian observed, impressed, as Benedict effortlessly turned around and lowered himself down into the crater along the cliff face, using his arms to support himself as his feet found his footing. "Have you done this before?" Sebastian asked.

"Have I scaled the side of a rock face before, or have I attempted to use this way out before?" asked Benedict, not even a strain in his voice as he lowered himself another inch.

"The second thing," replied Sebastian.

"Once. I'm sure I remember how to do this." Benedict glanced over his shoulder and then looked back at them. "Another thing, don't look down." He lowered himself farther still until his head was now below the brim of the volcano. Sebastian worked hard to memorize each foot placement, each movement of the hands as Benedict inched his way down the rock face. The problem, of course, was that Sebastian was watching it upside down and Benedict's body often blocked what his feet were doing below.

"Who's next?" asked Evie, but Sebastian didn't look up. He kept watching Benedict go, and then about seventy feet down, Benedict disappeared into the side of the wall.

"He made it!" said Sebastian, more with relief than celebration. He pushed himself up onto his knees and looked at the other two. "What did you ask?"

"Who's next?" repeated Catherine. "I'm going last." She glanced over her shoulder, and Sebastian noticed then that her right hand was at her hip, holding on to the handle of her bullwhip.

"Okay, okay," he said, looking at Evie.

"I'll go," she said with that fiercely determined look of hers.

"No, I should," said Sebastian.

"Why?" She looked at him, clearly confused. "I can do it."

"I've memorized the steps Benedict took. I think if I'm below you and can see your feet better, that'll help me help you more."

Evie thought about it for a moment. "But if I went first, you could talk me through it even though it would be a little harder from above, and then I could talk you through it from below. If you go first, then no one can help you. And you can't see your own feet."

They stared at each other for a moment, and Sebastian thought hard. He'd forgotten a bit what it was like to not be making all the decisions by himself. Things took longer. But at the same time, better decisions could result. "Yeah, you're right."

"Okay, kids. The teamwork is lovely and everything, but we don't have time for elaborate discussions. Evie, it's your turn," said Catherine.

Evie nodded and turned around so that her back was toward the chasm. Sebastian could see the concentration in her eyes but also the fear.

"You can do this," he said.

"Okay," she said back.

"You climbed up the side of a building, rappelled off a tower with a rope. You ran along the edge of a bear pit. You're like a cat or something." He said it both because it was reassuring and because it was true.

"I am really impressive, aren't I?" said Evie with a twinkle in her eye. She slowly lowered her right foot over the edge of the cliff while Sebastian positioned himself, lying flat on his belly with his head down over the side to see her better.

"Okay, so I just realized something," said Sebastian.

"Yeah?" asked Evie. Her voice was strained and she was flailing her leg around, reaching for a foothold.

"Benedict's a lot taller than you. I can't tell you where to put your hands and feet, because it won't be the same."

Evie looked up and then understood. "Well, I guess there's no point in trying to copy him, then. Just got to do this my own way. Watch and learn, photographic memory boy," she said.

She scratched at the wall with her foot until it found a spot that held it fast, and she grinned at him. Then she did the same with her other foot, and stood there for a moment, the top half of her body still propped up on the ground.

"I guess I have to let go now," she said, more to herself, it seemed, than to him. She slid her body toward the edge inch by inch and then began to crouch, reaching her right hand down along the cliff face and feeling for something to grab hold of. When she found it, she took in a deep breath and then slowly released her left hand. This hand was slower to find something to hang on to. It inched over the edge and down close to her side. Her hand was steady and still. Then a sudden movement. She'd found a small outcropping of rock. She smiled and released her breath.

So did Sebastian.

She was squatting, crouched in the air, and it was time for her feet to find a new home. And so she extended her right leg out, feeling blindly about for another groove or crevice. And when she found one, she reached with her left.

And so she continued, as Sebastian watched hard, encouraging her as she went, offering the odd suggestion—though it was hard from his perspective to see. It was arduous, and took time, but this was not something to rush. And then, finally, she was there, she'd made it. Benedict's arms appeared from within the hole in the rock wall, grabbed her, and pulled her inside the mountain. She was gone for a moment, and then her head poked back out.

"Okay, Sebastian. The first one is directly below you for your right foot!" she called up to him.

Sebastian nodded. It was his turn. He could do this. He had to do this. He turned around and lay down on the ground, facing Catherine. He looked at her, and she smiled in that not-quite-convincing way of hers. But it was enough. He started to slide himself backward and discovered that it was one thing to offer suggestions to someone else about how to do this, but to do it himself, that was something else. As the world disappeared around him, he realized he was holding his breath. And even with that realization, he just couldn't release it. He dangled over the edge, feeling the nothingness as he searched with his right foot for the foothold Evie had told him about.

"You've almost got it, just an inch more to the left," he could hear her say. He moved his foot to the left and found it. A small insubstantial crack in the wall, no deeper than his big toe. Well, that didn't inspire confidence. "Now your left foot is just above where it needs to be," said Evie.

Great, thought Sebastian as he slid his torso farther along the ground toward the edge and certain doom. His left foot found a jutting-out rock. This one fit almost his entire sole. That made him feel better.

Sebastian remembered where he had told Evie to put her hands on the wall, and he reached down with his right hand, blindly feeling for it. He got hold of it, and then with one last look at Catherine and one more not-quite-encouraging smile from her, he slowly slid his full body off the ground and grabbed for the rock.

His right foot slipped, and the world fell away. He could hear Evie scream from below and Catherine call his name from above. Only one thing stayed true and firm, and that was his grip with his right hand. When his body slammed hard against the rock wall, he was jarred back into the moment and saw that he was dangling for his life by one hand.

Catherine was now leaning down over the side, offering her hand to him, and he reached up with all his might to grab it with his left. Together they pulled him back up to where he'd been, and he felt around with his feet for their footholds. He found them. He was okay. Now if only he could tell his heart that it could settle down.

"Are you okay?" Evie called up.

"Yup. Yup, I'm fine," he called back, still trying to calm himself down. "Just need to try again. Okay. Okay. I'm ready. Let's do this."

"Okay. The next foothold is a little more toward the right," instructed Evie.

And so they went like this, very slowly, very carefully, Sebastian hugging the wall for dear life, following Evie's directions, and every single time he took a new step, the sensation of the world caving in below came swimming up to him in a nauseatingly accurate memory. But he fought it. What choice did he have? It was either go down or . . . go down but faster and more painfully.

When he reached the hole in the wall, he lowered himself so that his legs dangled over it, and Benedict grabbed them and helped pull him inside. The relief that washed over him was even more than he'd felt the many times when he'd landed safely after a crazy leap. There was something easier about falling and hoping than about climbing and sensing that at every possible moment something could go wrong.

"You made it," said Evie. She had a knack for stating the obvious. Then again, so did he.

"So did you," he said back.

"Move aside!" said Benedict as Catherine's legs appeared from above.

"Already?" asked Sebastian, astonished at her speed. She lowered herself a bit farther down past the hole so that her full body was dangling from her arms. She started to pump her legs like she was swinging on an invisible swing. And then she launched herself forward and into the cave.

"Cool," said Evie.

"Let's go," replied Catherine.

➤ CHAPTER 36 ⤙

In which we go into
the deep dark.

A deep black hole. That's what it looked like. That's what it was. This wasn't blackness like when you go to bed and your parents turn out the light and your eyes adjust and, thanks to a streetlight beyond your window blinds or the sliver of light under the door from the hall, shapes slowly start to take shape. No. There was no light once they turned that last corner, leaving the entrance behind them. None. Evie's eyes could not adjust to anything. There was nothing to adjust to. This was all there was.

And then someone turned on a light switch.

"What's that?" asked Evie, stunned by the sudden brightness, and blinking hard.

"The portable LED light I use with my camera. I turned it on. We'll need something to help us," said Benedict, as casual as ever.

Evie nodded, feeling relief but also still slightly traumatized by the suddenness. It took a moment for her eyes to readjust now to the brightness. When they finally did, she took a good look around. They were in a very narrow but tall cavern that just fit the four of them. It rose up above their heads. Almost, she imagined, to the top of the volcano.

"This way," said Benedict. He walked slowly along the cavern farther into the side of the volcano. "I think."

"You think?" said Sebastian from behind Evie, but Benedict didn't seem to hear, or at least didn't seem to find the question worth answering. Evie glanced back, and Sebastian shook his head.

For a while, a longer while than she would have thought, they walked in silence, pressing their hands up along the walls of the cave on either side to steady themselves. The ground was uneven. It wasn't really ground, actually. It was rocks that could trip you up, sharp edges sticking up here and there, always, seemingly, in your way. In the artificial light, Evie could see the pitch black of the walls, volcanic rock formed eons ago when the volcano had been young and much more active. Spiderwebs glistened in the light, and their owners were not particularly shy around humans. Evie learned this when she walked right into a web and, as she attempted to extract herself, the spider whose trap she had just destroyed meandered slowly along her arm and down to her hand. She was so stunned, she didn't even flinch, just watched it. Finally it jumped off onto the rock wall and wandered away, almost with a sigh: *Back to square one*.

After that, Evie began to notice more spiders along the walls, and some creepy crawly things that would disappear into the stone crevices the second she looked directly at them. She now wondered if having the light was a good thing after all. There was something to ignorance being bliss. Or being not nearly as creepy.

It got cooler as they went deeper into the earth, farther away from the sun. Evie had thought maybe it would get warmer, considering they were in a volcano, but they weren't going toward the magma. They were heading through the wall to the outside.

It was also damp. And claustrophobic.

And then Benedict stopped. He turned, and Evie threw her arm up, shading her eyes from the LED light of the camera now facing her. Benedict quickly turned it to the side and said, "It gets a little narrow here. Headfirst."

Headfirst?

Evie stood in alarm as she watched Benedict lower himself to the ground, and that's when she saw what seemed to be a tall rock wall dead end. She looked down, and realized that Benedict was slowly lowering himself headfirst into a hole not much larger than his body. She had an instant flashback to when this whole adventure had begun. To escaping the Andersons' burning home through their tunnel. Immediately her gut contracted. It was like she was back at the house, pushing her way to safety, leaving the Andersons behind, terrified that the tunnel was going to collapse on her. Slowly Benedict's body was engulfed by the hole, and Evie stood there and watched.

"Are you okay?" whispered Sebastian from behind her.

She just nodded. She had to be okay. What other choice did she have? She took a step forward and then sat herself on the ground. She looked into the hole. Now that Benedict had made his way all the way through it, his camera LED highlighted what was beyond. The hole opened into a small cavern, big enough maybe just for her and him.

"You can do this," said Sebastian.

I've already done this, Evie thought.

She lay down on her stomach and reached through

the hole, grabbing on to the sharp rock on the other side. Then she started to pull with her arms and wiggle her legs at the same time. As her head went through, she realized she'd have to turn her body a little to the side now to avoid a protruding rock on her right. She used it to propel herself forward even more, sliding along her side. Finally her head poked out into the small cavern. She reached out and grabbed for Benedict's extended hand, and he helped her as she slid the rest of her body through. In short order she was in the small cavern with Benedict.

"Good," he said with a relaxed smile. "Now you help the boy." And he turned and started to crawl through another tight crevice, taking most of the light with him.

Evie prepared herself. Then, just as Benedict had done with her, she grabbed Sebastian's extended hand. She helped him crawl through the hole to join her. In the dim light she could see the sparkle of his outfit, and it made her smile. Reminded her that the world wasn't always scary. It was often kind of silly, too.

"What?" he asked, furrowing his brow.

"You're so sparkly."

He shook his head. "Go on. I'll help Catherine."

Evie nodded and turned to follow the diminishing light through the narrow crevice, Benedict waiting on the other side to assist. And on it went much like this. A chain of helpfulness. And they continued. And they wended and wound and worked their way through, deeper and deeper and farther and farther down.

Hopefully toward an escape.

Time passed. At least it felt like time passed. It was really hard to tell in the dark deep. It did feel like they were really heading somewhere. They were now getting quite good at this cave-crawling thing.

Benedict stopped suddenly, and so did the rest. No one bumped into anyone else. They knew how this worked. He turned to them, and Evie waited for some kind of instruction. She couldn't see behind him. Would they go down? Up? To the side?

"We have to go back," he said.

"What?" asked Catherine from the end of the line.

"It's a dead end."

Evie felt her heart in her throat. "I thought you knew the way," she said, trying to keep her voice calm.

"I thought I did too. I made a wrong turn somewhere. We need to turn back. Find the spot. Try again."

It helped that he sounded so relaxed about it all, but since that was how he always sounded, Evie didn't know if it meant that he was confident they would find their way or simply that he was always relaxed.

There was much shuffling as Benedict and Catherine switched places so Benedict could lead them back. Evie was now behind Sebastian, and they began to return the way they'd come. It was both easier and harder to do. Easier in that Evie knew what to expect, harder in that everything they'd done they now had to do in reverse. There was also a lot more climbing upward, which she wasn't used to.

Benedict stopped again.

"Let's go this way." He turned the opposite way this time inside a tight cavern, and they each followed behind. They clambered for a bit, and then the tunnel started to get narrow. And more narrow. And Evie had to turn sideways, and if she had to turn sideways, she wondered how the adults were managing it. And then, once again, they stopped.

"Go back?" asked Sebastian in front of her.

"Go back," agreed Benedict.

Catherine led them back this time. When they arrived in the tight cavern again, they decided to continue to retrace their steps. Up and back.

Up and back.

And then Benedict suggested they climb up a wall to a hole some six feet above their heads. So they tried that. He went first, then helped hoist Evie up. Then

Catherine came up and helped Sebastian. And they crawled on hands and knees there.

Evie was getting tired. Her eyes were getting heavy. It almost felt like the world around her was getting dimmer.

Or was it that the world around her was getting dimmer?

"Benedict, the battery," said Catherine.

"I know," he replied, almost wistfully.

"Do you have any more?"

"I do."

"Good."

"In my camera bag."

There was a long pause as the light of the LED dimmed just a bit more.

"And your bag is . . . ," said Catherine slowly.

"Back on top of the mountain."

At first it didn't quite sink in for Evie just how dire the situation was. Okay, so they'd have to go along in the dark. It wasn't like it was easy going to begin with. But as the light dimmed yet again, it finally hit her how bad this was. They couldn't look for holes and caverns. They couldn't properly seek a way out. They would have to stumble blindly now. Feel their way along. What if they missed the exit? They couldn't even retrace their steps. They could be trapped inside the volcano. Forever.

It was only then that Evie registered the silence around her. It seemed quite obvious to her that she wasn't the only one having this thought. In the silence in the mountain, the light dimmed again. And again.

And then went out.

➤CHAPTER 37◄

In which the blind lead the blind.

Sebastian knew that his memory of what he had seen on their journey underground was woefully inadequate for the task at hand, considering he now couldn't see anything, but he also knew that his memory was pretty much all they had.

"I think . . . I think I can get us out," he said to no one or everyone. It was freaky, talking into the blackness like this. "I think I can remember the way. But it would take us back up, not down. And the men are waiting for us."

"I think at this point it's a risk we have to take," replied Catherine's voice.

"Then we need to turn around and I'll take the

lead. And we need to all hold on to each other," said Sebastian, not feeling sure of this plan in the least but thinking it really was the only one they had.

First, though, they had to crawl back out to the cavern in order to switch spots. It was tough enough turning around in such a small space, but then to climb down six feet in the darkness? It was truly terrifying. Fortunately Catherine was brave and found the edge and was able to lower herself comfortably to the ground with ease and then help the others.

Even after they were upright, Sebastian discovered a new challenge. He didn't really know where the front was. He stretched out his arms and felt for a wall and then carefully moved forward, tracing with his fingers as he went, until he finally came upon the exit.

"I found it," he said with relief. "I guess it's time to get in line."

He felt Catherine's warm firm hand on his shoulder as he inched forward, bit by bit, his hands on the walls beside him. It was feeling more impossible to translate his visual memory into something tactile. He touched a small jutting-out bit with his left hand. Was it what he was looking for? He felt around some more, and his hand slipped into an open space. Yes! Okay. This was getting them somewhere. They could do this. They could . . . He reached out farther and hit a wall.

This wasn't the space he'd thought it was. And he'd been so sure. He felt around a little more, beginning to get a bit frantic. Okay, so maybe this wasn't the opening. But the opening had to be here somewhere. He reached around more, but he couldn't find it. Why couldn't he find it? He took a step forward and could sense the line behind him moving likewise, and he was filled with guilt that they trusted him when he wasn't trusting himself right now.

That scared him more than anything else. More than the dark, more than the possibility of staying down here forever. He couldn't trust himself.

This was too hard. And he was getting too flustered. Breathe. Breathe.

Oh no.

He couldn't control it.

He was having one of his panic attacks. It was the university park bench all over again, or like when he'd confronted the men in black at the Reptile Realm. But this one seemed even worse, and at the worst possible moment. He had done so well up until now, had fought it so well. He had thought he was really getting the hang of this adventuring thing.

His chest got tighter, his breath shallower, he was getting dizzy, though in the darkness, mercifully, the world couldn't spin. He leaned against the wall.

"Sebastian, are you okay?" asked Catherine.

"I . . ."

"What's that?" asked Evie from farther back.

"She asked if I was okay. I'm having a bit of a panic attack," explained Sebastian, a lot more calmly than he felt.

"Oh no. Okay. Just try to slow your breathing if you can. Take your time, there's no rush. But what I meant when I asked 'What's that?' was, what's that to the right, sort of ahead? I feel like I can see something. Can anyone else see that?" Evie said.

Sebastian looked forward while trying desperately to slow down his breathing. And sure enough it was almost as if he could see the faintest outline of a wall ahead. He stumbled toward it, and he felt Catherine's hand slip off his shoulder. "Sebastian!" she said.

"I see it too." He walked quickly forward, and it felt like if he kept walking, he'd be okay. He'd be able to breathe again. It was getting lighter. He could see shadows. Could he see shadows? Was it just his imagination? Was he seeing things? Had he lost enough oxygen that he was hallucinating? But Evie had seen it too. He moved toward the shadows. This would help him. This would calm him down. He just had to . . .

A blinding white light.

Sebastian staggered backward.

"What's going on?" said Catherine loudly, and Sebastian was relieved that he wasn't the only person experiencing this. It was not a hallucination after all.

"Is that you, famous explorers?" said an unfamiliar voice. The light swung to the side. "It *is*! It *is* you! Ah, see? Great minds think alike."

"But fools seldom differ," muttered Sebastian to himself, completing the saying.

"What was that? Who are you? Where did you come from?" asked the voice.

Sebastian looked up finally, and now that his eyes had grown accustomed to the light again, he saw a young man standing before him, with wide eyes and wearing a friendly smile.

"I could ask the same of you," Sebastian replied.

"Peter!" said Catherine. "What are you doing here?"

"I came to find you, to warn you. There's been an incident outside of town in the jungle. On the path to the top of the mountain. A helicopter crashed and they did not have permission to be here. They're bad people. I think they're the bad people after you, Mr. Barnes," said Peter.

"That they are, Peter," said Benedict. "Do you know the way out?"

"Of course. Follow me, follow me," he said with a smile. Then he turned to Sebastian. "I'm Peter."

"Uh, I'm Sebastian."

"Not now, Peter," said Benedict, though he didn't sound remotely frustrated.

With Peter as their guide, and with a light to see by now, the five of them worked their way through the mountain quickly and efficiently. It wasn't easier going. It still required a lot of crawling and climbing, and at one point walking along a narrow edge over a deep chasm. But they made it through the mountain, and finally Sebastian could smell the fresh air just around the corner.

Sure enough they climbed up, one at a time, through a narrow crevice out into the lush jungle. Sebastian had never been happier to see daylight in his life.

They stood for a moment, gathering themselves. Sebastian wasn't certain whether the others were thinking what he was thinking—that if it hadn't been for Peter, they likely would not have made it out, they quite likely would have perished inside that mountain—but he could feel a palpable sense of relief wash over not just him but the whole group.

"We need to go to the house," said Benedict after a moment. "We need to get you the map and letter."

Sebastian was a little surprised by that. For some reason—and he realized there was no evidence to support his hypothesis, but still—he had assumed that

Benedict would be coming with them, would be actively helping them. Not just giving them what they needed.

"To the house!" announced Peter, and he assumed the role of leader again, taking them back through the jungle.

➤ CHAPTER 38 ⬳

In which everything comes to a head. Or whatever body part you feel like, really.

It had certainly been a long day. Of course, days couldn't actually be different lengths from one another,[17] but climbing mountains on both the outside and inside could make any day seem truly overwhelming. Evie's muscles ached, her body was completely exhausted, and she was pretty sure she was out of adrenaline. Could one run out of adrenaline?

But Evie and the others couldn't rest. They had to keep going. And keep going they did. How many hours had they been scrambling through rock and now dense trees? How many hours climbing over, ducking under,

---

17 Except that one September 26 in 1957.

and going to the left and right of things? She should have worn a watch. Then again, did she really want to know?

All she knew was that the light was getting warmer in tone, hued with orange, and she could tell the sun was starting to think it might be time for dinner. Dinner. How long had it been since she'd eaten anything?

So it made sense that the relief she felt as they emerged onto the narrow path that led into town was so strong that she nearly wept. And the small cheer that went up in the square as they arrived moved her even more. Even though she had no idea why they were cheering in the first place.

Evie was quite surprised to see the town square so full compared to earlier in the day. She was even more surprised when one of the boys around her age who'd been playing soccer ran up to her and gave her a big hug.

"We won!" he said with a smile in a thick accent.

"Oh, congratulations," said Evie. She supposed they took soccer very seriously. She knew that many countries did.

The teenagers who had directed Evie and Catherine to Peter earlier in the day came over. "He means we defeated the helicopter," said the teen boy.

"You did what?" asked Catherine.

"It kept flying around. They did not have permission to be here," explained the teen girl.

"Isa and I called the authorities, but the children, they thought they could help," said the teen.

Evie glanced over at the boy her age. He'd been joined by his friends, and they stood nearby, grinning, draping arms over each other's shoulders and looking quite proud of themselves.

"We made a . . . a . . ." The boy stopped. He didn't have the word for it. He gestured with his hands, pulling his right hand back and aiming for the sky.

"A slingshot?" asked Sebastian.

Oh yeah, thought Evie, *that's what he's miming.*

"Yes. A big one. We sent our ball. And the helicopter fell," said the boy.

The other children laughed at that and gave each other high fives.

"You brought down the helicopter?" Benedict was obviously surprised. Evie was too, for that matter. It made no sense. How could something as small as a soccer ball bring down such a large machine? Then again, she did recall Sebastian saying something about that earlier.

"We told them it couldn't have really done that," said Isa quietly to just them. "But they said they saw it. So we will allow them to believe it."

"No, it's true. I was in the helicopter. It wasn't the ball, but the ball was the thing that threw off the pilot. It was a tree that actually brought us down. But without the ball, nothing would have happened," said Sebastian.

Evie smiled. She was happy that the kids were right. She was happy in general when her peers were right, especially around adults. She felt vindicated.

"You were in the helicopter?" Isa's expression turned dark. Evie looked around. The faces of the other townspeople were likewise suddenly suspicious.

"He was kidnapped! He's one of us. He escaped," said Evie quickly. Their expressions softened, though they didn't appear entirely trusting. "But right now we have to leave quickly because soon those men will know that we're not up the mountain anymore. They'll come for us."

"When they come, we're ready," said the boy her age, looking rather fierce. He placed his hands on his hips, and his friends followed suit. If they could take down a helicopter, Evie was quite confident they could stop the men when they came to town.

"Thank you," said Catherine.

"Come on!" said Benedict.

Evie gave a smile to the boy, who nodded at her very seriously, and then she, Sebastian, Catherine, Benedict, and Peter darted through the square and back toward Peter's house.

They flew across the clearing and up the stairs and inside, and Benedict disappeared into a back room. He returned in an instant with two pieces of paper. "Map." He held up one. "Letter." He held up the other. Then he passed them over to Catherine. She looked at them closely for a moment, then looked up at him.

"The seal isn't broken," she said, holding up the letter.

"I didn't read it," replied Benedict. "You should go, quickly."

Catherine took a step toward him, and the two adults looked at each other for a moment. "You should read it, Benedict."

Nothing happened. No movement, no reply from Benedict. Evie was feeling antsy. Benedict was right, they really should go. He was also right about them probably needing to do it quickly.

Finally, with a not-unhappy sigh—though Evie was

starting to think that Benedict did have a range of emotion; he just didn't show it the way most people did—he took the letter out of Catherine's hand and broke the wax seal.

And read.

It was very quiet in the little house on stilts.

Benedict looked up at Catherine.

"So?" she asked.

"So he asks about the weather and wants to see my latest work," replied Benedict, passing the letter over to Catherine.

"Can I see it?" asked Evie softly.

Catherine nodded and handed her the letter. Evie read it over.

It was as Benedict had said. More talk of weather. This time a storm out west. Just like he'd written to Catherine about the . . . north . . . wind. What was it that Alistair had said in his letter to the Andersons? "The four directions point to home."

"The four directions," she said quietly. It was like she was talking to herself more than to anyone else in the room.

"Four directions?" asked Benedict.

"Like he wrote to the Andersons. Catherine, could I have your letter?" she asked. Catherine nodded and, taking hers out of her pocket, passed it over. Evie examined it again closely. "Look." Everyone gathered around, and she held the two letters from Alistair side by side. "He mentions north in his letter to Catherine, and west to Benedict. Surely that has something to do with finding him. With pointing to him."

"In what way?" asked Catherine.

"I . . . don't know." Evie sighed hard. She felt so much closer, and yet it was so far.

"Is he giving coordinates?" asked Catherine.

"There aren't any numbers," replied Benedict.

Think, Evie, think. "Four directions. Like on a compass." She said it aloud even though it didn't solve anything.

"What if it isn't about words? What if . . . ," said Sebastian slowly. "The puzzle box."

"The puzzle box?" asked Evie.

"Yeah, Alistair's puzzle box, the one that I found with all the info about the Filipendulous Five in it. He likes physical puzzles."

"He does!" said Catherine.

"What if we're meant to build a compass, from the letters?" As he said the words, Sebastian started to sound more confident.

"Build a compass?" asked Evie.

Sebastian laid Catherine's letter on the table vertically. Then he placed Benedict's on top but horizontally.

The two pages created a backward L shape. "Imagine two other pieces of paper. You get a cross, with the end of each paper sticking out facing one direction. North is top, east faces the right, south is upside down facing the bottom, and west is facing left."

"Interesting," said Benedict, leaning down.

"What now?" asked Evie.

"Um . . ."

"Wait!" she said without letting anyone answer. "The darker letters!" Carefully, she picked up the pages, maintaining the L shape, and held them to the light. Where the two pages overlapped, the lighter letters faded away and the darker ones almost seemed to grow more pronounced. The letters *A, N, D, A, D, A, T,* and *R* from Catherine's paper were clear. But even more amazing than that were the letters from Benedict's paper. They were two Zs when read upright, but with the paper sideways as it was, the Zs turned into Ns and filled in the holes between Catherine's letters. Creating . . . well, creating mostly gibberish.

"NANN DAD AT R," Evie read slowly.

She looked up at the explorers to see if anything registered on their faces. They looked just as confused as she was.

"I don't know what that means," said Catherine, furrowing her brow.

"Me neither," said Benedict.

"It doesn't matter," said Sebastian.

"It doesn't?" asked Evie.

"Don't you see? Look at the way the letters are spaced. Some are close together, but there are wider spaces between some as well. That's for other letters. It has to be. Once we have the other two letters sent to the Kid and Doris, once we have east and south, the words will make more sense. This is the clue. This is where he is!" Sebastian had that look on his face that Evie recognized well. It was the look of pure joy he got when a problem had been solved.

"You're right. We don't know what it means now, but we will. And at least we know how to solve the riddle!" Evie too was feeling a great sense of joy.

Catherine looked to Benedict. "Well, what do you think?"

Benedict was quiet for a moment, looking as calm and relaxed as ever. "I think Alistair has a flair for the theatrical, that he wastes time with riddles like these, that I still am not interested in ever being his friend again, and that I am going to go with you," he said. He took his letter back, pocketed it, and disappeared once more into the back room.

"What? He is?" said Sebastian, surprised. Evie was too. She hadn't expected the sentence to end that way.

"I don't understand, but don't question it," replied Catherine. "This is good. We now have two parts of the map. And the key." She smiled at Sebastian. Evie looked at him and smiled too. Everything was coming together as it was supposed to. Even though she still had no idea why Benedict, who really seemed to hate her grandfather, was doing any of this.

Benedict returned in that moment with a large duffel bag over one shoulder. "Peter, I need you to collect my things from the mountain and keep them safe," he said.

"Of course, Mr. Barnes," replied Peter in a tone that suggested he would not only keep them safe, he would keep them safer than anything had ever been kept safe in the history of safely kept things.

Evie decided there was nothing more for it, she had to ask. She quickly followed Benedict outside. "Why are you doing this?"

"Because he needs my help," replied Benedict, and though it was a perfectly good answer to her question, it was not remotely a satisfying one for her. Especially as he hadn't seemed to care that her grandfather had needed his help before now.

She didn't bother to question him further. They didn't have the time. Instead she walked quickly, keeping pace with him, as the others followed close behind.

As they approached the town, Evie could see that something was up. The crowd was thick along the far side of the square. Then there was a scream, and there was some kind of scuffle.

"They're here," said Sebastian.

"We'll take care of them," said Peter, breaking off from their group to join the crowd.

"Come on, let's go," said Catherine. She quickly led the way into the square and turned to head around the commotion. As they passed the crowd, Evie caught a glimpse of Mr. K and his melted face. He was holding his old-fashioned gun and aiming it toward the boy her age.

Evie stopped in her tracks. "Those men are going to hurt the townspeople," she said. "We can't let them do this!"

She turned back to the standoff just in time to see the boy do one of the most impressive high kicks she'd ever seen, sending Mr. K's gun flying out of his hands.

"Oh, okay. Maybe they're going to be fine," said Evie, changing her mind.

"You!" called out a sort of familiar voice, and Evie could see Mr. M standing to Mr. K's left, being blocked by Isa. He pushed her to the side and came charging right for them across the square.

"Run!" said Sebastian.

"I agree with that," replied Evie.

And that's exactly what they did. They ran.

Evie realized her well of adrenaline had filled up once more, because, man, she was totally able to do this running thing again. She glanced over her shoulder. The townspeople were marvelously getting in the way of the men. Engulfing them like a wave engulfing an explorer who had just rescued a little shark. Evie thought, *This is our chance!*

If they could get to the fake house, if they could get there first and slip through before the men noticed, that would give them time. The men didn't know about the fake house. They would think that Evie and the others had just disappeared. Or something. Evie looked over her shoulder, expecting to see the men appearing around the corner, but clearly the crowd was doing a good job at detaining the men in black.

"The house!" said Catherine, pointing. They'd almost run right by it, but they turned and darted down the narrow alley.

Benedict immediately grabbed the side and pulled the house a few feet along its track.

"That's bizarre," said Sebastian.

"Let us help," said Peter. Evie turned to see that Peter and Isa, as well as the soccer team, had managed to escape the crowd and come find them.

"We'll close the door behind you," said the fierce-looking boy.

"And," said Isa, grinning to herself, "once we close it behind you, I will lean up against the porch to make it look really real."

Evie laughed at that suggestion and thanked them. "You guys are amazing," she said.

"Any friend of Benedict Barnes is a friend of ours," Peter said.

The four of them quickly crossed over the track, and Benedict started to slide the house shut behind them. "Thank you, Peter. You've been an excellent apprentice," Benedict said. Peter smiled so widely and brightly that Evie felt a little emotional to see it.

Then the wall of the fake house slid fully closed, and he was gone.

➤CHAPTER 39◄

In which decisions are
made, and some aren't.

Sebastian sat on the bus, squeezed between Evie and Benedict on a bench that was clearly meant to be sat on by only two people. Still, it was so much nicer being squished between people you liked than between people who wanted to cause you harm.

"We need to find Doris and the Kid," Catherine was explaining. "But I don't know where they are."

Benedict nodded. "I think the Kid was in California, but I can't say if he's there now. I think our best bet is to find him first. He'll know where Doris is."

There was a charged silence at that.

"I haven't seen her in a long time," said Catherine softly.

"Yes," replied Benedict.

Evie leaned over and whispered to Sebastian, "Ever feel like you're missing a big part of the story?"

Sebastian nodded.

"Hey, are you okay?" she asked.

He nodded again.

He didn't know what to tell her. That was because he didn't know what he was thinking himself. He knew that the right thing was to go home. Call his parents, tell them he was okay, and get himself back to the city and to his regular life. Which would likely involve years of being grounded—and deservedly so. The mention of California, though. And the need to find the Kid. And then Doris. It made him feel upset. It made him kind of sad.

He didn't want to miss out.

There was no way his parents would give him permission to adventure like this, not with all the danger he was constantly facing and such. No way at all. He certainly wouldn't allow such a thing if he himself had a kid. But he couldn't not let them know he was okay. How they must miss him, how terrified they must be. But if he let them know, they'd make him come home.

Unless . . .

Unless he just didn't go home.

Unless he called them and said he was fine but didn't tell them where he was.

Well, now. Things were getting more inappropriate, it seemed. And maybe not in an appropriately inappropriate kind of way.

Sebastian didn't want to think about it anymore, not while he was stuck on a small bus and couldn't do anything about it now anyway.

"Uh, so do you think the Kid will be able to help us?" Sebastian asked the explorers. "I mean, he's all right, right? The men don't know where he is either, so he's not in any kind of danger like Catherine was or you were?" He was joining the conversation and driving his angst from his mind as best he could.

Catherine smiled to herself in a contained kind of way. Benedict too smiled and said, "Well, that's all a matter of context, but I am pretty sure it's safe to say that the Kid is doing just fine."

Meanwhile . . .
on the West Coast
of America . . .
this . . .

He was driving so fast that, even though he was following the winding road that twisted around and around the desert mountain, it almost seemed like he was unfurling the road after him in a ribbon of dry gray asphalt. They weren't far behind, and although he was more than aware of his current situation, he couldn't help but marvel at how beautifully this Lexus LFA handled the curves.

The Kid glanced in the rearview mirror. There was a sudden flash of bright light off a windshield in the distance behind. They had made up ground. He quickly adjusted his aviators, and then, with a grin, he slammed his foot hard on the gas. The Lexus burst forward with

renewed energy,
and the Kid
easily wound
around the next bend.

It was an adrenaline rush, that was for sure. It felt good, but it also felt dangerous. Which also felt good. The Kid grinned as he took the next bend, and the next.

And the next.

DANGER. ROAD CLOSED.

A bright orange sign, a wooden makeshift fence running across the pavement ahead. He slammed on the brakes and crashed right through the barricade onto the unpaved road. He spun the wheel furiously. The car fishtailed in the dirt, and dust rose up around him, swallowing the car. It wasn't until the dust settled that he noticed that the vehicle had been so turned around that he was now heading right for the cliff face. There was no time to stop. There was no time to think. Writing all this right now has taken more time than the Kid had in that moment. He tore off his seat belt and flung himself out of the car as it charged on, flying over the side.

The ground was hard and his body was a rag doll

as he rolled and rolled, slowing down but still maintaining momentum. He grappled with the dusty earth, reached his arms out, tried to grab at anything that might stop him, that might slow him down. And finally, finally, he found it.

The side of the mountain.

The Kid dangled over the edge, legs swinging below him, the fingers of his left hand white from the effort of holding on for dear life. The world was quieter now.

He could feel the breeze, even hear the cry of a hawk some distance off.

Don't look down, don't look down.

He looked down.

Oh, look. The ground. Was that the ground? It was so hard to tell, it being so far away and everything.

He looked back up.

He reached out with his right hand, grunting with the strain, and finally the tips of his fingers grazed the edge. He held on fast. And then—then he wasn't sure what to do next. He tried to pull himself up, but the dust beneath his fingers was slippery and the effort almost made him lose his grip. The side of the cliff curved in away from his body, so his feet had nothing to rest on. He stopped trying to pull himself up and just kind of hung there. Waiting.

Hanging.

Waiting.

Hanging.

Waiting.

And also . . .

Hanging.

➤ ACKNOWLEDGMENTS ◄

Check out *The Explorers: The Door in the Alley*—those folks acknowledged there? Still awesome, and still worth acknowledging!

In other words: Ditto.

Huge additional thank-you to screenwriter Young Il Kim, author and zoologist Jess Keating (who didn't mind my taking a few liberties with shark family dynamics), and Kuku Yalanji woman Larissa Walker. Your assistance with this book is so greatly appreciated, and your insights helped make it what it is today!

LEFT YOU HANGING, DIDN'T WE?

Turn the page for a sneak peek at the epic conclusion to the series!

➤ CHAPTER -1 ◄

In which we begin before we begin.

The best kinds of stories, as we all know, start with pigs in teeny hats. Then some continue and take you to far-off countries and involve great white sharks and K-pop bands, also maybe reunions and lots and lots of running. Some stories start in the middle of the sentence and with brand-new characters you've never met. And still others are then divided up into "parts" for some reason.

And if you're really, really lucky, some stories combine all those things.

And also maybe involve me getting to play the French horn.

No?

No French horn?

You sure?

Okay. No, that's cool. That's . . . cool.

PART 1

The Quest for the Kid

The Kid sat staring at the chart of faces. Little circles showing different expressions ranging from very happy to very sad. "Using this scale, how much pain are you in?" read the bubble letters printed just above them.

He stared at the palms of his hands. They were wrapped in white gauze. Some red could be seen on the bandage of the right one. He wiggled his fingers. Then he balled his hands into fists. It stung but felt kind of right.

"Dangerous business, stunt driving," the doctor said.

The Kid nodded. But of course, it wasn't. Not really. It was far less dangerous than what he had been through in his former career. On this occasion, though, things had gone wrong. How had the crew not seen the unfinished road? How could he not have taken it upon himself to check out the set? Time pressures. "Get it all done in one take. We only have the helicopter for a day." Stupid excuses. All of it was so stupid. He'd almost fallen to his death over the side of a cliff. All for what? For a movie? Not even a very good movie, if the script he'd glanced over was anything to go by. Thank goodness for fast-acting second assistant directors rushing to save your life.

"Well, you're good to go when you're ready." The doctor smiled at him briefly and then left the room.

The Kid sighed and slipped off the table and onto the floor. Time to put himself back together. He reached for his jeans and slipped them on under the hospital robe before taking it off. Then he put on his shirt. Then he reached into his pants pocket, not an easy thing to do thanks to the gauze around his palm, and pulled out a small vial filled with water attached to a thin leather string. He stared at it for a moment.

There was a knock on the door. Quickly he put the vial around his neck and hid it under the shirt. "Yeah," he said.

A man entered. Someone he'd never seen before.

"Charles Wu?" asked the man, with a smooth British accent. If the man hadn't used his stage name, the Kid might have been suspicious. But he was used to Hollywood types showing up out of the blue, and he just rolled his eyes inwardly.

"Yeah."

"I have a job offer for you," the man said, getting straight to the point.

The Kid almost burst out laughing. "Dude, this is so not the moment or the place. Talk to my agent."

"Your agent seems to be MIA." That was true. The Kid hadn't been able to get in touch with Annalise for two days, now that he thought about it. "How would you like to work on a project that's low risk and well paid? And very easy."

"Never been a fan of any of those things," said the Kid.

"Yes, we know, you have quite the daredevil reputation. But we thought that maybe . . . possibly . . ." The man stopped when the Kid gave him a look.

The Kid tucked in his shirt and grabbed his leather jacket off the back of the chair. He walked past the man to the door.

"Think about it," said the man, reaching into the inside pocket of his tweed blazer. He pulled out a business card and passed it to the Kid. "Call me if you're interested."

The Kid slipped the card with some effort into the back pocket of his jeans without looking at it. He grabbed his sunglasses and put them on. "See ya," he said, then walked into the hospital corridor.

He strode with purpose and a little swagger as he made

his way to the outside world and took a deep breath of cool nighttime air.

Yes, breathing was a nice thing to still be able to do. He flashed to a mental image of himself dangling off the side of the cliff that morning. The memory was so vivid, he could feel the fear rush through his system as if he was still there.

Low risk.

Very easy.

The Kid crossed in front of the taxis and made his way to the parking lot, and eventually reached his bright red BMW 4 Series convertible. He smiled when he saw it. His agent's assistant had brought it for him, knowing full well that there was no way the Kid was taking a taxi home.

After slipping into the driver's seat, he adjusted all the settings. He took a deep breath and sighed once more, long and hard.

Low risk.

Very easy.

He turned on the engine.

Good money.

The Kid peeled out of the parking lot and roared toward the freeway, the wind in his hair, his palms, stinging a little, holding the wheel.

➤ CHAPTER 1 ◄

In which there is a phone.

Sebastian stared at the phone in Benedict's palm, held out toward him, a kind offer. The buzz of the Los Angeles International Airport dimmed as Sebastian focused on the small black box.

He didn't know what to do.

Well, that is to say, with the phone.

He knew in general what he was supposed to do. Or at least, what his friend Evie needed him to do: she needed him to help her find and rescue her grandfather Alistair, her only living relative and the leader of the formerly famous exploring team the Filipendulous Five.

Sebastian knew they had to put the team back together, then use the information hidden in the letters Alistair had sent each of the former explorers to rescue him. Evie and Sebastian had already found and recruited two of the four explorers—animal expert Catherine and cartographer/photographer Benedict. All that remained was the pilot/driver the Kid, and Doris the engineer.

Sebastian also knew that he had to personally stay away from the scary trio of thugs in black leather jackets who had shown up about a week earlier and were also after Alistair. The men wanted a map that the team had that led to a waterfall that was supposedly a fountain of youth.[1] He knew he had to stay away from those men because he had memorized the key to the map before destroying it and was therefore very important to the bad guys, who had tried to kidnap him. Repeatedly.

All this he knew.

What he didn't know was what he should do with the small phone sitting in a cartographer/photographer's palm.

Now, it wasn't about knowing how phones worked. That was obvious.

Or why Benedict wanted him to use it—he wanted Sebastian to call his parents.

It was about knowing whether or not he *should*.

The thing was, Sebastian had put off calling his parents for a long time, coming up with explanations that pushed reasonable boundaries at every opportunity.

---

[1] While I understand why a fountain that has water in it that would keep someone young forever is pretty cool and I guess worth searching for, I have to confess I'd really prefer finding a chocolate fountain that never gets empty. But that's just me.

There was the fact that he and the others simply had to keep running away fast from the men in black who wanted his brain, so that he didn't really have a second to stop and make a phone call. There was the fact that when he had had a moment, it was while he was accidentally being held hostage by the manager of a K-pop band and wasn't allowed to make a call. The truth was, though, all that was behind him, and Benedict had a phone and Sebastian could have called by now.

But when they'd been in the capital city of Newish Isle and Benedict had been busy forging a passport for Sebastian to get him back home, and they'd had to sit around waiting for that—instead of maybe looking for a phone, Sebastian had decided to focus his mind on the moral question of breaking the law by using a fake passport, taking into consideration the fact that kidnap victims certainly were allowed a little bit of leeway to get back to their home country. To be fair, he had, for a moment, thought that maybe he should get his parents to send him his passport instead. But that would have meant talking to them, and that would have meant he'd have had to make the decision about whether he wanted to call them. So he hadn't bothered making the suggestion of having his parents send him his passport. At the time he had known that he'd be calling them soon enough. From American soil. When he was safe and sound. Which he'd thought might freak them out less. Maybe only a hair less, though.

It was interesting that Evie hadn't made the suggestion to call home either.

He'd hoped no one would ever actually say anything to him about the whole parents issue. He, Evie, Catherine, and Benedict had made it to Cairns, Australia, and then to Sydney. But when they were waiting for their connecting flight home, Evie had finally broached the topic.

He'd said he didn't want to talk about it.

She hadn't bugged him about it since.

Which was weird, because, of course, she was very good at bugging him about things.

Now they were in LA, ready to seek out the Kid. Not that they knew for sure he was here, but Benedict seemed pretty confident. The Kid had always wanted to be a stunt car driver, evidently, and Benedict said that he'd once seen the Kid very briefly in a movie when his face had been accidentally visible.[2] So they'd traveled thousands of miles on a hunch. Definitely not something Sebastian would ever have approved of before. Not really something he approved of now.

But the voyage had given him time to think.

---

[2] I too have once been seen briefly in a movie where my face was accidentally visible, which is weird because I don't remember filming that movie....

Time was up.

"It's really time, I think," said Benedict, no judgment in his tone of voice, though Sebastian was starting to suspect that regardless of tone Benedict did have opinions and wasn't always mildly ambivalent.

"You're right. . . ." Sebastian glanced around the airport as if looking for a way out, some kind of magical solution to his situation.

That was when he saw it.

"I think I'll use that, though." He pointed at the pay phone on the wall near the restrooms. It looked a little out of place, sad and lonely, unused and unloved. And just what Sebastian needed. Why did he need it? He wasn't sure. Clearly his consciousness wasn't quite up to speed with his problem-solving subconscious.

"How strange," said Benedict, but he withdrew his phone and allowed Sebastian to wander over to the pay one.

"I'll come too!" said Evie, joining him with a bright smile. "For support," she said a little more quietly, so as—he imagined—not to embarrass him in front of the grown-ups.

Sebastian appreciated the gesture, but he'd really wanted to do this alone. With no witnesses.

Witnesses.

As if he was about to commit a crime or something.

What a strange thing to think.

They approached the phone and then stared at it for a moment. Sebastian almost felt sorry for it. Nobody used public phones anymore. This one had become kind of a museum piece, but it had not been treated half so respectfully. Someone with a white marker had tagged it with a flourish of initials. Others had left behind a couple of stickers peeled off bananas. Still someone else had evidently taken something sharp to it and carved away at the dark plastic, not really creating anything particularly profound, just using the phone as an outlet for some seriously pent-up frustration.

"Are you going to call them?" asked Evie. Sebastian glanced at her. She looked very Evie. Wide-eyed, hopeful, generally excited. But there was something beneath the surface that he couldn't read exactly. It was weird. He had missed her so much when they'd been apart, while he'd been kidnapped, until she'd come to rescue him, and he had been so happy when they were all finally together again. But he'd forgotten just how much pressure it was having her around, him not wanting to let her down. His life wasn't just about him and his plans anymore.

He didn't really answer her question. Just kind of shook and nodded his head at the same time. Then he turned back to the phone.

Sebastian picked up the receiver. It felt a little sticky.

"Do you need some change?" Evie's voice sounded far away, small and thin, like it was coming through the speaker of the phone. Sebastian peered at the phone carefully. He noticed a question mark drawn on it, black on black, almost invisible.

"Or . . . should I let you have some space, maybe?"

Sebastian looked at her again, still with no idea what to say. They stared at each other for a moment, and then he nodded. She gave him a quick smile and wandered back toward Catherine and Benedict.

This was it. This was the moment of truth. He had to make this call. But what did he want to say? What did he really want?

Deep down.

I think I have to ask them if I can continue to adventure, Sebastian thought. *If maybe I make it sound like extra credit for school or something, they might think it's worth it. Seeing the world. Experiencing different cultures.*

That sort of thing.

It had been the one hope Sebastian had. That his parents would consider such bold exploits a most excellent educational opportunity. But it was a small hope. His parents weren't that interested in alternative forms of education. Even sending Sebastian to a special math-

and-science school had made them a little uncomfortable.

The biggest problem really was that his parents were smart people. If there was a convincing argument against Sebastian staying with this adventure, they would make it. And there were plenty of those types of arguments. He knew a ton of reasons himself.

He put the phone to his ear and inserted several coins. He raised his fingers to the keypad and held them there, not pushing down. Instead he ran his fingers over the buttons, feeling the texture of the metal and the bumps of braille indicating to the visually impaired what the numbers were.

Just do it.

Or don't *do it.*

But do something. Even if it is nothing.

The anxiety of not knowing what to do was probably at this point worse than any bad news his parents might share. He'd never felt like this before. It wasn't quite like his usual panic attacks—though his heart was racing fast, it was more surreal. The numbers seemed to be dancing around before him. Were they trying to escape his fingers? Were they trying to entice him?

He felt like every choice was the wrong one.

He felt trapped.

Sebastian hung up the phone and stared at it, mindlessly wiping the stickiness off his right hand and onto his pants.

"Well, what did they say?" asked Evie.

He turned around, flustered. He hadn't heard her come back.

Sebastian felt oddly on the spot. Which was probably why he said what he did. "They are glad that I'm safe." He gulped quickly before forging on. "And said that they'd tell the school what was going on, and that as long as I stayed in touch, this seemed like an excellent learning experience." He widened his eyes in shock at his own lie, wondering whether Evie could tell what he'd just done.

But she apparently didn't notice the guilt written all over his face.[3] Or, maybe, chose not to notice—he wasn't sure. Instead she smiled broadly. "Oh, yay! That's fantastic!"

And true to form, she launched herself at him. He was used to her hugs by now, and better prepared, but this hug didn't make him feel better the way they usually did. Instead it made him feel even more anxious. She released him and said, "I'm going to go tell Catherine and Benedict! Next stop—find the Kid!" She flew off, leaving Sebastian alone with his thoughts and the sticky phone.

---

[3]   Obviously not literally. That's not a thing that people have written on their faces. Except, that is, for Gerald Haversham, the infamous bank robber, who had a giant tattoo of the word "guilty" on his face and still managed not to be picked out of the police lineup.

What had he done? It was one thing to lie to bad guys, a lesson he had come to learn was occasionally necessary in a life-and-death situation. Or to lie to managers of famous K-pop bands, which might be a matter of self-preservation. Even, well, to lie to himself if he needed to make himself feel braver. Sometimes, as he was slowly realizing, lying wasn't always so bad. But there were certain lines that surely should never be crossed. And lying to a friend? To Evie? That felt like a big no-no.

She waved him over then, still grinning that big toothy grin of hers, and Sebastian's feet felt like they were sunk deep in quick-drying cement.[4]

If he said something now, maybe it wouldn't be a big deal. If he told her the truth, he could be forgiven. But then she'd try to convince him to call his parents for real, and then he would have to, and he'd likely get yelled at. He would probably have to go home.

He'd tell Evie later. Maybe after. Or maybe a perfect time would present itself. Conveniently.

Besides, she'd understand. She was the one who'd wanted to go on this whole adventure in the first place. She was the one who had wanted his help. She knew

---

[4] Slow-drying cement, on the other hand, feels pretty much like you're standing in a puddle. Which is totally fine if you get out of it right away. But if you are enjoying the feeling of cool liquid against your ankles, you might end up stuck about twelve hours later. Trust me on this one.

how important all this was. And she'd been the one to teach him how to lie in the first place.

Yes.

Sebastian mentally unstuck his feet from the imaginary cement.

She would totally get it.

She just had to.

THIS IS ONE OF THOSE STORIES THAT STARTS WITH A PIG IN A TEENY HAT.

Then there is danger and adventure. There are hired thugs, a lost map, famous explorers, a risk-averse boy, and a girl on a rescue mission. It's not for the faint of heart, but if you enjoy derring-do (and doing dares), this just might be the story for you!

READ THE WHOLE SERIES!

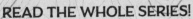